Ascension at Antioch

Ascension at Antioch

RC White

Copyright © 2008 by RC White.

Library of Congress Control Number: 2008903751
ISBN: Hardcover   978-1-4363-3821-9
               Softcover   978-1-4363-3820-2

All rights reserved. No part of this book may be reproduced or transmitted in any form or by any means, electronic or mechanical, including photocopying, recording, or by any information storage and retrieval system, without permission in writing from the copyright owner.

This is a work of fiction. Names, characters, places and incidents either are the product of the author's imagination or are used fictitiously, and any resemblance to any actual persons, living or dead, events, or locales is entirely coincidental.

This book was printed in the United States of America.

To order additional copies of this book, contact:
Xlibris Corporation
1-888-795-4274
www.Xlibris.com
Orders@Xlibris.com

47977

CONTENTS

Antioch 7
Annette Cobb 15
The House 20
Another Closet 28
The Ascension 37
A Home for Berniece 43
Nicky 53
Clyde 63
Charity 67
Erwin 72
A Test of Faith 79
Home 87
The Committee 89
A Cry in the Night 98
The Package 103
Choices 108
Virgil's Story 116
A Parable 120
Surprises 127
The Big Day 134
Afterglow 142
Hidden Words 147
Forgiveness 155
Truth from Fiction 162
Green Lights 169
DNA 177
Eagle Valley 184

Antioch

Situated halfway between Hattiesburg and Jackson and offering little in the way of big city excitement, Antioch is the kind of town you have to mean to go to unless you stumble on it as I did. I had left Atlanta with memories of a bright chrome gun pointed squarely at my face, and when a flat tire intervened, I stopped at the town's only service station.

While I waited, I wandered down a wide concrete sidewalk toward a meager collection of shops facing Main Street, the only street as far as I could tell. Faded signs announced businesses that were attempting to survive in this odd collection of buildings, some dirty stucco, others composed of haphazardly painted brick supported by a patchwork of wooden beams and arches. All had seen better days.

I stood for a moment looking through the rippled window of an antique store. Iris-patterned Depression-era pitchers, embroidered dresser runners, a heavy-looking blue churn, complete with its wooden paddle—the road show's influence felt everywhere. I strolled on to the next window with its scant offerings of spring styles. That day, I wasn't interested in antiques or fashions, but the aroma of deep-fried lunch beckoned from the little café up the street.

Before I could move that way, however, a farmer's pickup stopped in the middle of the wide street, devoid not only of other traffic but also of signals and blinking lights and the fumes of diesel buses and automobiles. He called out to a pretty middle-aged woman on the opposite sidewalk, and she stopped to smile and call back to him. As their familiar words and laughter floated across the nearly deserted street, my pulse idled, just like the truck, and I took that as an omen.

Within a couple of months, I had returned to Atlanta, sold the house I'd probably never make enough money to pay for anyway, and exchanged it for my own piece of small-town America. Antioch has been my home ever since, but neither the town nor I are the same. Credit Berniece Messer with that.

The first time I saw her, she was coming down the steps of the post office with those long legs stretched out as a racehorse's, energy bursting from every pore. At the time, I was still new in town and didn't know any better, so I smiled and spoke as she approached. A mantel of wiry black hair peppered lightly gray framed her granite face, and her piercing blue eyes drilled into mine for a brief second.

"Mornin'." She nodded, the granite crumbling ever so slightly. Then as fast as it had happened, the eyes withdrew, and Berniece was gone.

I turned on the steps to watch her stride the brief distance down the street to her nondescript four-door Ford, gray and faded with age, all the while feeling something I couldn't quite place, something I wasn't even sure existed. I don't know how long I stood there while she got in, backed out onto Main Street, and headed out of town, but I watched until the car topped the hill and disappeared from sight. It was all such a simple event you'd think hardly worth remembering, but if I'd known then what I know now, maybe I would have at least talked to her before it was too late.

Berniece's father, Mr. Virgil, as the locals called him, had inherited the neat white farmhouse out on Jordan Road from his parents, who came to Antioch by wagon, they say from Florida, some time around the turn of the century, the last one. When Old Man Messer died, his son Virgil took over, and soon those two hundred acres produced the best cotton the state of Mississippi has ever seen.

Although little else ever changed about the appearance of the farm down in the holler, Mr. Virgil's reputation as a cotton grower soon spread across the state. Succeeding where others had failed, he was sought after. More than one farmer trekked out to Jordan Road to talk to the expert, and more than one left mystified. Using techniques of an era gone by, Mr. Virgil simply defied the odds.

Mrs. Messer, along with Berniece when she was old enough, tended a garden that supplied them with their needs, and with the exception of holding down the back pew of the New Hope Baptist Church every Sunday morning, the family rarely ventured out. Folks said it wasn't that they were unfriendly. Around Antioch, lots of people stay to themselves out of necessity. When there are crops to plant, tend, and harvest, not to mention animals to feed and cows to milk, you can't go gallivanting around. But in the stories I'd heard, folks also said there was something about the Messers they couldn't put their fingers on, something mysterious.

All the stories sounded fairly normal to me, and I passed it off as part of a local myth. That is, until I heard about their disappearance. Sheriff Johnston told me. Berniece had just walked past us on the sidewalk, and he looked back at her, shaking his head. "Odd bunch," he mumbled.

"Bunch?" I asked innocently. "Doesn't Berniece live alone?"

"Oh, she does now," he said, his eyes lighting up. "I keep forgettin' you weren't around back then." He licked his ample lips. I hadn't heard the story.

"You see, one Sunday, they just didn't show up for church," he told me. "Nobody thought too much about it, but when they didn't show up the second Sunday, folks got worried."

It seems that the church folks subsequently sent Brother Ira Peake into town to talk to the sheriff who, in turn, took along his single deputy, Oscar Dewitt, and wearing their official uniforms, they drove the town's only patrol car out to the farm. It was no less than their Christian duty, not to mention their civic obligation, to see what might be wrong.

The Messers' gravel drive turns off Jordan Road at the top of the hill and runs almost straight downhill for a hundred yards or so, makes a circle in front of the wire gate, and turns back again. Positioned behind oaks that probably sheltered Choctaws long before they did the Messers, the house does, I admit, look a bit like a mirage. With its tall porch and carved valence running the length of the front, when the shade's just right, you can't see the windows or the door. Makes it all look more like an outline missing the details.

But anyway, Sheriff Johnston and Oscar went out there. Berniece herself appeared at the door and waited while the sheriff stood there hat in hand while he offered his apologies for bothering her. Then he came to his senses. He wanted to know if everything was all right because nobody had seen the Messers lately, and the townsfolk, particularly the church folks, were concerned.

They say Berniece looked back as calm as could be and told them, "They're fine. They've gone back to where they came from."

The sheriff figured that didn't make any sense at all, knowing full well that Mr. Virgil had been born right there, so he asked if he could go into the house. Berniece escorted the sheriff and Oscar into the living room and even fetched hot tea for them in her Blue Ridge cups on a little matching tray. Try as he might though, the sheriff never got a single word out of her about their whereabouts except what she'd already told them. The sheriff finally replied that he was mighty sorry, but he was "going to have to look around."

The sheriff said Berniece didn't even object. For days, he and Oscar scoured the farm. Not only did they fail to find hide or hair of Mr. Virgil and Mrs. Messer, but they also failed to find a single thing out of the ordinary. The garden was still brimming with beans and tomatoes, the chickens were still laying out in the barn, and the cotton bolls were still lying open in the fields, waiting for somebody to come and pick them.

Sheriff Johnston finally called in the Mississippi State Police who, in turn, questioned Berniece and poked around on the farm for days. They even talked to neighbors and townsfolk, none of whom were able to offer a single lead.

When those efforts yielded no clues, they brought in dogs trained to sniff out bodies, or so I'm told. For sure, they sniffed every square inch of the farm. Periodically, the hounds would look up at their handlers, no doubt asking for clues themselves before resuming their futile task. All in all, no person and certainly no dog found any evidence whatsoever to indicate that Virgil and Mrs. Messer were on the premises.

Sheriff Johnston decided to make one last effort. "If you won't tell me where they are," he pled, "at least deliver a message for me, will you?"

Berniece glared right back with those steely blue eyes. "I can't do that, Sheriff. But I'll be going there myself some day."

Since the sheriff didn't have the vaguest notion of what that meant, he let the statement lie and accepted the obvious. He wasn't going to find the Messers that day or any other day.

Eventually, the state police gave up and went back to Jackson, satisfied at least that no bodies could have escaped their search. And around town, interest finally waned. Although people surely thought Berniece was nutty, she hadn't done anything to merit being locked up for either. So it boiled down to the fact that nobody had seen or heard anything out of the ordinary, and with absolutely no evidence to indicate otherwise, the police were forced to conclude that the Messers had indeed taken up residence elsewhere.

Of course, this all happened long before I got to town. Many years had passed with never a sign of the Messers. Berniece continued living in the farmhouse down in the holler although the garden was a fraction of the size it had been, and nature, mostly kudzu and honeysuckle and blackberry vines, took over the once-prized fields.

Neighbors said that every few years, Berniece would come into town and buy some paint. For six days straight, finishing up in time for Sunday church, she'd work out there in the broiling sun until the white house sparkled again. And every Sunday morning, she'd park the old gray Ford on the east bank of Poorhouse Creek and, just as the service was about to start, take her seat alone on the last pew at the New Hope Baptist Church. Then without fail, week after week, she'd deposit a crisp once-folded ten-dollar bill in the offering plate when it came around.

Folks began to say you could mark your calendar by Berniece, beginning with every first Friday when she made her brief appearance in town. She'd mail off her bills from the post office, walk to the hardware store to pick up a can of wasp spray or some such, then drive on to the Piggly Wiggly, and leave with always a single brown paper bag full of groceries. When she was done, she'd get back into the Ford and head home.

To the best of anyone's knowledge, Berniece never had a visitor, and she certainly didn't belong to any of the organizations that the other ladies did, even I after a while. For all those years, Berniece lived in that house with no telephone and, as far as anybody knew, no television. My guess was that she read a lot, but without a proper town library, I really don't know what she could have been reading.

By the time of my own brief encounter, Berniece had become a legend, complete with nickname.

"Demon Lady," the children sniggled and called her behind her back.

They couldn't think of any other reason that a person, let alone a woman, would live way out there on Jordan Road all by herself. I had to admit that my meeting with her had engendered some sort of eerie feelings within my heart of hearts, but I wouldn't have called it demonic.

Standing there on the steps to the post office, I felt it, and after all this time, I've finally decided it was sadness. I've felt it a couple of other times in my life being around somebody so filled with grief that it seemed to rub off on everybody close, like a sort of tangible sorrow. Berniece gave me that same feeling. When she'd passed by, I couldn't help turning to watch. She walked erect, but with an aura of aloneness, a space between her and the rest of the world. Surely, that was no demon lady unless she was a really sad demon.

I guess most people were so accustomed to Berniece that they didn't feel her sadness anymore, or at least they ceased to care. Anyway, the rumors started about a month after my encounter. As the town's only pharmacist, folks considered me their version of a medical expert, so I was hardly surprised when Ethel Downey leaned across the counter and started whispering. Expecting details of some intimate physical discomfort, I must have looked funny when I realized what she was saying because she stopped in midsentence.

"Go ahead," I urged.

"Well, like I was sayin'. Scott Carruthers's boy and some of his friends were drivin' by that house around midnight, and they say there was a glow all around it. I'm tellin' you, that woman's up to something."

"What could she be up to?"

"You know about drugs and all that stuff. I'll bet she's makin' meth, whadda you call it, meth-whatever out there."

My first thought was that any drugs involved must have been inside the teenagers. Secondly, if she were indeed mixing drugs that produced a glow, it would have been preceded by an explosion the likes of which this county has never experienced. And those thoughts still ignored the most obvious flaw in her story, that Berniece hardly fit the role of illegal drug manufacturer. There had to be something else.

"Go on," I ordered again.

Ethel finished her story with more of the same, and I held my tongue. I intended to find out more, but as soon as she left, I got really busy and forgot all about it. That is, until Sheriff Johnston came into the store to get me.

It seems that Scott Carruthers's father had overheard the boys' wild story about lights out on the Messer place and determined to find out for himself what was going on. He reasoned that there'd always been something really weird about that woman, and before he'd let her get his son into any more trouble than he'd already managed to get into by himself, Mr. Carruthers would put a stop to it. So around one o'clock that same morning, he drove out to Jordan Road. What he saw brought him to the sheriff's house before daylight, banging on the door and yelling alternately about flying saucers and witchcraft.

Sheriff Johnston said he had quite a time getting the boy's father to calm down and make some sense. Once he got Mr. Carruthers past the glowing house and strange objects in the air, the sheriff agreed to wake up Oscar and go back to the farm for a look. Mr. Carruthers though had seen enough and would sit right there until they got back.

Day was breaking when the sheriff and Oscar opened the gate at the top of the hill and proceeded down the lane. When no one answered their knock, the sheriff thought it appropriate to take action and bashed the door into splinters and entered Berniece's house. That's what brought him back into town to fetch me. My guess is that he wanted somebody with a scientific education to see it too, so folks wouldn't think he was crazy, but if he's crazy, I must be too.

The sheriff went ahead of me, and from over his shoulder, I could only see Oscar, whom he'd told to stay behind to keep guard, sitting alone on the couch, hat in his lap. His mouth hung open, and his eyes were glued to the ceiling as if the angels might summon him directly through it at any moment.

When the sheriff moved aside, I too entered the room, and I followed Oscar's gaze. Helplessly, my own mouth dropped, and hairs on my arms stood erect.

"Oscar!" the sheriff called again. "You seen anything at all?"

"No, sir," he said numbly, glanced at us, and then returned his gaze heavenward.

Berniece's simple living room, where the sheriff and Oscar had once sipped tea, was now an artist's palette. Overhead, indigo planets glided through golden galaxies that stretched into infinity while magentas and teals and lemon yellows swirled across every wall, every windowsill, and even the old wooden floor.

Without interruption, one scene flowed into the next. Innocent children built castles on seashores that melded into forests thick with life where purple bears climbed vanilla trees and conquistadors sailed off into azure horizons.

Snatched from a mind too intense to share in any other way, Berniece's colors pulled me into their grasp, and I don't know how many times Sheriff Johnston said it before I recognized my own name.

"I think we might oughta look through the rest of the house," he urged, this time including Oscar in his jerk of the head.

We followed him from room to room, all easels for Berniece's dreams. Then we reached her bedroom. Gone was the sadness I'd felt when Berniece passed by me at the post office, and in its place, I felt something more akin to longing. After my first really big paycheck, I'd visited the Caribbean, and once home, quite illogically found myself homesick for a place I hardly knew. I felt it again in that room.

The room was all white, not as if by paint and brush, but more like Mr. Virgil's cotton had taken root in Berniece's bedroom with a white so intense it seemed to breathe. The only color came from a brick fireplace on the outside wall where a lone robed figure beckoned us forward with a knowing smile and outreached hand. Blue veins all but pulsed in sunlight that poured through the window.

The steely eyes sparkled now, and the features, once hard, were soft, understanding. The black wiry hair still waved untamed about her face, but now in juxtaposition with graceful wings poised above her head.

The sheriff and Oscar and I left everything like we found it, boarded up the door as best we could, and went back into town. For days, the sheriff tried to find Berniece. He even tried to find relatives, but all with no luck. Oscar quit his job and moved to Hattiesburg, and the whole town eventually went out to Jordan Road and saw the house, but nobody could explain it, not for a long, long time.

As for me, I still live in Antioch. Wouldn't live anywhere else. But we're all different people now. Part of that is because of what happened to Berniece, and the other part is because of what happened to me.

Annette Cobb

Annette was the first person in Antioch to see how much I needed this town. I met her even before I actually moved here and long before the events out on Jordan Road. Now that I think back on how easy it was, I know this move was meant to be, and she had a lot to do with it. Once I'd made the decision, the rest fell into place, and all I had to do was tend to details.

I left Antioch and went straight back to Atlanta, home for most of my life, with visions of the country life dancing in my head. I started my online search. Several things in Jackson and a couple in Hattiesburg looked promising, but I nearly fell off my chair when I spotted an ad for Antioch itself. I guess they weren't overwhelmed with applicants because when I called the number listed, the storeowner sounded quite surprised. By the time I actually made it back to town, the interview with Edwin Wilks proved little more than an exercise.

Edwin owned the drugstore along with the town's two other most viable businesses, a combined feed and hardware store and a catfish restaurant out by Pep's Lake. The last in a long line of family from Antioch, Edwin's interests had expanded beyond the town, but he retained the businesses that kept his pockets lined and his name in local politics.

That left only the question of where I would live, and that's how I met Annette. When I asked Edwin about homes for sale, he thought for a moment, scratching his bald head with a stubby finger. Then he smiled.

"I just might have something for you," he admitted and reached for the phone.

I listened, all the while thinking it too good to be true. But I also knew that everything had worked so far. Why not this too?

The house belonged to Annette Cobb and her husband, Azariah Bartholomew, thankfully nicknamed Bart. He worked as an electrical engineer at Mississippi State University in a program called CAVS, which

I learned later had something to do with advanced vehicular systems but, like most everything else pertaining to engineers, remains a mystery for me. He came home on the weekends, and Annette kept the place going. The house in question became Annette's when her mother died a couple of years before, but she'd never put it on the market. When Edwin told her I was looking and assured her that I wasn't a status-seeker from Jackson or Hattiesburg looking for a bedroom community, she agreed to show me the house.

Edwin gave me directions to Annette's, and I drove to her farm and stopped midway in a driveway running a hundred yards or so from the county highway and consisting of two parallel ruts of pinkish gravel separated by a raised median of lush grass.

Annette, or the person I assumed to be the owner of my desired home, rode an old tractor across the rear lawn, intent on the job at hand. When I got out of the car and walked toward her, she saw me and cut the engine. She climbed down from the machine and ventured me a smile as she whisked away grass clippings scattered over her front.

Annette wore an old straw hat stenciled around the wide brim with faded blue and red patterns and held beneath her chin by a matching strip of cloth tied in a haphazard bow. A pair of oversized sunglasses covered what the hat didn't, and she wore a plaid flannel shirt rolled up to the elbows beneath a real, honest-to-goodness pair of well-used overalls.

She undid the bow at her chin and took off the hat, releasing a thick mane of red hair just about the color of a worn penny. She tossed the hat back toward the tractor and then turned her attention to me. Annette stood several inches above me, and when she took off the sunglasses, the smile that had begun on her lips spread to the greenest eyes I'd ever seen.

"You must be the new pharmacist."

"That would be me. Lila Dawkins," I said and offered my hand.

"Glad to meet you, Lila Dawkins," she said simply and pulled a towel out of the side pocket of her overalls. "Hope you'll excuse the dirt." She wiped her hands with the towel and then offered the right one to me. "We're glad you're here. This town can sure use you."

"I hope so," I answered sincerely. This Annette was much prettier than the version I'd seen on the tractor. And she was older. She didn't move like someone with close to six decades under her belt, but there was something in the eyes that said she'd seen that much of life. "I think I'm going to like working and living here."

"Well, in that case, you've probably come to see me about the house."

That's Annette. She doesn't waste time—gets right to the chase. And that's one of the many things I've always liked, even loved, about her.

She asked me into her home, made sure I had something cold to drink, and then excused herself for all of two minutes while she cleaned up. When she returned, Annette had rid herself of the overalls and flannel shirt and exchanged them for a pair of jeans and a maroon tee shirt that proved her to be also thinner than I'd estimated.

"Way too hot with all that on," she explained. "But I can't work in the sun without some protection. You know how it is."

I mumbled agreement, and she responded by removing a set of keys from a hook over the kitchen door and motioned for me to follow. My soon-to-be house is only five miles from Annette's farm, but I probably would have spent an hour trying to find it on my own, especially by the circuitous route Annette followed. She insisted on driving her car, and I soon found out why.

Annette drove the same way she does everything else: with a purpose. With Annette waving at each driver we passed, the five miles flew by, and we soon entered what would become my driveway.

Edwin had told me the basics of the house, but still I wasn't prepared for seeing a near-replica of the one in my favorite movie. The two-story white farmhouse on top of the hill at the edge of town had my name written all over it. And the real phenomenon was that in a few days it could be mine. I was increasingly sure too that, like the town itself, this house would become a part of me.

Annette's grandparents had built the house around 1908, shortly after their marriage. Back then, it was surrounded by fields laden with profitable crops, but by the time Annette was born, adjacent land had been sold to the big farming concerns, and Annette's father had set up shop as the town's only lawyer. All that remained of the huge farm were several acres of pecan and oak trees, rolling, green hills, and a small lake behind the house that she assured me was filled with bream. Good. Maybe I could get some feed for them from Edwin's store.

I followed her onto the covered porch that extended the length of the house front. A wide railing, painted gray-blue, bordered the porch and encircled a wooden swing on one end and two rocking chairs at the other. Overhead, a ceiling fan waited for the afternoon's breeze.

Again, I followed Annette, this time into her childhood home. Our footsteps echoed lightly on old wooden flooring as we passed down the central hallway, and I already knew I was home. She walked straight through to the rear of the house as if she knew that's where I'd want to be and then stopped in the middle of the big airy kitchen, turned around, arms akimbo. "So whadda you think?"

"It's gorgeous. I love it."

Annette chuckled and shook her head. "You're not supposed to say that. You're the buyer, remember?"

"Does it matter? I do love it. And something tells me you're not gonna sell it to me if I don't, so why pretend?"

This time she laughed out loud, and her arms fell to her sides. "So how'd you learn so much, being from the city?"

"They don't teach human nature in the city or, for that matter, in the country either."

"How true," she agreed. "Still, you must be observant."

"I've learned a few things even if I am from the city."

"That you have," she said and headed toward a rectangular oak table at the other end of the kitchen. Its polished surface was the color of molasses, worn lighter at either end of the table.

She pulled out a chair and slid her tall frame between it and the table and then squared those green eyes on me. "So, what brings you here to Antioch? I mean, what *really* brings you here to Antioch?"

"I guess I've had all the big city I need." I'd asked myself that question a hundred times, but how'd she know?

Those eyes didn't believe me for a second. She leaned further my way. "And?"

"And, here I am."

"Lila, there's one thing you need to know about me."

I didn't know how to respond, so I waited.

"I know that everybody's got a story. And whatever your story is stays with me. Kinda like the old saying, what happens on the Gulf Coast stays on the Gulf Coast."

I couldn't help laughing at the simile, and I laughed too because I knew at that moment, Annette had become my friend.

So I told her the real story. "The whole time I was in college," I began, "I had a friend, a male friend, who was also in pharmaceutical school with me. We were never romantically involved, but we were about as close as any two friends can be, and we had a plan. Once we got our degrees, we were going to buy a drugstore somewhere in the outskirts of Atlanta, you know, the American dream and all that. And we were going to make it into something special."

"So what happened?"

"We did it. We both worked for a few years for the big guys so we could save enough money to buy our dream store. He married his college sweetheart, also a friend, and we finally bought the store out in College Park. We offered people the kind of service and human contact that they used to have before Wal-Mart and the big drugstore chains. We even had a little soda fountain. It was working like a dream—until I found out what he was doing."

Annette's lower lip poked out in anticipation. "He cheated you." It was a statement, not a question.

"Yeah, but that wasn't all." I continued. "I found him padding insurance claims. Not just little bits, mind you. I was convinced that if he'd been caught, I'd go down with him, so I figured there was only one way out. I waited till everybody was gone one night, and I showed him what I'd found. I mean, Johnny and I'd been friends for so long."

"What'd he say?"

"It wasn't what he said. It's what he did. My own partner, my best friend, pulled a gun on me."

"Dear Lord! Did he hurt you?"

"No. He didn't, but he said if I told anybody, he'd follow up. I took that to mean he'd kill me. All I wanted was to get as far away from him as I could, as fast as I could. Never mind the investment I had in the store. I figured I'd get him to buy me out, but I'd do that from long distance. I just got into my car the next day and started driving."

"And that's when you wound up here," she said, shaking her head slowly.

"Yeah. That's how I found Antioch."

"Do you think you're safe here?"

"As long as I don't report him."

"How about family?"

"I told my parents that I needed a change. Wanted a different lifestyle. There really is nobody else. Not now anyway."

For long seconds, the only sound was the gentle ticking of the clock above the stove. She finally asked, "And will you report him?"

"I don't think so." I looked across at Annette, at those eyes the color of spring. "I'm hoping it'll eventually work out, but I can't risk going back. I can't take any more hurt."

"I understand. I wouldn't either."

In that moment, I knew that Annette would indeed never tell. And in that moment, I knew that my secrets, past and present, would always be safe with her.

The House

Once I bought the house, life for me in Antioch took off. The fashionable monster in Atlanta produced enough in equity to buy Annette's house outright, so everything moved quickly.

Moving day turned out to be little more than a month after my original encounter, one of those marvelous days that only spring can bring. Anybody who's ever spent much time in Mississippi knows that later, summertime, is meant for growing stuff, for playing baseball, and for heading for the Coast, but not for moving. I was lucky things happened when they did.

Spring had arrived with a green vengeance and peppered the yard all around the house with jonquils and daffodils. Even the dandelions looked pretty. While folks in Detroit and Buffalo dug out from the latest blizzard, I gleefully acknowledged my wisdom in moving to this part of Mississippi. Come August, it would be their turn to laugh, but the dogwood beside the driveway made me forget all about it for the moment.

I spent the night in Hattiesburg, knowing that the van would be in Antioch early the next morning. Although I had met only a few people in town, they all had offered assistance in moving should I need it, but I still imagined myself to be self-sufficient and politely refused. Before the day was out, I welcomed anyone who crossed my threshold.

The first to do so would be Sheriff Johnston. The moving van was late as I soon learned the norm, and by the time they began unpacking, it was nearly noon. That meant that unless I wanted to pay even more for their services, I had to make up my mind quickly about where I wanted everything placed. Although I'd penciled sketches from memory, the house had a few surprises for me.

One of them was that the living room dwarfed my meager furnishings. The huge desk I'd inherited from my grandfather and that I'd just sent upstairs would have to come back down. And the bedroom furniture I owned didn't look right in a farmhouse, no matter what the configuration.

I was standing in the hallway considering an alternate plan when the front door opened, and what my mind first envisioned as a brown bear entered, official hat in one hand and a covered bowl of something in the other. He was big, not fat, but big in the way that a bear is, and he moved with all the ease of an animal with little to fear. He presented a friendly but imposing face centered by a bushy moustache and topped by thick generously salted brown hair. The uniform in varying shades of brown only added to my initial impression.

I shook my head to dispel the image and then pulled myself away from the furniture problem to the more interesting diversion in the hallway.

"You must be the sheriff," I said, closing in to get a look at the badge. I stuck out my hand. "I'm Lila Dawkins."

His shoulders visibly relaxed as a smile warmed his features, and he shifted the bowl to the other hand.

"Glad to meet you Ms. Dawkins. I'm Ward Johnston." He looked down again at the bowl. "My wife asked me to come over and give you this," he said and held the offering my way. "She wanted to welcome you herself but figured she'd do that in person later."

"Thank you, Sheriff. What a kind thing to do."

His purpose accomplished, he stepped back. "Sure thing. Hope you enjoy it. Dolly made up that gumbo this morning when she heard you were movin' in today. Thought you could use it."

"I'll say." The grumblings in my stomach weren't all caused by hunger, but the aroma emanating from that bowl sure made me think they were. I lifted the lid gingerly and lowered my face to savor the aroma. "Would you like to join me while I sit down for a minute? I've got to taste this."

He glanced out toward the official vehicle parked in my front drive, then back toward the living room where two men struggled with the desk.

"Sure. I'd like that."

"Let's go back to the kitchen then. It's quieter."

At my request, Annette had left her mother's old kitchen table, and it was fast becoming the center of my new life. Even though Annette's mom had brought the kitchen up to modern standards of efficiency, I felt safe and warm there. And the hub of it all was the table on the eastern side, surrounded by a row of windows that looked out over the pond and the barn. Perfect for watching sunrises that didn't include my neighbor's imposing house.

As we entered the kitchen, I was tempted to eat the gumbo right out of the bowl he'd brought it in, but manners kicked in, and I offered to share my portion with Sheriff Johnston.

"Oh, no. I couldn't do that," he explained. "Dolly'd kill me. That gumbo's for you."

"Well, thanks again." I rummaged in a box I'd already opened, retrieved one of my own bowls, and then looked around on the counter for the plastic spoon brought in with my takeout breakfast. "Please sit down." I motioned toward the table and then took my seat at what would become known as my place.

He eased his large frame into the same chair that Annette had chosen on my first visit and rested his hat formally in his lap.

I couldn't wait any longer and poked my spoon into the stew. All previous versions of gumbo vanished as I brought up chunks of okra and tomatoes and crabmeat swimming beside plump oysters in a thick spicy roux. My taste buds were on fire for more, and although a bit afraid of making a pig of myself in front of a guest, I plunged the spoon back in as rapidly as I had deposited the latest portion into my mouth.

"Excuse me," I managed between mouthfuls. "I must be hungrier than I thought." I inserted another spoonful and all but smacked. "This is divine. You say your wife made it?"

"Yep. Dolly's a mighty fine cook. Nothin' fancy, just good Cajun, you know?"

"Oh, I know now," I said sincerely and filled my mouth again. "So your wife's name is Dolly?"

"Yeah. Sorry. We've been here so long, I forgot you didn't know."

"That's okay. I imagine as soon as I start working, I'll get to know everybody pretty fast."

"That you will. When do you think that might be?"

"Get to work?" I asked, pausing to lift a crab claw from the stew and strip its meat off with my teeth.

"Yes. To the drugstore."

"I'm going to try to make it in tomorrow. At least for a while."

His eyes widened as he looked around the kitchen and its stacks of boxes. "You don't have to go rushing. Looks like you got some work to do here first."

"That I do. But it'll all get done. I'm anxious to start meeting people."

"Well, whenever you can get there will be good for everybody. Nearest place for prescriptions is almost to Hattiesburg."

"I know. Edwin told me. Kinda hard to believe in this day and age, but the flip side is that your town still has some personality. You've still got plenty of beautiful woods, and there's no gray-and-blue concrete monster looming over the town."

"Not yet anyway," he said a bit uneasily.

"It's good to know I'll be useful here." I looked down at my now-empty bowl. "Thanks for bringing this, Sheriff. You probably saved my life."

"Glad to do it."

I stifled a belch and sat back. My whole body had melded into the chair and begged me to remain. I wanted nothing more than to continue my conversation with this kind person in spite of the work I had yet to do. "So you've been here all your life?"

"Yep. Except for a few years in the army. Did my bit in 'Nam, you know. Dolly's a Louisiana girl. Met her down at Fort Polk before I went to 'Nam. Couldn't wait to get back before somebody else claimed her."

"What a neat story," I said, meaning it. I glanced back at the larger bowl he'd brought, but again, I forced myself to wait. "So how long have you been sheriff here?"

"'Bout as long as I've been married to Dolly—last twenty-seven years or so." His thick moustache curled up at the corners.

"I guess folks around here respect you. Otherwise, they wouldn't keep electing you."

"Either that or nobody else wants the job."

His honesty surprised me. I'd seen too many other cases of unwarranted pomposity, especially with big fish in small ponds. "Now don't tell me you never have opposition in an election."

"Oh, there's been some opposition. I always figured people think it's easier to stick with what you've got though. You know, the tried and true."

"Still, that says a lot about you. You must do a good job."

Ward shifted in the chair, lifted his hat from his lap, and laid it on the table in front of him. "Well, it helps that we don't have much crime around here. We've had a couple of strange things happen through the years, but nothing like you have happening all the time in the city."

"Strange things?" I could tell by the way his eyes left mine and sought some place over my shoulder that there was more to this story, but at that precise moment, a crash sounded in the living room.

Ward's hand ran across his face, and he reached for the hat. "That'd be my cue," he said and rose from the table.

The moment was over, and I led my guest down the hallway and thanked him again with a plea to share my gratitude with Dolly. Then I returned to the living room.

The disaster turned out to be only a glass I'd lent to one of the workers who stood staring down at the shards on the floor as if he'd done irreparable damage. I assured him nothing of great value was lost, but he insisted on helping me clean up the mess.

The man was older than the others, but his thin body remained as taut as piano wires. While a droopy eye in his dark face made him look sleepy, his work was anything but. He worked right through breaks the others took, always at the same metered pace. He told me that his name was Walter, but a couple of times, I heard the others call him something that sounded like "Squirrel." Maybe I wasn't the only one who'd noticed his inability to remain still.

I went to the closet off the kitchen to dig out a broom and dustpan that I had placed there earlier, reached to the back of the closet, lifted the broom off the little hook, and started to close the door. But something caught my eye. The closet was lined on both sides with shelves, and on the top one on my left, almost out of sight, I spotted what looked like a piece of thick paper slightly curled up at the corners.

I slid it to the edge of the shelf, and as motes of dust filled the air around me, I looked down on the single sheet of paper, the kind used for watercolor paintings. Heat and time had warped it a bit, and I lifted the tail of my shirt to brush dust from the surface.

In spite of its age, the colors remained vibrant. The more I dusted it, the more I saw the beauty of the simple church depicted in the painting. Before the month was out, I'd see the building for myself, but for the moment, I could enjoy it as some idealized representation of life in small-town America.

It was a small church, mostly brick with white trim, positioned amidst a grove of oaks and pines, and around the steeple, playful angels circled in an imagined game. Below, churchgoers dressed in their Sunday best filed into the building, Bibles in hand. The characters were real looking enough, but like the angels circling the steeple, they appeared playful as if going to church were some sort of game.

Intending to look closer, I took the picture to the table, but before I could examine it, Walter called me back to the living room. By the time he and I solved the latest dilemma, night was fast closing in, and I didn't want to pay overtime. The work wasn't nearly finished, but it would have to do. I paid Walter and made sure that he shared the praise as well as the pay with the rest of the crew.

When everyone had left, silence crept in through the walls, through the windows, and with darkness erasing my splendid view I soon found out what it's like to be alone, all alone in a new home. Before I fell into any sort of melancholia, I forced myself to go into the bedroom to make up the bed, a chore that somehow makes things right for me. I'd pulled the last stubborn corner over the mattress when I heard a familiar voice coming from the front door. Did I leave that door unlocked?

Then I heard, "Lila, it's Annette. Where are you?"

"I'm in the bedroom," I instructed, and in a second, she stood at my bedroom door, hands on hips and wearing her patent grin.

"So had a big enough day?"

"You could say that." I looked around the room at the stacks of towels on the dresser and the boxes of personal stuff awaiting my attention. "Looks like another big one tomorrow, doesn't it?"

Her only response was a nod as she went to the chair where I'd laid the comforter, brought it back to the bed, unfolded it, and draped it evenly on all sides. "Maybe I can help," she suggested.

"Don't say it if you don't meant it."

"Oh, I mean it." She stood straight up and looked directly into my eyes. "People around here like to help. You'll see."

Suddenly the night didn't seem as threatening and the distance between my previous life and me so far. She helped me put the towels into the bathroom closet while I emptied and put away both boxes in the bedroom. Now, I could at least take a bath and sleep in comfort. The rest could wait because I'd done all I could manage for the day.

My bones ached, and I felt as if I'd wallowed in a dust bowl. Unable to go any longer, I finally asked her if she would like to sit with me in the kitchen for a few minutes before she had to get back to Bart.

Thankfully, she agreed, and I found the bottle of wine I'd saved for that very night. It was really a dessert wine, but it was what I wanted for such a special occasion—Moscato de Asti, sweet, bubbly, and thoroughly pleasing.

She took her place at the opposite end of her mother's table, and as she did, she glanced down at the picture I'd left there in the afternoon. I was pouring glasses of wine, and I'd already forgotten about the picture, but I could tell as she picked it up that she'd seen it before.

"Where'd you find this?"

"In the broom closet, on a shelf. Do you know who did it?"

She nodded and picked up the picture. Her face changed from mere remembrance to something else, and her brow knitted as she studied the picture.

"What is it?"

She shook her head and then looked back at me. "I never noticed this before. But of course, I didn't know you then."

"Notice what, Annette?"

"Here, you look. I knew you looked familiar for some reason."

Now thoroughly curious, I took the picture into my own hands. Once again, I stared at the innocent churchgoers.

She added, "Look at the woman stepping up onto the porch. Her head's turned this way."

I followed her lead and blinked away my own disbelief. There I was, stepping onto the portico of the little church. No, it was not like a photograph, but the resemblance was still unmistakable. The smiling face was my own.

"Who did this, Annette? I mean, how could anybody paint me into this picture? I wasn't even here when it was done."

"I know. Mother bought this at a church auction years ago. But look, the person in the picture is about your age now. I'm sure it's just a coincidence. Anyway, Berniece had no way of knowing what you look like."

"Berniece?"

"Berniece Messer. She lives out on Jordan Road. She did this painting for a church auction one time. They were raising money for a new Sunday School Building, and Mother thought it was good. Kinda folk art. She bought it, probably as much to help Berniece as to help the church, but she had it up in this kitchen at one time. I don't remember when she took it down. She must have used the frame for something else."

I stared down at the unmistakable rendering of my own face, and Annette repeated that it was probably a wild coincidence.

"But, Annette, I don't really believe in coincidence, do you?"

The green eyes blinked, and she said, "No. Not really. But I also don't have any other answer about how your face came to be in Berniece's painting."

"Can we ask her about it?"

"We can try, but she's not exactly the easiest person in the world to talk to."

"I don't understand."

"We'll try," she said again without much faith. "But I doubt she'll have any answers either. Probably if she says anything, it'll be what we've already said. Coincidence, pure and simple."

Annette stayed a while longer, and we talked about other things, each of us knowing all the while that there was really only one subject we wanted to discuss. There simply wasn't anything else we could say about it for the moment.

I walked her to the door and turned again to face the empty house and all of its questions. I intended to put the picture first on my agenda for the next day, but true to my word to Sheriff Johnston, I went into the store instead. Although I stayed for only a few hours, the day after that turned into a full one, and before I knew it, a month had gone by. And that's when I passed Berniece on the street.

Another Closet

The day I first saw Berniece began like all the others since I had moved to Antioch. As I said, I was standing in front of the post office, about to go in myself, when Berniece came out and passed by me and spoke. I watched her get into her car and leave, but instead of going into the post office right away, I remained there while I tried to put a name to the elusive mixture of feelings that our brief encounter had evoked. Several seconds passed before I could shake myself free from the moment and return to my present business.

The post office was an old brick building on Main Street, between the hardware store and the café. As such, it served as a sort of meeting place, which still offered the best view of the whole town's goings-on from its wide front windows, not to mention the daily confluence of citizens with real or feigned business. Ron, the postmaster, himself a longtime fixture, was a strange mix of hyperactive humor and cynicism. Although nearing retirement age, he perpetuated a unique custom of daily badinage with anyone who came to his window, most of whom not only expected it but also looked forward to it.

One day the topic could be national politics while on another, he might light into a series of Hollywood-celebrity-gone-wrong jokes. All in all, his witticisms kept him out of notorious headlines, and they kept the townspeople coming back for more. Although he'd been a bit soft on me at first, he soon made up for it. Apparently, Ron enjoyed my semifame as the newcomer and big-city refugee.

"Where else could you get such a captive audience?" I first teased. This day though I was more concerned about something else.

Once we'd shared the daily joke, I asked, "Ron, you know that woman who just left here?"

His eyes rolled behind his thick glasses and his mouth scrunched up into a question as he clicked off the last few customers on his fingers. "You mean Berniece?"

"A tall thin lady, dark hair?"

"That'd be Berniece. Berniece Messer."

I looked behind me to make sure I wasn't delaying anybody and then went on. "What do you know about her, Ron?"

The question caused him to turn his head to the side as he stared up into space and groaned audibly.

"Gee, that's a tough one, pill lady. Her family's been around town forever, but I can't say as I know much about her. Why do you ask?"

It was my turn to be puzzled. Why did I ask? "All I can tell you is that when she passed by me, I felt something really unusual about her. That and the fact that I found a watercolor painting of hers in my house." I debated about sharing that my face was in the painting but, for once, kept the thought to myself.

"I didn't know she was an artist."

"Apparently so. And a good one at that."

"Well, I'll be. You never know, do you?"

As we spoke, a plan formed in my head, and I soon ended the conversation with Ron. Since the painting had been left in my house, and since I was now a member of her hometown, I'd go talk to Berniece. But there were a few other things I had to do first.

I went back to the store to finish my afternoon's work, closed the doors at six, and took off. Ethel Downey had been more than glad to share directions to the New Hope Baptist Church; although it was on the other side of town from where I lived, I could still make it with plenty of daylight. Before I talked to Berniece though I wanted to see the place for myself to figure out why she thought I belonged in that church. Even more than that, I wanted to lay a foundation of trust with this woman who had remained a stranger in her hometown. She had talent, but I suspected she had something else that kept her distanced from other people. And I suspected that something else also sustained her. At any rate, I had to see the church, and obsessive or not on my part, I had to talk to Berniece.

I found the church a few hundred yards off Highway 49, exactly as Ethel had said, on a slight bluff overlooking a bend of Poorhouse Creek. Although paved, the road that led away from the highway was rough and full of unexpected curves, so I welcomed the sight of the little church.

The building didn't qualify as pretentious, but it was well kept. The small red brick church was trimmed in white that looked recently painted, and the unadorned portico that I'd seen in Berniece's painting was as inviting as somebody's front porch. Three large, clear glass windows ran down the side of the building facing me. In the center of each was a colorful stained glass symbol: three crosses, a gold chalice, and a stylized fish. I wondered what was on the other side, but from there, I could see only a small asphalt parking lot that met the surrounding forest. I made a mental note to check it out before I left, but I didn't realize at the time that it would be after dark when that happened.

On the right, a wide grassy area held a tiny cemetery surrounded by a low white fence. Behind that, I saw what Ethel had described as the parsonage—a wood frame house painted the same green as the pines towering over it. However, someone had gone to a great deal of trouble to distinguish the house by adding attractive taupe shutters, a wreath of purple irises and yellow daises on the matching door, and a row of soft pink azaleas on either side of the porch.

I had intended to go straight into the church, but when I heard a noise, a clinking sound, I followed it to the rear of the building where a late-model Buick was parked with its hood raised. A tall dark-haired man leaned over the engine and tapped gently with a metal tool on something inside the car's workings.

"Hello!" I called out as I rounded the corner.

The man stopped what he was doing and looked for the source of the voice.

"Hi! Are you the minister here?"

His blue eyes matched a deep blue shirt, and paired with a precisely creased pair of khaki pants, he didn't look the part of a mechanic. But then he didn't really look like a preacher either.

"No, I'm afraid that's not me," he answered with a smile. "I'm just the mechanic. But you've got the right house." He took a white cloth from his pocket and methodically wiped his hands and then offered one to me.

A dimple in his chin deepened when he said, "Nick Reynolds."

"Lila Dawkins. Glad to meet you."

"Same here, Lila. How can I help you?"

I looked toward the parsonage and tried to explain. "Nick, I'm sorry to interrupt you, but I came here to see the church, I mean inside. Do you think it would be okay if I looked around?"

"I'm sure it would, but I don't know if the church is open." His eyes never left mine as he added, "Brother Sciple is home though, and he'd probably be glad to show you around."

"Then Brother Sciple is the minister?"

"That's right. Most of us call him Jimmy though. You must be new around here."

"I moved to Antioch about a month ago, but I guess that's still new."

"Yeah, I'd say that's new, especially here. And since we don't get many newcomers, I'm guessing you're the pharmacist."

"Guilty as charged." I didn't like the sound of my voice at that moment, but I couldn't stop. "Do you live here too? I mean, here in this house?"

The eyes crinkled into a broad grin. "No. Sometimes I work at the office, but when a car won't start, it's easier for me to go to it."

"That's nice. And different. I'm not accustomed to mechanics who make house calls."

"Probably not many do, but it works for me. Besides, we like to help each other if we can."

"You're not the first person to tell me that," I admitted, "and I'm beginning to realize how true it is."

"Then maybe you'll hang around."

My ears burned as I said, "Thanks. I plan to."

"Good. Good enough." He half turned toward the parsonage. "Come on, and I'll introduce you to the Sciples."

The woman who answered the door was tall, model tall, and her looks were striking enough to qualify her for a New York runway too. She'd swept her blonde hair into a simple ponytail, but stragglers around her face softened the effect as did well-worn jeans and a denim shirt, sleeves rolled nearly to her elbows. Still, she was pretty, remarkably so.

"Hey, Nicky!" she drawled. "Are you finished with the car already?"

"No, not quite, but I wanted to introduce you to someone." He laid a hand gently on my back. "This is our new pharmacist. Lila Dawkins."

"Glad to meet you," I again offered my hand.

"Oh, I've heard all about you, Lila. We don't get too many newcomers. I'm Becky. Becky Sciple. Listen, my husband's out on the patio with Sarah. Would you like for me to go get him?"

"If you don't mind, Becky," Nick answered. "Lila wants to see the church, but she didn't know if it was open. So we came back here first to ask the preacher."

"Hmm. You know, I'm not sure either, but I can get Jimmy. Won't take a minute," She gestured toward the living room, immaculate except for a couple of toys. "Please, you both make yourselves at home. I'll get him."

Becky and a little girl of five or so followed the Reverend Jimmy Sciple back into the room. The child's kinship with her mother was apparent. The same blond hair, the same lithe figure, but added to it was a bounce in her step that made her seem to skip across the room.

The pastor towered over both of them as dark as they were blonde and a good ten years older than his wife. The only thing that made me think "preacher" was the patent smile that they must teach at seminary.

He held my hand in both of his own to personalize the smile. "How nice to meet you, Lila. I've heard all about you."

"Hopefully, some of what you heard was good."

"All of it, in fact. We're mighty glad to have you here in Antioch."

"Thank you. It already feels like home."

"Good, good. Please, have a seat." He motioned toward a flowered Queen Anne chair.

Sarah jumped onto the sofa beside her father and giggled when he hugged her to him.

"Antioch's a good place to live, Ms. Dawkins," he said and kissed his daughter's forehead. "So what might I do for you this afternoon?"

I decided to spill it all and began telling him about the picture. "But it has me intrigued," I continued. "Annette Cobb told me that Berniece Messer painted it for an auction at the church years ago. Do you remember that?"

"No, I'm afraid I don't. I've only been here three years, but I do know they had quite a few fund-raisers to complete the Sunday School Building."

"I see. Well, there's something odd about this picture, Reverend. One of the people in it looks a lot like me, and I hoped maybe you knew why. Maybe somebody who used to belong to your church—somebody who looked like me."

Sarah's upturned face studied her father as he asked, "Do you have relatives who might have lived here?"

"No, that's just it. My family's all from Georgia, and until I stopped here a few weeks ago, I'd never heard of Antioch."

"I see the reason for your curiosity. And I don't know how much a tour of the church will help, but I'll be glad to show you around anyway."

Nick excused himself from our tour to finish his work on the car, and the reverend escorted me to the church. Inside, a plain white wall with doors on right and left and centered by a light oak table separated the vestibule from the sanctuary itself. On the table was a vase filled with the same pink azalea blooms I'd seen across the front of the parsonage. On the right wall was a recessed coatrack and, on the left, a pair of smallish upholstered chairs in shades of burgundy and rose situated on either side of another smaller table.

He swung open the door on the left and led me into the sanctuary. I listened while he highlighted the history of the church from its inception in 1905, all the while pointing out objects donated by faithful members throughout its century or so of existence.

Rows of honey-colored oak pews filled the sanctuary in three neat sections with aisles on the left and right, but none in the middle. Seats of the pews were covered with burgundy velvet cushions that matched tiny specks in the otherwise gray carpet that ran the length of the aisles and covered the altar area. Space beneath the pews was a flecked ceramic tile of the same colors. On the back of each pew, wooden racks held hymnals, also burgundy and stacked precisely, two to each section; three small circular holes to the right and left accommodated what I assumed to be the Protestant version of communion cups.

The reverend hadn't turned on any lights, but sunshine still filtered through the western windows and gave the church plenty light. The air was filled with the overly sweet smell of leftover flowers.

Midway down the aisle, he stopped walking and turned around. "Ms. Dawkins, I have a bit of a confession to make."

"A confession?"

He smiled at his own unintended allusion and continued. "You see, when you asked me about Berniece Messer, I was truthful when I told you I didn't know anything about that picture. But I didn't tell you the rest of it." He pushed his hands into his pockets, and change jingled noisily. "Have you ever met Berniece?"

"Not really. I spoke to her on the street, but I haven't met her to talk to her. Why?"

"I see."

I waited, and he finally added, "Come on back here for a minute, will you? I've been debating about whether to show you something, but I think now I should."

He led me down a short hallway behind the sanctuary that stopped in front of an unmarked door. He fished out a key, opened it, and flicked on the light. It was a large storage room with several cabinets, painted institutional green, and a big black safe on the opposite wall.

"Too bad we need these in churches," he said and took his place in front of the safe. He spun the dial right then left. "But it's a fact of life now. Even in Antioch."

He swung the door open to reveal empty bank deposit bags, stacks of silver communion plates, several crystal vases, and on the bottom shelf, where there was more room, a dozen or so large flat objects wrapped in plain brown paper.

"This," he said, taking the top one from the vault, "is what I wanted to show you."

He took the object to the cabinet surface and carefully undid the tape at the back and then held the picture up for me to see. The frame was a simple varnished rectangle, and I recognized the style. Its brilliant colors and interest in faces were the same as the picture I'd found in my closet.

The focus this time was the interior of the church I'd just seen. Some faces were familiar, but most were not. Most conspicuously, however, my own image was missing from the church scene entirely.

"Did Berniece Messer do this too?"

"Yes. She brought these up to me about a month ago and asked if I'd hold onto them for a while. I didn't mind, and we had the room to spare, so I agreed."

"Did she happen to say if she's going to try to sell them?"

"No. And to tell you the truth, I only looked at this one. She told me they were all about the same, so all I could do was to tell her that I thought it was really good. I encouraged her to do some more." He thought for a moment and added more softly, "Berniece is a very private person. I figured she didn't want to share them with anybody, so I agreed to keep them safe. If you hadn't told me about the picture in your house, I never would have mentioned it to anybody."

"I understand." I could tell that is was getting dark outside, but I turned back to the stack of pictures. "Do you think we could look at the others?"

For a moment, I thought he would refuse, but his curiosity must have gotten the better of him too, and we unveiled them one by one and leaned them against the walls until we were surrounded by Berniece's art. The town unfolded before my eyes. She was right about their being more of the same, but she hadn't told the entire truth. A couple more did indeed picture the church, but the others were far more private in nature.

One picture, he told me, depicted her farm, busy with workers in a field white with cotton, their backs sloped from the weight of heavy bags while a woman picked long green pods of okra from tall stalks dotted with intense yellow blooms. The same wiry black hair framed similar strong features, not unlike the person I'd passed on the street.

One by one, we viewed scenes from Antioch—the post office, the drugstore, what the pastor called the old swimming hole, and even my farmhouse on top of the hill.

In each picture, the scenes were as fresh as daylight itself, and each one almost whimsically mixed reality with flights into fantasy. The result was the creation of a world in which angels and cotton pickers knew each other well. Her world drew me in until I no longer was surprised to see playful angels lifting a dog into heaven while its sad owners grieved for him down below.

I became aware that the better part of an hour had passed, and the pastor and I hadn't spoken except for our comments on the paintings. It was as if neither of us wanted to break the spell, and neither of us knew how to express openly the passion that Berniece's paintings displayed silently.

I finally asked, "Do you think she knows how good these really are?"

"I don't think so. They are rather miraculous, aren't they?"

"That's a good way to put it. They say everything good about this town without a single word."

"Yes, they do." He nodded agreement.

"So what are you going to do with them?"

"Nothing right now. It would be a great breach of trust if I told her I'd shown them to anybody else, especially somebody she's never met."

"I understand. But you can't let a talent like this stay hidden."

"Lila, I can't do anything else. You must understand that I'd be breaking her trust, a trust I take very seriously. Maybe the two of us can think of some way to encourage her, but in the meanwhile, these pictures have to remain our secret."

I agreed and then helped him put the pictures back into the vault all the while squelching my inner protests. We closed up the room and its secrets, and I thanked him with a promise to keep our pact. But as I left the church, I still wasn't sure I could keep that promise. I'm a firm believer in confidence being held, and this was no exception. But at the same time, I was bursting to share my discovery of a rare talent.

Berniece, for all the world to see, chose her life of solitude. But was her art a way of communicating that she had yet the daring to share? Or would she resent the intrusion into her world to the extent that she might withdraw even further, never to return?

My whole drive home, the questions swarmed in my head like the bees over Poorhouse Creek in one of her pictures. If I told and we lost Berniece forever, it would be my fault. There was only one way I could figure out to solve the dilemma, and that was to talk to the artist herself. I had the reason with the painting in my house. I wouldn't have to break any confidences that way, and perhaps my enthusiasm would lead her to share others with me. I would just take it from there. Typical for me, I had it all figured out. What I hadn't counted on was how soon my chance would slip away.

The Ascension

I went home from the church and pulled into the gravel drive that goes around behind my house. The moon, a thin sliver on its back, was high over the pond and making little iridescent shadows as a dragonfly swept down and hovered over the surface for a moment. A chorus of cicadas that competed with tree frogs in the trees hanging over the porch stopped when I got out of the car. They seemed to watch until I'd entered the house and then resumed their chorus to the night.

Dining alone has never been my favorite thing to do, but I was much too tired to call anybody or go out for anything even if the café was still open. I made myself a big salad and sat down at the table, but I hardly tasted it. How would Berniece picture my house now with me as its occupant? Where did she get the image of my face? I was tired, but my mind still buzzed with possibilities. There had to be some unknown connection, and I wanted to find out what.

When I finished dinner, I followed my usual routine of showering and propping myself up in bed to read until sleep overtook me. But night was turning into daytime before that happened. I'd seen too much and anticipated even more.

I went in to work as usual, but the day was not half done when Ward came to get me. He told me only that something strange had happened out at the Messer place, and he'd really appreciate it if I'd go out there with him.

We made the trip out to Berniece's place in a shaky silence. Ward had come to trust my judgement, and I'd come to respect his equally. But when we walked through that door, neither of us was equipped to say what had happened, much less where Berniece had gone.

We went back into town, deposited Oscar at the station, and drove back to Ward's house where Mr. Carruthers waited. He was tired, and he was still vague on what he'd seen, but at least he'd settled down enough to make some modicum of sense by then.

He admitted that the lights around Berniece's house were really more of a glow than anything else and that they could have been a reflection of moonlight on the tin roof. And he admitted that he really didn't see any objects rising from the house. But it was still obvious to both of us that Mr. Carruthers had indeed seen something extraordinary. So had we.

When he asked us what we found in the house, Ward stole a look beneath his shaggy eyebrows at me before he answered. "We didn't find anybody in the house, Carlton." His words lay flat in the distance between the two men, but he wouldn't elaborate any further.

"You didn't find that Messer woman?"

"Nope."

"You didn't see any strange lights?"

Ward's head bowed, and he rubbed his eyes. "No, Carlton, we didn't find Berniece or anybody else for that matter."

Carlton Carruthers's mouth twisted into a near snarl, and he lifted his large frame from Ward's sofa. "Look, Ward," he began and then softened when Dolly entered the room and placed two new cups on the coffee table. "My boy didn't make this thing up. I know 'cause I saw it myself. But I guess it doesn't matter all that much anyhow. So I'll be off if you don't have anything else to tell me."

Ward nodded and reached for the steaming mug set before him. "I reckon not. That's about all there is to tell."

Carlton nodded toward Dolly and headed for the door. As he opened it, he turned back toward us once more. "One of these days, somebody's gonna find out what that woman was up to, and you can mark my words. It ain't gonna be normal." He shook his head and then turned and left.

Ward fell back onto the sofa and propped the mug on his chest just below chin level. I'd been too busy to notice how tired he looked, but the morning's activities had worn on him. And I had to admit that I felt as if somebody had pierced my inner being and drained me of all previous experience. The only thing that I could feel at the moment was wonder. I didn't know what I'd seen, and I had no earthly idea what it all meant.

Dolly sat down beside her husband. Her petite frame was a contrast with his, but she filled the room with her presence. I could see that in her youth, her dark hair and vibrant eyes could easily have had every boy in southern Louisiana seeking her attention. Now the youth may have gone, but the vitality and the music of her voice had not. In a rich Cajun accent, she summed up the morning's events with, "I reckon Berniece knows all about it now."

Ward couldn't hide the surprise. "What? Knows all about what?"

"Heaven."

Ward's brows raised. "Heaven? Do you think that's where she's gone?"

Dolly took his hand into her own and said patiently, "Where else could the woman have gone?"

"Well, I always kinda thought that somebody had to die before he went to heaven."

"How do you know she didn't?"

This time, Ward shook his head and, with a sigh, added, "Honey, there's nobody, live or dead."

"I know that. But I also know the Bible's full of things that can't be explained away. Look at Lazarus. What makes Berniece's case so different?"

Ward looked to me for help, but all I could manage was, "I guess that makes as much sense as anything else, Ms. Dolly."

"Exactly," she said. "Now, how 'bout some lunch? I made some fried green tomatoes and boudin."

Dolly's slant on life was that if food couldn't fix the problem, it would at least make it bearable. At that moment, I couldn't disagree.

Later in the day, when I went back to the store, word had spread, and the store soon filled with the curious and those who relished a good story. Everybody knew that I'd been on the scene, and everybody asked me questions that I had no way of answering. I think they all assumed I was being evasive, but honestly, I didn't know what to say.

If I told them that I'd seen walls filled with luscious art, most would say, "So what?" If I told them that I'd seen a portrait of Berniece so alive, so ethereal that I suspected she'd taken leave of this earth through it, they'd lock me up.

When it came down to it, what we'd seen begged description, but we'd both agreed that we wouldn't share any particulars until we had time to sort through it. Ward wanted to get some experts from Jackson to come out and look for clues, and I wanted to find an expert in art to verify what I already knew—that Berniece's art was priceless.

But for the moment, I told them the truth. Yes, Berniece apparently had a talent for art, and no, we didn't find her on the premises. The truth would take time, and time was something I didn't have at the moment.

Ethel Downey was bearing down on me like a tank on a mission. Her eyes were lit up with the fervor of the story, and her skinny mouth was working before she reached the counter.

"Hello, Ethel. How are you today?"

"I'm fine. Just fine." Her head swiveled as she took in any would-be listeners. "Didn't I tell you?"

"I'm sorry. Tell me what?"

Her smug smile made the mouth stop for a moment, and I grabbed the lead. "Oh, you mean what happened out at the Messers?"

The gray head nodded. "I told you, there was something funny goin' on out there."

"Ethel, we still don't know what happened. After all, we haven't had a chance to talk to Berniece yet. She's probably out of town somewhere, and when she gets back, I'm sure she'll answer all our questions."

"Oh, I don't think so. I mean, those folks of hers left years ago without so much as a word. You just wait and see. That'll be the last we ever see of Ms. Berniece."

Two others had by now entered the store behind her, giving me the excuse I needed. I glanced over her shoulder to the front of the store then back at her. "It'll all work out, Ethel. What can I do for you today?"

Air left her sails, and she said, "My husband's prescription is about due. Can you go ahead and fill it for me?"

"Let me check."

As I suspected, the prescription couldn't be filled for another two months, but by the time I checked on it, the line had grown, and Ethel went elsewhere to do her stirring. Even Edwin made it by later that afternoon, but at least he had the sense to avoid asking the same questions I'd heard all day. His eyes sparkled though when he said, "Guess you're not exactly the newcomer anymore, are you?"

I made it home shortly after six, fixed myself a tall vodka and tonic with lemon, and went to sit on my screened-in back porch. My first purchase in Antioch had been the four rocking chairs made by a Mennonite fellow up in Mount Olive. Annette and I had since made two more trips up there, and as a result, my house displayed several baskets and a pair of beautifully carved wooden candlestick holders on the mantel.

My glass was sweating, and I got up to go inside for a napkin, but as I turned, movement caught my eye out at the barn. It could have been a cat or a dog, both of which wandered onto my property from nowhere and disappeared as easily. But I didn't think it was either. This looked more like a man.

Bunny rabbits on my grave, I thought and shivered. The day had already had enough adventure for me. Anyway, while I was inside, I heard the crunch of gravel on the driveway. I suspected that Annette could read my mind, so I wasn't surprised when the shiny silver pickup rounded the corner.

Annette's truck stopped at the back steps, but instead of Annette getting out of the driver's side, Bart's gray head appeared. She got out the other side.

"Hey!" I called from the porch. "Guess you heard about all the excitement too."

Annette's mouth was a firm line across her face as she climbed the stairs, her usual smile absent and worry in her eyes. "We came by to see if you're all right."

Bart stopped right behind her and rested his hand on her shoulder. Bart's the kind of person everybody calls when trouble strikes. "Thought we'd hear it before it got blown out of proportion." He was still handsome in spite of thinning hair and a slight paunch, but more importantly, Bart always had a way of making me feel better with his unassuming confidence.

"Sure. Why wouldn't I be?"

"Oh, nothing," Annette laughed. "You just helped the sheriff break into somebody's house, found a treasure trove of art, and witnessed the disappearance of one of the town's stranger citizens. Why should that disconcert you?"

I had to laugh myself. "Don't forget fending off Ethel Downey."

Bart added, "That would do it for me."

"Ah, she's not so bad. Just likes to stir up things a bit."

Annette chortled and plopped into her favorite rocker. "Huh! That's like saying Brett Favre likes football a little bit."

"Now you've got a point."

"I know I do." She pushed the rocker into motion. "How about offering your best friends a drink."

I gladly made Bart's whiskey and Diet Coke along with Annette's perennial chilled wine and then returned to the porch. "What has you in town in the middle of the week?" I asked Bart.

"I was on the way to a meeting in Jackson when we heard about your little episode." He took a sip of the drink and leaned back. "Any excuse, you know," he said and held up the glass in mock toast.

I always could see why Annette chose Bart. His calm was a perfect match for her spirit.

Annette watched him for a moment before she added, "Lila, we're concerned about you. This kind of stuff can wreak havoc with your psyche."

"Don't worry about my psyche. I'm tougher than you may think."

"This town's had more than one strange occurrence to sort through. They'll survive this one too. We're concerned that all the talk might affect you."

"Don't be. I'm okay. Really, I am."

We shared a laugh about my tee shirt that bore the same caption beneath a cow lying upside down with its feet in the air, obviously quite dead.

We rocked and talked for a few minutes when Bart asked, "Lila, have you seen anybody poking around your place today?"

"No." A fleeting image that disappeared behind the barn flickered through my consciousness. "Why do you ask?"

He never broke the rhythm of his rocking as he sipped and talked. "Oh, nothing much. You know how it goes. Mrs. Garner told Peggy at the grocery store, and Peggy called us to say that some stranger was poking around your place—about the time you were out at Berniece's. Just thought you might have seen who they were talking about."

I gulped to force the quiver from my voice, determined that they not hear it. These two people were the only ones in town who knew that I might have someone to fear. "Since you mention it, just before you got here, I thought I glimpsed something behind the barn. But you know, it could have been anything, including my imagination. I was pretty wiped out."

The sun had gone down by then, and only the outline of the barn remained visible, dotted by shadows of trees. Our rockers creaked in near unison. I asked, "How about some homeless person looking for a place to spend the night?"

"Could be," Bart said without enthusiasm. "At any rate, harmless enough, I'm sure."

"Lock your door anyway, will you?" Annette asked. "I'll sleep better."

"Like you lock *your* door?"

I could feel her smile all the way across the darkened porch. "No. Like I *should* lock my door."

Bart laughed aloud. "At least she's honest."

Annette urged again, "Please do it, Lila. If somebody's lurking around here, it's somebody who doesn't know about small towns. Somebody who isn't interested in stealing an old lady's antiques."

I had no answer for that one because I knew she was right. After all, it was my property with the stranger lurking. And I was the one with a past I'd as soon not come looking for me.

A Home for Berniece

True to his word, within a week, Ward had investigators out at Berniece's place looking for some clue as to her whereabouts. He was working on what few clues he possessed in memory and from the slim notions of what the town could piece together about her past.

He remembered Mr. Virgil's telling him that his family had come to Mississippi some time around the turn of the twentieth century, and he thought he'd told him that their origins were somewhere around Tallahassee. So he made a contact with an old army buddy who made his current living in that city as a private detective.

The buddy promised to look into it without costing the town of Antioch a lot of money it didn't have and get back with him as soon as he knew something. And it turned out that it didn't take long indeed.

Within a week, Ward showed up at the store wanting to know if I could go to lunch.

I glanced at the clock and at the slim stack of prescriptions waiting for me. "Sure. Give me ten minutes, will you?"

I met him at the café, and once we ordered, he told me what he'd found out.

"Randy found a woman living there who says her grandfather had a brother named Warren Messer. Says he took off with his wife some time around 1905—she thinks to Mississippi. She remembers them coming for a visit one time when she was a little girl, but she couldn't remember anything much about them, just that they were old folks. You know how a child sees things."

"Did she know anything about Berniece?"

"No. Didn't know anything about any family he had here, but she said she has a cousin that kinda kept up with Mr. Virgil and his wife. I'm still trying to get in touch with her."

"Well, it's something," I conceded. "Do you think there's a chance this cousin knows anything about Berniece?"

Ward made a sucking sound through his teeth and shook his head. "I wouldn't count on that. But she might know something about Mr. Virgil and Delores."

"Delores? Is that his wife's name?"

"Yep. Funny. Nobody ever called her by her name. She was always just Mrs. Messer."

"How did you happen to know it?"

"When they disappeared, I found it on the paperwork that I got Berniece to help me fill out. No county records of births or deaths or even marriage licenses. At the time, I didn't know about the Florida connection. And," he said lowering his eyes to the table, "I guess I just left it to the state police."

"I can see why you would have." I dumped two artificial sweeteners into my iced tea and stirred while I thought about how to say it. "But Ward, that was before you knew about Berniece. Now we have a whole different reason to look for clues. If her parents disappeared twenty-something years ago, that's one thing. Berniece could hardly have killed them and done away with the bodies without leaving a single clue behind. Maybe they did go back to Florida. Maybe Berniece really did follow them there."

"Could be. Stranger things have happened."

"And if that's the case, I really need to find her. I want to show her art. It deserves it. But I could be in a heap of trouble if I talk some museum into showing her art and she shows up one day with a lawsuit in hand."

The waitress set down a steaming plate of corn and peas and fried okra in front of me. Ward's was the same except for the added hunk of fried chicken. When she'd left our table, he continued, "That's why I thought you might wanna go with me down to Tallahassee."

"For real? You're going to Tallahassee?"

"I can't think of any other way to get to the truth. Talking on the phone isn't always satisfactory, kinda hard to build trust that way. Besides, you've got a stake in this too. You've got a good head on your shoulders, and I could use the help."

My heart raced right along with my mind. "When, Ward?"

"Soon as I can get somebody to replace Oscar. I've got a handful of applications on my desk right now, but I'm not sure any one of 'em could find his ass with a road map, much less fill out a report."

"No Harvard grads then?"

"Hump! No high school grads that I can tell."

"Surely, there's somebody in town who'd like the job and would make a good deputy."

Ward nodded as he dug into the pile of peas on his plate. "There is, but so far he's not interested."

"May I ask who?"

"I don't mind telling you. Maybe you can talk him into the job. Nick Reynolds knows this town better than anybody else, and he's smart. Real smart."

"You mean Nick the mechanic?"

"Yep." He stopped chewing and gazed at me. "You don't know, do you?"

"Know what?"

"Nick's more than just a mechanic."

"I know his father was the town's only physician for a long time, but I didn't think too much about it. I only met Nick one time out at the church. I think Edwin told me that his father had been the town's doctor."

He smiled as he picked up the chicken breast and tore off a chunk with his teeth. "Nick was gonna walk in his father's footsteps. Finished college and went on to medical school up in Nashville. They say he was doin' real well too."

"So what happened?"

"Don't know for sure, but at some point, he started drinking. And then all we ever knew was that he'd quit school and come home. His daddy was as tight-lipped about it as an old maid and her sex life. Doc wouldn't say a word to anybody about it, still won't. He and his daddy still don't get along worth a damn. Nick lives all by himself out there on the river, and his daddy lives in town. Damn shame, that's all I can say."

"Does Nick still drink?"

"Not that I can tell. Every time you see him, he's neat as a pin, smiling at everybody. And he's learned a hell of a lot about cars—even brought in computers to check things out. He just won't have much to do with people."

I fought to squelch that smart-woman syndrome that said I could fix it. I hardly knew Nick, much less should I think that I could fix whatever was wrong between him and his father. I asked, "How about his mother? Is he in contact with her?"

"No, Doc's wife died about four years ago. Nick and his mamma saw each other on occasion, but you could tell, whatever happened had broken her heart. I don't think she ever got over it. That's what killed her, you know. Heart attack. Doc did what he could, but by the time the medics got there, she was already gone. Musta been hard on him not being able to do anything for his own wife."

I nodded agreement. "So how did Nick come to be a mechanic?"

"The old fella who owned the service station got tired of it, fell behind the times you know, and was looking for a way out. Nick went to work there when he first came home, and I guess he learned the business and liked it. He bought out Frank Mercer and been there ever since."

By that time, I'd nearly finished my vegetables, and Ward plucked the last of the chicken from the bone. I'd almost forgotten what started his talking about Nick.

"Is there any chance you can get Nick to work with you, maybe part time?"

"I don't know, but I'm gonna try one more time. I really need somebody like him. Then I can let the reins go for long enough to go over to Tallahassee and talk to those folks."

I considered talking to him myself, but it wasn't my place to go asking him favors. Folks would call that meddling. But then maybe Ward could use the help. I'd have to think about that one.

Ward saved me though from perhaps making a fool of myself. A couple of days later, he called me with the news that Nick had agreed to help him out on a part-time basis, and Ward was headed to Florida by the end of the week. And he wanted to know if I could go.

I made a few phone calls, filled the orders I knew would be due, and asked Annette to keep an eye on my place. In the short time I'd been there, I'd already managed to put up two bird feeders and a birdbath that would need refilling. She appeared more than glad to help, but she wanted some information too. "How about Dolly? You and Ward going off together might not sit well with her."

"I thought about that. But Ward says it's not a problem."

"Hmm. I wonder about that," she said and let the matter go.

I wondered too right up to the time we were in his car headed west toward Jackson rather than in the opposite direction. I thought the plan was to drive to Tallahassee, talk to the people we needed to see, spend one night, and drive back.

But when he turned onto the interstate headed west, I had to ask, "Ward, where are we going?"

His eyes never left the road. "Jackson. Why?"

"But Florida's the other way."

"Not if you're goin' by plane. I haven't flown much, but I do remember where they keep the planes."

"Who's paying for this?"

"The county. Official business, Lila. I've got the FBI breathing down my neck on this one. Smart guy was in town yesterday, reminding me that this isn't the first time somebody's disappeared from my town. If I can talk to these relatives, get some idea where Berniece is before the feds get a hold of it, it'll go a long way toward making me look less foolish. Not to mention, I'd really like to know where it is these Messers keep disappearing to."

He had a point. What I finally said was, "Ward, I'll have to pay my own way though. We could both get into a heap of trouble. We don't need any scandals about who paid my way." The corners of his mouth turned up, and I knew I'd been had. "*You* did it, didn't you?"

"Dolly and I agreed," he admitted. "Besides, if we didn't have five kids, we'd be rich."

"Ward, that's just not right. I insist on paying my way. Berniece is my project, remember?"

But that sealed the matter. Like everything else that he and Dolly agreed on, it became a matter of law. I'd have to think of some other way to pay them back. I was learning a lot in the way of small-town behavior.

Our destination in Tallahassee turned out more correctly to be about an hour out of the city in a place called Alligator Point, a coastal area that, as far as I could tell, deserved its name. Berniece's relative still lived in her own home on the beach, but I could already see the developers circling, waiting for her to pass on. That prime property would make an ideal site for a high-rise.

Rows of beach houses filled every square inch of available sand, interspersed with five- and six-story condos. Her property was situated on a point of land that jutted into the Gulf of Mexico and offered views from every angle. Surviving hurricanes probably hadn't been easy, but the old house, although not especially pretty, was built like a fortress.

Round pilings as thick as a large man lifted the house a good ten feet off the sand. Rough-hewn cedar covered the exterior walls, and thick wooden shingles gave the house a brown sameness, but it impressed nonetheless.

We drove straight from the airport in a rental, and when we turned into Vivian Bastrop's driveway, a knot formed in my throat. What if she wasn't lucid? What if all we found after all this trouble was an old lady who remembered nothing but the past?

We parked in the drive behind a recent model SUV that filled the only space left under the house. The rest of the area was paved in concrete and filled with neat stacks of beach furniture, a portable bar, an enclosed area, probably a bathroom, and a barbecue grill covered with a heavy black tarp.

Ward's eyes told me that he thought the same thing I did. This didn't look like an old lady's house.

We were halfway up the stairs when the front door opened, and a large pleasant-faced woman, somewhere in her sixties, called out a greeting. Before we could respond, a little sandy-haired boy squeezed by her in the doorway and scampered down past us on his way down the stairs.

"'Scuse me," he said without looking up at us as he rushed past on the stairs.

"Thirty minutes, Michael. Remember how to tell how long that is?"

"Yes, ma'am. I remember," his voice drifted over his shoulder as ran toward the nearest house, a trim blue one tucked between the rows of those on the beachfront and the ones that faced the highway.

She watched until he reached the house and then turned her attention to us. "You must be Sheriff Johnston."

"Yes, ma'am. I'm Ward Johnston." He started up the stairs again, and I followed.

"Forgive me for that intrusion, Ward, but you know how kids are. When they've got something in their heads, you might as well tend to it. We can talk better this way anyhow."

Ward nodded with a smile. "I've had five of my own, so I understand."

Neither of us asked the obvious question of whether the child was a grandchild or just somebody else's, but she soon supplied the answer.

"Michael's adopted. I had twelve children, all of 'em grown now," she said, leading us into her living room. "It's kinda interesting when the grandchildren come though."

"I'll bet," I added.

"Michael's parents were members of my church, and when they were killed in an automobile accident three years ago, I couldn't resist. My husband had died just before that, and I was lonely."

"Parents like you are rare," I said. "Michael's a lucky boy."

Ward told her, "I understand. You did the right thing." He added, "Mrs. Bastrop, this is Lila Dawkins, the pharmacist in our town. She came along because she's tryin' to find Berniece too. I hope you don't mind me bringing somebody else."

"No, of course not. I'd love to help if I can," she added and offered her hand. "Glad to meet you, Lila. And please, I'm Vivian. Let's sit in here," she said and led us toward a bright living room where a row of nine- or ten-foot windows looked out over the Gulf of Mexico and filled the room with sunshine. In front of the windows hung a type of hammock, more like a bed covered in old-fashioned chenille, strung from ceiling hooks. Every wall bore bold abstract paintings.

"Are you an artist?" I asked.

She smiled and lowered her large frame onto the butter yellow sofa amid a collection of cushions in bright sunny colors. She moved with the grace of someone much smaller and much younger. "I used to paint quite a bit, but I haven't done anything since Michael came." She laughed softly. "He takes up most of my time."

"That's understandable," I answered. I made my way around the room, openly admiring her work. "You've done some beautiful things," I said and meant it. "Perhaps you can go back to painting soon."

"Perhaps," she said but didn't elaborate. "I understand that you're both trying to find a long-lost relative of mine, and I'd like to help. Life is too short to lose touch completely with relatives, don't you think?"

"Absolutely," I agreed. "Anything you can tell us about Virgil and Delores might help us find Berniece. And," I glanced at her work displayed on the walls, "she has something in common with you that I think you'd find interesting."

"Oh?"

"Your art. My reason for being involved in this search is because of *her* art. I'm new to Antioch, but I first discovered a sample of her work that was left at my house, and then I got to see a whole collection. I was going to talk to her about trying to find a showcase for it when she disappeared."

"What's her work like?"

"Very different from yours. I'm no expert, but I'd call it more folk art because of her subject matter, but the style doesn't have the simplicity of folk art. Almost all the ones I've seen are watercolors, and they're filled with strong colors and lots of movement." I struggled for descriptions. "My best comparison would be either Van Gogh's *Starry Night*, but because they're watercolors, they lack those strong brush strokes. But the passion's there all the same."

"Oh my! I'd love to see her work."

"I hope you can too. Apparently, the talent runs in the family."

"Thank you," she said softly. "I see what you're up against. You need Berniece to pursue this goal, don't you?"

"Yes, I do. And Ward needs to find out what happened to her and, ultimately, to her parents so he can close the books on their disappearance."

"I'll do what I can. But I still think Pearl might be able to help you more. Actually, she's not doing badly for somebody who's ninety-eight, but some days, she's sharp as a tack, and others, she thinks we're all kids at our grandparents' house."

"That's not uncommon," Ward said. "Seems like our minds take us back to a time when we were happy."

"I think so too, but we'll just have to see how it goes. Anyhow, I'll tell you what I know, and then we'll go to see what Pearl can add."

"Good enough. So you never actually knew Virgil and Delores?"

"No, Virgil and Delores lived in Mississippi. I know they came for a visit one time, but I was too young to realize who they were at the time, and I don't really remember anything about it." She sighed as she reached into her memory and began the recitation. "There were three boys: Warren, Bobby, and Loel Messer. Warren took his family to Mississippi around 1905, and you already know, his son Virgil was born there. His brother Bobby married Katherine, and Pearl is one of their children. My grandparents, Loel and Ruth, had six children, one of them my father, Johnny. My mother was Elaine.

"Even though Pearl and I are cousins, there's still quite an age difference. I guess being the oldest, she felt it was her duty to keep up with family, so if anybody would know their whereabouts, Pearl would. But I still can't imagine why she wouldn't tell me if she knew about their returning to Florida."

She looked down at her watch. "That child will spend the day if I don't keep tabs on him. Will you excuse me for a second?"

She made a quick phone call and then waited at the door to watch Michael's return. When he was safely back, Vivian tucked him into the SUV, and we followed in our rental. To catch our flight at nine that night, we wouldn't have time to return to the beach house.

The drive to the nursing home took nearly an hour. It was nestled in an older middle-class neighborhood and, without the signs, could have passed for a larger nicely kept residence. Made of blonde brick, the house spread out over the better part of an acre and had wings that jutted out in three directions.

Previous experiences with nursing homes had braced me for the inevitable smells and sights that make us all want to die young. But this one was far better than most, and apart from the fact that wheelchairs outnumbered other types of furniture in the meeting room, I might not have known.

Pearl's room was at the end of one wing, and it was sunny and warm—too warm for those of us still ambulatory but pleasant nonetheless. And Pearl herself appeared the same. The tiny woman sat propped up on her bed, waiting for the company she'd been told was coming. Her hair was as white as Virgil's cotton, and her eyes glittered with interest as she watched the little boy who had taken a chair by the window and amused himself with a computer toy.

"Pearl's having a good day," Vivian told us and looked fondly at her cousin. "Pearl, these people are here to ask you about Virgil and Delores, and also Berniece. You remember her too, don't you?"

The eyes returned from the little boy and squinted in thought for a moment. "Yes, of course, I remember Berniece. She's old enough for school now, isn't she?"

"Pearl, Berniece is a grown woman now. She's nearly as old as I am."

Pearl smiled at her cousin. "Of course," she said and knotted her hands on her chest. "Is she coming for a visit too?"

"I'm afraid not, Pearl. But that's what these nice people are here about. They need to find Berniece, and they're hoping you can help."

"Oh? How can I help?"

Ward answered, "Ms. Pearl, we've got a bit of a mystery on our hands. Berniece just up and disappeared one day, and we don't have a clue as to where to look for her. Her parents did the same thing twenty-odd years ago, but Berniece kept telling us they were okay, so we left it alone. Figured it was family business. But with Berniece gone, there's nobody except us townsfolk to look for her. Is there family in some other place that she might have gone to see some relatives? Somebody we don't know about?"

Pearl listened to his explanation without stirring, and for a moment, I thought she'd drifted off. Then she said to Vivian, "I thought I told you about all that."

"Told me about what?"

"What these folks are asking about. Virgil and Delores."

"Pearl, if I knew about them, I wouldn't have brought the sheriff to see you. What do you know about Virgil and Delores?"

She chuckled and, with a smug smile, added, "That place they went to live."

We all looked at her, waiting for the rest of it. Vivian prodded, "What place, Pearl?"

"I don't remember where it was. I never went there. But it was one of those places where a bunch of folks go to live and share everything they have."

She placed two fingers on her lips, tapping as she thought. "A commune, that's what you call it. Now, Vivian, I know I told you about that."

Vivian's smile flickered with exasperation. "No, Pearl, I'd remember hearing about a commune. When was this?"

The old lady thought again. "Back some time in the eighties I think. I remember that because I thought it was too late to go off and be flower children." She chuckled at her own joke. "And they were way too old."

Vivian asked her cousin, "Was this commune somewhere nearby?"

"Don't think so. I wanna say it was in Tennessee. In the mountains maybe."

Vivian turned to Ward and said, "I didn't know about this. I'm sorry. If I had known this much, I could have saved you a trip."

"Don't worry," I assured her. "Now at least we've got a clue."

"Yep," Ward nodded. "This is the first solid clue we've heard in all these years. Now we at least have a place to start looking."

Pearl closed her eyes, and again I thought she was asleep. We began to make our exit, but Pearl wasn't through. "I'd go with ya'll, but I'm a little weak, you know. Good luck with finding her."

"Thank you, Ms. Pearl," Ward said and picked up her slender hand. "We'll let you know how she's doin' when we find her."

Pearl nodded and closed her eyes again. Vivian followed us into the hallway where we stopped for a moment. She whispered, "I guess she's lucid about this commune thing. Believe me, it's the first I've heard about it. Maybe they didn't talk about it because it wasn't the kind of thing my family would approve of." She shrugged. "I just don't know."

"Not your fault at all," I offered. "Besides, we came here looking for a clue, and we got one. I know about family secrets, believe me. That generation told only what they thought people needed to know."

"How true that is," she agreed.

We thanked her once again and left the home. We made our way back to the airport and, over hamburgers in the terminal, finally had time to talk. Berniece could be some place in Tennessee. The operative words there were *could* be and *some* place. Mighty big ifs in my book, but I didn't want to put a wet blanket on Ward's enthusiasm at the moment. I had help in locating Berniece, and I wasn't about to discourage him. Somewhere, Berniece existed. All I had to do was find out where.

Nicky

Antioch looked the same, but for me, it had changed forever. I could never again look at the simple buildings depicted in her work without remembering how she had painted them. I could never again understand how this little town, my ultimate haven, had been too much for Berniece. What exactly was she looking for when she left? Did she leave in the middle of the night? Why did she leave? Was it the lack of human understanding, and how did she expect that to be better anywhere else? Or maybe there was something else entirely, something I couldn't yet fathom.

Questions pestered me and wouldn't let me rest. Ward told me that he'd follow up the best he could, but he couldn't afford, financially or time-wise, to go traipsing off to Tennessee to look for who-knew-what. Without some evidence that Berniece had met with foul play, he had a greater responsibility to the people living in Antioch. I couldn't really blame him. After all, it appeared that nobody had been hurt, and nobody in the town screamed for retribution.

Still, the issue wouldn't leave me alone. I spent the better part of my first night back home on the Internet researching communes of all sorts, not only in Tennessee, but also throughout the Southeast. Apparently, Berniece wasn't the only one disenchanted with life in her little berg because more than one such place existed. Should I so choose, I could join forces with all sorts of folks, from modern-day Druids to snake-handling zealots.

Whatever Berniece was, I wasn't sure, but her attendance at the local Baptist church led me more toward the religious clans than the pagan ones. Toward what goal she expected to move I hadn't a clue, but at least I felt I was getting closer.

A few days passed while I continued my online search. I made a list of communes scattered across the country. I felt that Berniece would have gone to one nearby if possible, but I couldn't really eliminate the others yet.

Then I arranged them according to type. I put three of them at the bottom of the list since they drew a much younger enthusiast, seemingly those with a Gothic inclination.

A second group appeared a little more promising although there were still some problems. While religious in nature, they went way over and beyond the teachings and practices of the Baptist Church. These two openly favored a verbatim interpretation of Old Testament scriptures, in particular those that dictated what to eat or not eat, specific rules of dress and decorum, exacting retribution for crimes against one's neighbor, and the assignation of women to a second class.

A third group was composed of all sorts of societal dropouts that had one thing in common: hatred and distrust for any form of government, in particular the federal type. These people scared me by their warlike stance on all issues relating to government's interference in everyday life, and they openly advocated arming one's self and family for warfare should the need arise. Although secretive, they were bold enough to let the trespasser beware. Shoot first and talk later.

By this time, I had a stack of those that didn't fit anywhere else. I looked away from the computer and out the window beside where I stationed the desk. Was I so different from these refugees from society? I mean, there I was living alone in an old house on the edge of nowhere, with my closest relatives five hundred miles away. My living room, usually comforting, seemed dark, and the glow of the screen created weird shadows on the opposite wall. I got up and turned on lamps at either end of the room, but even that couldn't fill the void. Was I in my own type of commune?

I turned back to my groups that didn't fit anywhere else. What common denominators did they possess? Only one thing became apparent. Part of this group wanted out of society because they viewed it as inherently evil. Somehow, I didn't get the feeling that Berniece fit into that group. While she didn't take an active part in the goings-on of the town, I couldn't see her painting scenes from it if she viewed it as evil.

That left me with one small stack. Only two groups remained in the stack, but their identity made my heart beat faster. Neither group had any particular religious affiliation, nor did they practice rigid adherence to the mores of some ancient society. Furthermore, both appeared indifferent at best toward government. What then made these people leave their homes and band together?

The more I read, the more I knew. Testaments from these groups, along with accounts of people living in communities nearby, told time and time again of the good that these people do. They apparently did not search to take their goodwill gospel to faraway continents but chose instead to focus on small-town and rural America.

These groups, it seemed, had donated time to sit with the very sick in hospitals when no family members were available. They had made anonymous donations of school supplies to children across the South, and they had delivered food to families during times of crisis.

I read every word I could find on the Internet. These people began to sound like modern-day saints. How did they find each other? The more I read, the more something else leaped out at me. Yes, their actions proclaimed a love for their fellow man, but within the confines of their small community, they practiced a love for art.

With that news, I knew where to start looking for Berniece. Love for fellow man, albeit not shown in the traditional interactive way, coupled with her passion for art would surely be enough to make her seek those with similar passions. One group lived as close as Virginia, but the other even closer. Pearl had mentioned Tennessee, and that's where I would look first.

My computer search filled any spare time in the days after our return from Florida, and as a result, nearly a week had passed when I dropped by Ward's office on Thursday about noon.

The phone held up to one ear, he worked the keyboard of his computer with a single digit of the free hand. He motioned for me to sit down and then finished his conversation.

He put the phone down on its stand and grinned. "This must be my lucky day." Then he made a show of holding his watch in front of his face. "Could it be lunchtime?"

"That it could. And it's my time to buy."

"Uh-oh. That means you've found something and need some help."

"Are my motives that obvious?"

He rose from the desk and reached for his hat on the hook by the doorway. "No, you're not obvious, just persistent."

I let the subject rest until we'd walked down the hill to the café and found a booth in front of the window. The café was usually full at noon, but somehow, a table always waited for the sheriff. Aware that people in small towns like to gossip, I made sure that we kept our distance, and if possible, I invited Dolly to our unplanned luncheons. But this time, I wanted his undivided attention.

When Patti had delivered our iced teas, I began. I told him about the lists I'd made, my criteria, and how I'd narrowed it to two possibilities although one really. He listened the way Ward always listens—intently without change of expression. But when I finished, I could see the answer coming.

"Lila, you know I want to solve this little mystery as much as you do, but so help me, I don't have time right now."

"I understand, Ward. I really do. I was just hoping you could go because, well, you know how to talk to people. You know what questions to ask."

"I take that as a compliment, Lila, but don't underestimate your self."

"Thanks. I won't. It's just that you're such a pro at talking to people."

A sly grin played with the corners of his moustache, and he said, "Now you're rubbin' it in."

"Rubbing what in?"

"Aw, Lila, I can't let you go up there by yourself talking to folks that run away from society. What kind of a sheriff would I be to do that?"

"Now I *am* confused. You just said you couldn't go."

"Yeah, but I didn't say I couldn't send somebody with you."

"If you're not going, who is?"

"Nick. I've already talked to him about it, and he's right anxious to go up there and see those Smokey Mountains."

Patti arrived with two steaming plates and set them in front of us. When we'd thanked her and she left, I asked, "Can he go on the weekend? I mean, that's really the only time I have right now."

Ward nodded with a punch of his fork into the mound of coleslaw on his plate. "Of course, you'll have to talk to him about the rest of it. I just figured you might appreciate my paving the way."

My mouth fell open. "You know I do." In spite of my appreciation, my stomach did flip-flops. "Ward, thanks. You know what this project means to me."

"Yeah, I think I do." He ducked his head and gazed at me over the glasses perched near the end of his nose. "If you think *you* wanna know where this woman went, imagine how I feel. People in small towns don't usually just vanish. And it's happened twice to me."

"I hadn't thought of it that way."

He continued eating, and I could see that with Ward, the matter was settled. I was going out of state with Nick Reynolds. I'd been a grown-up for quite some time, and we were going on business. So why did I find it nearly impossible to utter a coherent sentence in his deputy's presence?

We finished our lunch, and I went back to the drugstore filled with plans. The weekend was only two days away, but if I pushed it, I could still make the trip. Ward had given permission to pay Nick's airfare if I could swing mine, and flying instead of driving would give us far more time once we got there to find the place and talk to people. I spent the rest of the afternoon in a sort of haze, filling prescriptions, listening to the usual chatter along with complaints, and answering questions. But by the time I closed the doors, I couldn't wait to talk to Nick.

Ward had told me to call Nick to make arrangements, and I had every intention of doing that, but my cell phone rang as I walked into my house. I didn't recognize the number, one with a prefix indicating that the call came from the Jackson area.

I hit the green bar. "Lila Dawkins?"

"Yes."

"Lila, my name is Clyde Kennedy. I hope you don't mind if I call you at home."

My mind buzzed to connect any dots. Did she say Clyde? I finally answered, "No. That's okay." Then I waited until the deep but decidedly feminine voice resumed.

"I apologize for calling like this without any introduction, but Bart Cobb gave me your name and number. We both work at the university. He said he thought you wouldn't mind."

"I see. No, I don't mind at all. How can I help you?"

She sighed audibly and then regrouped. "As I said, I hate to intrude, but Bart and I are friends. We know each other through an organization on campus, and he told me about the artist you discovered in town. You see, I teach art here, and what Bart told me piqued my interest greatly."

I still hadn't told anyone, even Bart, about the paintings stored in the church vault, so I asked, "You mean her house?"

"Yes, her house. He said it's unique. I'm wondering if you would allow me to meet you in town some place and perhaps take a look at this house. It sounds absolutely fascinating."

I flipped on lights as I walked down the hallway toward the kitchen. "I don't know, Ms. Kennedy. It's probably not my place to say. The house doesn't belong to me."

"I understand that, and I certainly appreciate your position. But Bart said he'd talk to the sheriff and get his permission."

By that time, I'd taken the remnant of a bottle of Johannesburg from the refrigerator and poured half of it into a wineglass. "Well, sure. If the sheriff says it's okay, then I'd love to show you the house."

"That would be lovely. Would this weekend be convenient for you?"

Again, my head spun with unsettled details. I wanted to go to Tennessee, but this was too good a chance to pass up. I decided that a week's delay in getting to Tennessee wouldn't hurt anything, especially since the immediate chance to bring Berniece's work to the attention of the art world was too good to pass up.

I thanked her and made arrangements to meet her at the café on Saturday for lunch. From there, I'd take her out to the Messer place. Things were happening too fast for me to soak it all in. But first, I had to make that phone call.

The glass of wine was nearly empty by the time I worked up the courage to dial the number of the Sheriff's Office. I knew that Ward had gone home and left Nick on duty for the night. That was easier than calling Nick at home. But why did I feel like a silly teenager? I had genuine business with Nick Reynolds.

The phone rang a couple of times before he answered, and I tried to be as casual as possible. We got through the introductory phase of the conversation like pros, and I plunged into my reason for calling. "Ward tells me that he's already talked to you about going to look for Berniece, but I'm touching base with you. I guess we need to make specific plans."

"As a matter of fact, I was going to call you tonight."

"Oh?"

"Yeah. When did you plan to go?"

"I was thinking next weekend. Something's come up here for tomorrow, but if you're free next Friday, we'll go then."

"Sure. That works for me. Ward's told me to take off as soon as possible, and I've got somebody covering the shop. Shouldn't be a problem."

"Great. It's a date then."

He paused and then said quickly, "Lila, could you excuse me for a second? Somebody's calling in."

I agreed, mentally kicked myself for the word choice, and then drained the remnants of the wine while I waited. When he finally came back on the line, he apologized and then said, "Lila, if you don't mind, I think we might need to get together before we go. Think we could meet?"

"Sure. That's no problem. Name it—the place and time, that is."

He suggested that we meet for lunch at the café the next day; again, I felt like a teenager making a date. *Don't be silly*, I told myself. *The man is perfectly capable of making a date should he so wish.* This was business. But business or no, I made sure that I wore my best aqua-colored linen shirt over the white slacks the next day. With my blonde hair and blue eyes, it never failed to get compliments. Truth is, I also felt it camouflaged my worst figure fault, a bottom too wide for my liking. Mom always said it was for bearing children, but at the rate I was going, I had serious doubts about that ever happening. I'd been close once, but the bitter taste still lingered.

Nick was already seated at my favorite table, in the back away from all the commotion and beneath an air conditioning vent. He stood when he saw me come in and then slid out a chair for me.

"Thanks," I said and tried to look casual. "I hope I didn't keep you waiting long."

"No, not at all."

He glanced up as Patti came to our table. She was part of what kept people coming there, with knowledge of goings-on in Antioch and her ability to embellish even the most dramatic situations. Once a knockout beauty, Patti retained good looks even well into her fifties, but woe be to the man who suggested as much. "You wanna talk about that?" She'd quip. "You'll have to see Jimbo."

And Jimbo was a man that nobody wanted to take on. In his earlier years, he'd played college ball in the state and then gone on to a brief career in the NFL, shortened by a crushing knee injury. He was a giant of a man, and I always suspected that at the auto dealership in Hattiesburg, what his former reputation as a defensive lineman didn't accomplish in persuasion, his size would.

"What's on the grill today?" Nick asked.

Lunch with Ward usually included something fried, and it hadn't occurred to me that the café also offered grilled food. She told him about the special, a hamburger steak with salad, and I ordered the same. Patti left, and we looked at each other and grinned not unlike a couple of kids on a first date.

"Thanks for meeting me," he said and sat back. "I really prefer making plans in person. Things get too easily mixed up on the phone."

"Oh, glad to do it. I agree."

"Besides, I wanted to see you."

I tried the casual answer and lobbed back, "Thanks. Good to see you too." But my ears burned, and I suspected he could see the tinge from across the table.

"Well, that didn't exactly come out like I intended, but the truth's out now. I did want to see you. Antioch's not exactly a swinging place, but you must realize what a storm you've created around here."

Now he had my attention. "I'm not aware of anything except that people here have really been nice to me."

He laughed aloud this time. "That's not exactly what I'm talking about, but humility is a virtue. The few times we've seen each other, we didn't have much chance to talk."

I concentrated on stirring my glass of tea and said without looking up, "Yes, I know. And I appreciate your making this trip with me."

"Glad to do it."

"I'm not sure why I'm so intent on finding Berniece except that I think her art is rather spectacular. And of course, there's the painting she did of me."

"You're kidding! She painted you?"

"I thought you knew." I told him about the painting from my kitchen. "And it's not just that one work. All of her art touches me. It's passionate. I don't know how else to say it."

His eyes lost some of the mirth, and serious, I realized that he was even more handsome.

"There's nothing wrong with passion, Lila."

I nodded. "As long as it's for the right reasons."

"Of course. I'm talking about the passionate people who make the world a better place. The Albert Schweitzers of the world are passionate, and so are the Flannery O'Connors."

"I feel the same way. And Berniece was passionate about her art. It's obvious. And that's what I can't figure out. From her painting, I can tell that she loved Antioch and its people. So why would she go off without even telling anybody where she went?"

"That does seem to be the question, doesn't it?"

I agreed, and he continued, "So Ward tells me that you've found a commune for artists in Tennessee. Sounds to me like Berniece would be a perfect fit."

"That's what I thought. There's another factor, too. This group of artists does a lot of community work. Now I never knew Berniece, but from what I've seen, she'd fit right in. Anyway, it's a guess."

"Your guess is as good as anybody's. Ward told me he'd cover Saturday and Sunday, so if we can find her in a couple of days, maybe we can straighten some things out. I'm betting she never thought anybody would miss her, so she just left."

"You're probably right. I mean, I'm moving ahead with this project as if it's my own work. But I have a feeling Berniece might see things a little differently."

"Could be. Unfortunately, nobody knows enough about her to say."

"Yeah, and that's too bad, isn't it?"

"Especially since she lived her whole life around this town."

"Sometimes it happens," I said. "That road goes both ways, you know."

He nodded. "Well, at any rate, we'll give it a try. If we haven't found her in a couple of days, she's probably not there anyhow. I figured we'd rent a car in Knoxville and drive up to the mountains."

"I suspect that's the only way to get to the commune."

"Pretty remote?"

"Looks like it. But there is a town close by. At least we know there are roads leading to it."

He studied my face for a moment and then asked, "What do you plan to do if we find Berniece?"

I'd asked myself the same question more than once. "Talk to her. Ask her why she left like she did. And ask her how she came to know my face long before I moved to Antioch. And of course, ask permission to show her work, preferably back in Antioch. After all, it's her own hometown."

"You know we can't force her to talk to us."

"Yes, I know. But we can still ask."

"As long as you realize she may not be too generous with answers. For Ward and me, it would close the books. I know it still bothers him that he never found her parents. I think solving that one would mean a lot to him."

"Nick, do you think she'd confide in you? I mean, your father must have treated her family too."

"Sure. My father probably treated everybody in town at one time or another. But that doesn't mean she'd confide in me. Do you plan to ask her to come back?"

"I'm not sure. All I know is that before I can arrange a showing of her work, I have to at least try to get her permission. And hopefully her approval."

"I wouldn't count on that part. If she hasn't shared her work with anybody in the town all these years, I can't see her showing it to strangers."

"You're probably right. But I have to try."

"I understand. I just wanted to know what you had in mind. We'll fly into Knoxville then and take it from there. Stay wherever the road leads us. Sound okay?"

Suddenly my throat constricted. I hadn't thought about that part of it. My mouth worked on an answer, but all that came out was a sort of grunt.

We finished our lunch, and Nick left to make arrangements for the car. I'd buy my own airline ticket online since I still didn't want anybody to think I was freeloading on the county or the town. And I certainly didn't want to start the rumor mill.

In little more than a week, I was flying off to a commune for artists somewhere in the mountains of Tennessee with a man whose eyes drew me in like a bass to a lure. And I'd had a grand total of one lunch with him. In the meanwhile, I had an appointment the very next day with a woman who could make Berniece a celebrity in the world of art. And considering that we didn't even know if Berniece *wanted* to become a celebrity, my finding her was all the more imperative.

Clyde

She was easy to spot in the Saturday lunch crowd, a mixture of farmers taking the day off and a few strangers enjoying their weekends away from the city. Antioch hadn't yet become the bedroom community for Hattiesburg and Jackson that some nearby towns had, but it would happen. As they shared the café's offerings with locals, they stood out like beacons in a fog.

I was sure that Patti had placed Clyde there in the booth at the window so I could see her when I crossed the street, but I also suspected that she'd put her there for the rest of the town to see too. Patti thrived on creating interest. The former owners had hardly put the sale sign in the window before Patti was in there haggling over price, and she hadn't looked back.

Clyde Kennedy was what Southerners used to call a handsome woman, with gray hair the color of seed clouds pulled tightly to the back of her head in a bun. The result, rather than hardening her features, simply emphasized a huge pair of soft brown eyes that appeared to see into the life of things. She was thin although not gaunt and her hands moved like graceful monarchs as they flitted over her glass of iced tea, emptying pink packets into the glass and stirring the dark liquid.

I entered the café and walked straight to her booth. She was already looking up at me when I asked, "Ms. Kennedy?"

The face softened, and we introduced ourselves as I sat down across from her.

"Thanks for meeting me," she began.

"I'm quite glad to do it. And the thanks should go to you. I appreciate your making the trip, especially on your weekend. I think Berniece's work is special, but having an expert confirm my opinion will help."

"I don't know how much of an expert I am, but I am always interested in new talent. Can you describe her work?"

"Most of what I've seen is watercolors. She paints people and scenes from the town, but she does them in a style that's different. It's not really what I'd call folk art, but it's not impressionistic or wholly realistic either."

"I can tell you this much already. Watercolors for the subject matter you've mentioned is a bit unusual in itself."

"Oh?"

"Most prefer oil or acrylic mediums. When Bart told me this woman painted watercolors, I couldn't resist. You see, I've spent a lifetime working with them, so I can't resist the temptation to see what someone with no training has done. I guess, truth be told, we art teachers live our lives in search of one truly great talent."

"That surprises me a bit."

"Oh? It shouldn't. We're teachers, Lila, and any success of the student reflects on the teacher, or so they say."

I had to smile at that. This independent woman hardly needed a student's success to assure her worth, but that touch of humility engaged me. "In that case, why don't we order lunch so you can go to see for yourself?"

By the time we turned onto Jordan Road, Clyde and I had become friends. We discovered that we shared a love for impressionism, purple irises, classical music, and of all things, for football. The last was a fact that I kept stashed away unless somebody asked. It was purely by coincidence that we broached the subject, but when this refined woman mentioned in passing a local legend in that sport, I ventured forth. Before long, we had discussed not only the state's prospects for the upcoming season but also much of the National Football League.

I turned onto the drive off Jordan Road and asked her, "What is it that makes people like you and me who abhor violence love such a violent sport?"

"Passion, my dear. One must be quite passionate to throw his body about with such abandon, don't you think?"

"That makes sense. We just avenue our passion in a different direction."

"Exactly. And passion also accounts for my parents' odd choice of names for their daughter. You've shown great restraint in not asking. People usually do by this time."

I couldn't help smiling because I'd wanted badly to do so. "I must admit that I've never known a woman with that particular name. I figured it was family."

"Oh, it is," she said laughing, "but not like you might think. You see, I was one of those honeymoon babies, and my parents chose to spend theirs in a wonderful old resort on the Alabama coast called the Clyde."

I laughed out loud, and she quipped back, "All these years I've been grateful only that they didn't choose to spend their honeymoon in Memphis at the Peabody. Things can always be worse, Lila."

"How true, how true," I said between giggles. "I've always suspected that my mom had seen too many reruns of old Southern movies."

"So there you go. By the same token, you could easily be Prissy now, couldn't you?"

"I never thought of it that way. But you're right."

I slowed the car and stopped at the rickety gate in front of Berniece's house. Ward had gone out to make the doorway passable for us, but the whole house still looked forlorn and lost from the outside. Even the once pristine paint peeled in spots near the roof.

"Ready to go in?" I asked.

"Quite. Let's see this undiscovered talent, shall we?"

I slid the key into the padlock attached to the frame of the door and stepped back into the house where I'd seen something miraculous. Then I stood to the side to let Clyde enter. Speechless, she remained in the doorway as her eyes took in the room.

When I closed the door behind us, the noise seemed to bring her back to the moment. "Oh my goodness," she breathed. "You were right indeed. This is extraordinary. I've never seen anything quite like it."

She eased her way around the room as if sudden movement or noise might make the illusion disappear. Although I'd seen it before, I followed behind with a new reverence. Like a great work of literature, it required more than one reading. When she'd made her way around the little living room, I suggested, "There's more, if you'd like to see it."

I led her down the wooden hallway, dark without the presence of any windows. Its coolness reminded me of the old root cellar at my grandmother's house. It was never used in my lifetime, but I'd often hide out there for hours engrossed in imaginary games, and I could imagine Berniece as a child doing the same in that very house.

When we entered the bedroom, afternoon sun streamed through the windows that flanked the chimney and its angel, creating a sort of halo around her. Nothing had diminished its effect on me, and I held my breath. Once again, I looked back into those blue, blue eyes. Once again, I all but felt her pulse quickening through the painted angel.

Clyde took her place beside me, shaking her head and muttering again and again, "Such beauty. Such talent." She edged toward the wall and extended her fingers to lightly touch the angel's robe. "I expected it to be fabric. She looks positively alive. I haven't seen anything this exceptional in many years."

"I'm glad you think so," I admitted. "It's passionate for sure, don't you think?"

"Indeed. And quite beautiful." She moved in to examine details. "Such brushwork on this difficult surface. What could she have done with proper paints and canvas? And training. It boggles my mind."

My memory jogged for a moment, and I thought about telling Clyde of the cache hidden in the church. But I'd made a promise to Brother Sciple, and until I spoke with the artist herself, I would keep it. What I finally said was, "Who knows? Talent like this can't be denied by lack of tools. Even cavemen drew on whatever was handy, didn't they?"

"That they did. But this is far beyond what I expected. It shows a quality I've not seen very often."

"I'm so glad you think so. That only makes me more determined to find her. To convince her to share this with the world."

Clyde turned to face me, an obvious question on her face. "You don't intend to show her work unless you can locate her?"

"No, I don't. It wouldn't be fair. After all, Berniece created all this without a word to anybody else. She obviously never expected anybody to find it, much less to make it public. That's why I'm so intent on finding her and trying to convince her to let me show it."

"I see. Is there anything I can do to help?" She turned back to the wall once more, shaking her head. "Lila, I hope you find this lady soon. I feel as if I've discovered the treasure of the Sierra Madre, but I can't bring the gold out until you locate this woman."

"I know what you mean. Believe me, I'll do my best. We found a clue that she may be living in a commune in Tennessee with a group of other artists. I'm going up there next weekend, and I'll give you a call as soon as I find out anything."

"I'd appreciate that," she said turning around. "Now let's go back through the house again if you don't mind."

Charity

Framed and back hanging on my kitchen wall, my portrait haunted me like a good ghost. On the first morning it hung there, it startled me a bit when I walked in to make my coffee, but since then, I've come to look forward to these daily encounters. Seeing my own face mixed with other churchgoers, some recognizable now, never failed to produce a smile. As I left the house that morning to make the drive to the airport in Jackson, I took the initiative.

"Good morning, Lila's twin. I'm leaving now, but I'll be back Sunday. You go on to church now."

I sincerely hoped that no one ever overheard those one-way conversations. But I was off to look for the author of this mystery, and nothing could deter my enthusiasm. Nick drove us to the airport in Jackson, and after we drank coffee, made our purchases in the airport bookshop, and went through security, Nick Reynolds and I were alone on a plane with a hundred or so strangers for the next ninety minutes.

We talked some in a politely conservative way and then turned attention to our respective books. He pushed his seat back and soon appeared engrossed while I tried to concentrate. My eyes scanned the words, and I turned the pages, but the mystery I'd chosen remained just that. Nick had left the uniform behind, and for all the world, we could have been any happy couple off for a weekend in the mountains. His nearness intrigued me far more than the book did.

Once on the ground, we packed our two suitcases into the rental car and headed northeast, away from the log cabins, souvenir shops, and restaurants that dotted every crook and cranny of the Great Smokey Mountain National Park and into the heart of the Appalachians, to a place called Charity. My research told me that the founders had given it that name in the sincere belief that charity begins at home, a philosophy corresponding to their own.

Of course, I always thought that the adage meant first we should do good to those close to us, and the rest would follow naturally. I guess that's what they thought too, but having found so much need at home, they never tried to take their mission farther afield.

Nick took the first turn driving, giving me the chance to fill him in. By the time we reached the little town of Greenville, I had told Nick everything I knew about the commune, and I had repeated the highlights of my conversations with Clyde.

In spite of my careful planning, it wasn't long before we came to a four-way stop at a crossroad that I couldn't find on the map, and I was puzzled. My research indicated that the nearest town to Charity was a place called Liberty, but the road that I thought would lead us in that direction was blocked off with barriers. A detour sign pointed us toward Mt. Carmel, away from where we needed to be.

Unlike the old joke about men who never stop for directions, Nick suggested that we go into the log building housing a combination grocery store and gas station to do just that. He wandered off in search of a restroom while I waited in the doorway for a moment, letting my eyes adjust. Outside, the day was brilliant, but little sunlight penetrated into the store's interior, where concrete floors had soaked up the smells of cheese hoops and gasoline. The air felt cool and damp in contrast with the day outside.

An older woman that I hadn't seen at first stood up behind the counter and smiled my way. Gray hair mingled with a dirty brown curled wildly around her wrinkled face while a blue plaid shirt fell loosely on the toothpick frame covered in front by a bright red apron.

"Can I help you, honey?"

I told her that we were looking for a commune called Charity. The eyes, once wary, softened, and she answered, "You're headed the right way, but you're gonna have to go around a bit to get there."

"You mean the detour sign?"

"Yeah. That's right. Bridge over the creek's out 'bout a mile up ahead. But I can tell you a quicker way to get there anyhow." Visions of wandering the hills in darkness flitted through my head, but still I listened. "You see, honey, they put that detour sign up for folks that don't have no need to go up to Charity. But since that's where you're aimin' to go, I'll just tell you the quick way."

"Thank you. That'd be nice." Again I listened.

"You see, the detour's gonna take you all the way up to Limestone, but you don't need to go that far. So here's what you do. Go right on by that sign they got across the road. Don't pay it no mind. Like I said, it's just there for tourists passin' through."

"Yes, ma'am."

"Once you pass that sign, you just keep goin on until you get to a road on the right that's called Old Tusculum Road. Turn right there. It's a little bit rough, but trust me, it'll get you there."

"Okay. I'm with you so far. What then?"

"Well, you just follow that road till it gets to another one called Howard Pickens Road. It'll be on the left. Turn there, and it'll take you right up to Liberty. And once you get to Liberty, anybody around there can tell you how to get to Charity."

I thanked her profusely and went back to the car where Nick was waiting. We had agreed to share driving duties, so I took my turn behind the wheel. "I think I know how to get there."

"You think?" he asked.

"Well, I'm pretty sure the directions were good, but I'm not sure about the roads. If a local says it's rough, it probably is. But the alternative is going about thirty miles out of the way. Whadda you think?"

"I'm with you, Lila. Drive on."

Her directions proved to be good, but her estimate of the road was seriously underrated, and it wasn't long before I understood the brief life expectations of a rental car. Old Tusculum Road was paved but narrow and rough. Then we turned onto Howard Pickens. What at first was a broad expanse of finely leveled gravel soon morphed into a dusty washboard that went straight up the side of a mountain. Too late to turn around, I pushed the rental toward the top. Although it wasn't much as mountains go, it still offered a splendid view of the tiny town of Liberty nestled in the valley below.

From our vantage point, we could see the highway that normally cuts through the town, nearly empty now. Older houses lined the road on either side and eventually gave way to a scant gathering of small businesses around a tiny square. Only a few streets led away from the main one, each with its own smattering of houses and trailers arranged in no apparent order. Some faced the street while others were arranged at odd angles and distances from each other.

"That must be Liberty," I said. I momentarily relaxed my death grip on the steering wheel and dared to look down the steep dirt road in front of us. "And this looks like the only way to get there. Do you think we should try it?"

"I'm with you, Lila."

"Hang on then," I said and eased my foot off the brake. The road going up had been rough, but at least I'd felt somewhat in control. Going down proved to be another matter. Ruts crossed the roadway in haphazard patterns and came at us from nowhere. I swerved in one direction then the other until our descent felt like a ride at the fair. Maintaining a death grip on the steering wheel, I kept going jolt after jolt until the car, along with my stomach, finally leveled off at the bottom of the hill.

I planted my foot on the brake, let out the breath I'd held for most of the journey down, and dared look across at Nick. His right hand still gripped the support over the passenger door while his left was planted around that knee. For a long moment, he remained motionless as if waiting for the next jolt. The facial muscles began to relax, and I could see the corners of his mouth turn slightly upward as his fingers unwound from the support. Shaking his head, Nick sighed, "Ride 'em, cowgirl. That was some show."

"Sorry," I said, my own voice breaking into laughter too.

"Nothing to be sorry for. We're here, aren't we?"

"That we are. But now, I can't wait to see how we get to Charity."

The red brick building where we stopped boasted a State Farm sign over the doorway, but it appeared also to be a residence. It was Nick's turn to ask, so after we parked in the short driveway, I got out to stretch my legs. I'd no sooner closed the car door than I heard a sort of a snort apparently coming from the bushes that lined the driveway.

Was I being attacked? I backed toward the car, keeping my eyes on the bushes. They rustled, and I reached for the door. Then a head appeared, followed by the squat pinkish body of a pig. I didn't know much about pigs, but this one didn't appear to be the type likely to be served up for breakfast. The pig made more grunting sounds as it waddled toward me.

"Well, hello," I said to the pig uncertainly and leaned closer. "Where'd you come from?"

I'm not sure if I expected an answer, but before further conversation with the pig could continue, the front door opened, and a tall, thin bearded man came out onto the porch. "Nellie! So that's where you are," he called out and started toward the pig and me.

Nick followed him out of the house while the pig scooted through the grass, grunting merrily toward its owner's outreached hand. "I told you not to leave the yard," the man scolded. The pig flopped down on the ground as the man stooped over it, scratched its head, and then stood up again. He started to offer a handshake, and then thought better of it. "Sorry," he said. "Old Nellie here's quite clean, but most folks don't know that."

"Nellie?" I asked.

"Yes. Nellie Bly." He looked fondly at the pig as it stared up in rapt attention. "You familiar with that story?"

"Sort of," I said. "Wasn't she a reporter?"

"She was indeed. The first woman investigative reporter. Most folks don't know that. She was quite a spunky woman, too. This little pig had a rough start to her life—almost became somebody's bacon. Then I took her in, and she sorta saved my life too. I fell down the steps out back, broke my leg real bad. Old Nellie took off to the neighbors' house, squealing till they came over to see what was going on. Turn about's fair play, I guess."

I looked at Nellie with new respect. "I'd have to say you're right."

He shrugged and then added, "Anyway, I'm Trey Fisher." He looked at Nick. "Your husband here was tellin' me you're lookin' for Charity."

I stammered, "Yes, yes. We're looking for someone there. A friend."

"Friends are the only folks who come here."

The man's white beard bobbed in the sunlight as he talked. "You're in the right place. I don't know many of the folks up there, but I'm sure they'll introduce you around."

"Up there?" I asked.

"Yep." He turned and pointed toward a mountain opposite the one we'd just ridden down. "See that clearin' up at the top?"

Nick and I followed his hand to the indicated clearing where a thin waft of smoke lazed around the mountain's peak. "Is that Charity?" I asked.

"That'd be it."

"Is there a road leading up there?" Nick asked.

"You can follow a road about halfway up, but it's all by foot from there."

My stomach tightened as I added, "No wonder only friends go up there."

Trey's blue eyes glittered with humor. "Helps keep out the riffraff. That's for sure."

We thanked Trey, scratched the appreciative pig's head, and got back into the car. Trey had told us about a town a few miles away called Erwin. It was larger than Liberty and had a motel or two, so we decided to give it a try. Otherwise, the nearest string of motels lay along the major highway we'd come in on, but there was no way I was going back up and down the same mountain. And there was no way either of us was going to hike up a different mountain to get to Charity, at least not in the dark. Erwin seemed the logical choice—especially considering whom we found there.

Erwin

The little town was surprisingly alive with traffic. Both of us voiced conjectures about the cause of such, and by the time the third motel turned us away, we decided that tourist season must reach up this far from the Smokies.

By that time, my disappointment was coupled with even greater tiredness. My bones ached, and I wanted a hot shower and at least a semicomfortable bed. And I didn't want to drive into North Carolina to get either one.

At the last desk, I finally asked, "Is there any place else nearby?"

"There is a bed and breakfast just out of town, but Paul's probably full up too. Would you like for me to call him?"

"If Paul's the proprietor of the inn, yes. Yes, I would."

We waited while the conversation took place. It seemed that two of his guests had left early because of a crisis at home, and he'd be glad to rent the room to us.

"Room?" I asked.

The manager watched us as we exchanged questioning looks. "The room has a private bath and a deck area," he added.

I felt Nick's eyes on me as I asked, "About how far is the nearest motel?"

"Either in Johnson City or maybe Elizabethton. Either way, you're lookin' at thirty, forty miles. Of course, there's a shorter route through the mountains."

"That's okay. We've had enough of the scenic route for today," I added. "Would you mind calling the proprietor to let him know we'll be there in a few minutes?"

Neither of us spoke until we got back into the car. I backed the car away from the office, keeping my eyes well away from his. "I hope you don't mind," I said. "We'll figure out something. I just couldn't go any further tonight."

"Mind?"

"Well, that's pretty pushy of me to accept the room without consulting you. It seemed like our best choice."

"If anybody should mind, it's you. You're the one about to share a room with a world-class snorer."

I laughed at his way of excusing an awkward situation and vowed that we'd figure out something we could both live with once we got to the inn. However, the situation soon went from awkward to bordering on bizarre.

Paul Cranley waited for us on the front porch of the big Victorian house, and he wasn't alone. Rocking chairs lined the roomy front porch, and in each one, a happy septuagenarian rocked away. The house was nearly in darkness, but nothing dampened the spirits of the rockers. All eyes were on us as we got out of the car and went toward the house.

"Why do I feel like a kid on a date?" Nick whispered.

"Same reason I do. We *are* kids compared to these folks."

"You must be the people who called from the motel," Paul said as he stood up to greet us. Tall and lanky, he was no youngster himself, but still he had at least a decade before he reached the age of his guests rocking on the porch, and he moved with the ease of an outdoorsman. "Come on in, and we'll get you settled."

"You guys have fun," he said waving to the couple nearest the door. "I'll be back in a while."

They offered their versions of hurry back, and Paul escorted us into the house. Furnishings in the living room were all period but looked surprisingly new, and a large screen television occupied most of the opposite wall.

"Had supper?" Paul turned in the hallway to ask.

"No, but that's okay," I answered truthfully and then remembered Nick. "Unless of course, it's no trouble."

"It's no trouble," Paul countered. "I think my wife's got some of her beef stew left. That sound okay?"

"More than okay," Nick answered.

We made a date to meet him in the kitchen once we'd settled into the room, and we followed our host through to the back of the house and into what looked like an addition.

"We built this addition," he said as he flipped on the light, "when my wife's mother came to live with us. She couldn't take the stairs, so we added this on. Hope it's okay with you folks."

Nick and I both assured him that it would be more than adequate, especially the small deck adjoining the bedroom area. Then Paul said, "Good enough, then. When you folks are ready, just come on into the kitchen, and I'll fix you up some stew, and we'll get the paperwork done."

We both thanked him again and watched the door close behind him. Finally alone, I couldn't hold back the laughter any longer, and I fell over onto the tall plump bed, my hand held firmly over my mouth lest the whole house hear me.

Nick remained by the door as his eyes took in the entire room and then settled on me. "Lila, you may be the cause of my downfall."

"Me?"

"Yeah. I may have to start drinking again."

That comment sent me into throes of laughter again, and I struggled to keep it quiet. Nick finally sat down beside me, his eyes still scanning the room. The walls were covered in a dainty lilac pattern, in and of itself not so bad. But together with the curtains of a correlating flower, a comforter made to match with lots of frilly pillows, and even a row of silk lilacs bedecking the latticework that outlined the doorway onto the deck, I felt as if we'd entered into a lilac nightmare.

"I never saw so much purple," I managed. "I didn't even know there was this much purple in the world."

"Yeah. Kinda makes you wonder, doesn't it?"

"Wonder what?"

"Whether the old lady died of natural causes or got flowered to death."

"Stop it!" I rolled back on the bed and hid my face in the stash of pillows. I was determined that these nice people not be offended, but what were they thinking? I finally sat up and reached for a tissue, in a lilac covered box of course. The reality of the situation was that Paul had assumed Nick and me to be a couple. And in a very few minutes, we'd have to face him and explain how we were going to handle what he would no doubt consider a very delicate situation in that part of the world.

"So. What do we tell him?" I asked.

"How 'bout the truth?"

"Oh, I don't know, Nick. This isn't Atlanta."

He looked around the room again. "You can say that again."

We decided that honesty was our best course, and once explained to him, Paul had an answer. "The weather's still cool at night," he began. "And that deck's got a real nice lounger on it."

Nick took the hint and offered to spend his night gazing at the stars while I lounged in lilac comfort.

Business attended, Paul dished up his wife's famous beef stew. Debbie had retired early to their private quarters, so the three of us sat down at the kitchen table. One spoonful and I knew Debbie could cook. I longed for some wine or other appropriate spirit, but a look around the kitchen kept me from asking. The walls were filled with various versions of biblical quotes, from embroidery to varnished plaques. And most of them pronounced the virtues of sobriety.

"This is quite good," I told him, and Nick followed suit. "Thanks so much for feeding us too. You didn't have to do this."

"Can't let our guests go hungry," he said.

"Well, whatever, we appreciate it. It's been a long day."

Paul asked, "You two on business, then?"

Nick nodded. "Yes. I'm with the sheriff's department in Antioch, Mississippi. We came up here looking for somebody who disappeared from our town, and we think she may be close by."

His interest piqued, Paul asked, "That so? You mean around Erwin?"

"No, actually we think she may have gone to live in the commune up on the mountain."

His brows raised. "Charity? You think this person's living in Charity?"

I told him, "I did some research on the commune, and the person we're looking for is an artist. It would make sense if she's gone there."

"Well, I'll be," Paul said, shaking his head. "How 'bout that."

Nick stopped eating and studied our host. "Are you familiar with the commune?"

"That I am. I used to live there."

"You did! When was that?" I asked.

"Oh, it's been a while now. Back in the late sixties. But I only stayed there for a couple of years till I figured out what it was I wanted to do with my life."

"So you're an artist?" Nick asked.

"That depends on your definition. If woodworking is art, then I might qualify. I had all sorts of visions about making furniture by hand. Beautiful stuff that people would pass down from generation to generation."

"Sounds wonderful," I admitted. "What happened?"

"Same thing that probably stops most folks' dreams. Reality. I fell in love about that time, and I couldn't propose to Debbie until I could offer her some way of making a living. I figured it'd be years before folks knew my work well enough to pay me enough to support a family. So I got a job over in Asheville at a resort. I took care of the grounds there for thirty years.

Pay was real good, and my family had a real pretty place to live—everything they needed. When I retired, we bought this old house and fixed it up."

"Have you ever made furniture like you wanted?"

"That I have. Come on out to the shop tomorrow, and I'll show you. I only do a piece at a time, you know, on commission, so I don't have much around at one time. But I'd love to show you what I've got."

"And we'd love to see it," I assured him.

Nick agreed and then asked, "Paul, you said you were at Charity back in the sixties?"

"Yep. Guess I was a bit of a flower child."

I realized where Nick was headed as he asked, "Do you remember some of the people you lived with there?"

"Sure. You don't ever forget people like those. We were close as any family. Huh! Closer these days."

"I'll bet." Nick continued, "Were there by any chance some people by the last name of Messer?"

Again his brows raised. "Sure were—Virgil and Delores. That's right—you're from Mississippi, too. It's been so many years, I didn't even think about that."

"You knew Virgil and Delores Messer?"

"Sure I did. We all knew each other." I watched Paul's face as he inventoried. "Good grief. It's been a long, long time. I haven't thought about them for years. Did you know the Messers?"

"We don't know them," Nick said, "but we do know their daughter, Berniece."

"They had a daughter?"

"Yes, and we think she may have gone to live in Charity."

"Well, I'll be," he said again. "Is she an artist?"

"Very much so," I told him. "Unfortunately, we didn't find that out until she was already gone."

Nick asked, "Do you think Virgil and Delores could still be up there?"

"Afraid not," he said sadly. "They both died not too long after they got to Charity."

My heart sank as I asked, "Died? From what?"

"Folks in the commune said he had cancer when they came there. And it seemed like she just didn't want to live after he was gone. Knowing what I know now, it was probably her heart, but you know how kids are. It made a better story if she pined away."

"How sad," I said. Then it occurred to me to ask the question that I should have asked long before. "What type of art did they do?"

"He was a writer. Wrote some really good stuff too not like all that rebel crap we used to do. He wrote some novels, or at least one that I know of. We all tried to get him to work on getting published, but he said he wasn't ready. Then he up and died. I'm pretty sure Delores said she mailed some stuff to some relative."

Nick and I looked at each other. "Florida?" I asked.

He nodded. "Yeah, come to think of it. I think it was Florida. I haven't thought about all that stuff for so long, but I'm pretty sure that's what she said. Does that mean anything to you?"

"Yes, it could," I added. "We talked to some cousins near Tallahassee, but they didn't mention anything about letters. Certainly not a manuscript. But then the cousin who was closest to them is quite elderly, and she may have forgotten. We'll check back with her."

Nick added, "Anything else you think of might help us find Berniece."

"Sure thing. I'll work on it. But I didn't know they had a daughter. You said she just disappeared?"

"Yes. Virgil and Delores did the same thing back then. They all left without a word to anybody, and until now, nobody in the town knew where they'd gone. We'd just like to find their daughter, make sure she's all right, and close the books on her disappearance. You've already told us enough to close the books on her parents."

"There is more," I added. "Berniece left behind a whole treasury of her artwork, and I want to find her to get permission to show it."

"She's good, then?"

"Very." I looked at Nick. "And there's one other thing. Call it coincidence or whatever, but I moved to Antioch not too long ago, and I found one of Berniece's paintings in my house. That painting had my face in it. I'd like to know how she did that."

"I'll bet you would," Paul said.

For long seconds, the three of us said nothing, each savoring our own thoughts until Nick asked, "Paul, are Virgil and Delores buried around here?"

"As a matter of fact, I think they were. In a little cemetery out between Liberty and Erwin next to a church. Pretty place with all the mountains around it."

"Did any family come?"

"No, and that's why I was so surprised to hear they had a daughter."

"Who paid for the funerals?"

"Don't know that either. I always assumed Virgil had some money stashed away, but I don't know for sure."

"Well, it doesn't really matter," Nick said, pushing his chair away from the table. "Paul, thanks for everything. It's getting late, and we've taken up enough of your time. You've been a great help."

I agreed with Nick and started taking the dishes off the table, but Paul stopped me. "Leave those be," he told me. "I'll take care of it. You folks have a big day tomorrow."

A Test of Faith

In spite of my protests, Nick attempted to keep his word of sleeping on the deck. But around midnight, when I was sure that the entire house was deep under the influence, I crept outside where Nick was lying wide awake, staring up at the sky.

"Hey," I said, "let's don't be ridiculous. There's a perfectly good bed in there, and in the dark, you can't see the flowers."

"You think?"

"I know. Now come on inside. I promise I won't attack you."

We kidded through the next awkward minutes, but before long, Nick fell asleep by my side on top of the lilac comforter although I had yet to hear the first inkling of a snore. I'd slept through the first part of the evening, but as I lay listening to his breathing even into a regular pattern, I found myself more awake than ever. By the time first light seeped into the flowered room, I was up and ready to go.

I told Nick that I'd wait downstairs for him and went to meet my fellow guests. They greeted me as heartily as the breakfast they were consuming in the dining room. Waffles smothered in blueberries, crispy bacon, tons of scrambled eggs, and coffee that could have come from New Orleans. Suddenly, I was hungry and took my place at the table.

Introductions began. The couple across from me was from Birmingham. Another was from Biloxi, and the third, a pair of elderly ladies, said their home was in Florida, but they spent most of their time now in the mountains.

"We're halfbacks," Susan told me with a gleam in her eye.

"Halfbacks?"

"Yes. You see, after our husbands died in a few years ago, we moved from New Jersey to Florida. But the climate's so dreadful there in the summer, we're moving back up here to the mountains. Halfway back, you see."

"Oh, I get it. Is that what natives of the mountains call outsiders?"

She chuckled and pursed her mouth into a secretive smile. "They think we don't know, but we do."

"Then I guess it isn't derogatory."

"Don't care if it is. We're staying."

Before I could pursue that conversation further, Nick entered, and the introductions began anew. We finished our breakfast and prepared to leave, but not before Paul remembered his promise of the night before.

I'd just put my suitcase into the car when he came out onto the porch. "Nick, you two have time to see my shop?"

Of course we did. His shop was behind the house a good hundred yards, sheltered by a copse of sweet gums and dogwoods. Originally a barn, the shop was large enough to accommodate tractors, horses, and anything else that the farmer might need. But what Paul had inside was far more exciting to me.

Neatly stacked shelves on both sides of the barn held wood in assorted sizes and types. A tack room had been converted to hold a variety of saws, everything from handheld ones to a router, table saw, and one I couldn't identify. Everything was pristine in appearance, but the scent of sawdust said that he used them frequently.

He proudly showed us through each phase of his woodworking, saving the best for last. He unlocked the last door on the right where an air conditioner hummed loudly. "This is where I put the finished products," he said and flicked the light switch beside the door.

Only two finished products occupied the room, but they were adequate to take my breath away. He walked toward the large oval table in the center of the room. It would seat ten or twelve people with ease. Its warm wood was the color of honey with streaks rippling through that reminded me of sand dunes, natural and dramatic at the same time.

"May I touch it?" I asked.

"Sure. You can't hurt good wood by touching it."

Nick joined us, asking, "Is this maple?"

"Yep. Got that piece from Vermont."

I lightly slid my fingers over the surface and then backed away until I could see the twin pedestals at either end. Formed like tree trunks, larger at the bottom and separating into facsimiles of branches for support beneath the table at the base, they resembled roots ending in gnarled fists.

"I've never seen anything like this," I said honestly. "It's absolutely gorgeous. Will you make chairs to go with it?"

He laughed. "Eventually, but we're a long way from that. The owners are still deciding exactly what they want. It'll probably be some sort of upholstered chair with a basic wooden frame. You know how folks in Asheville are." I must have looked puzzled because he continued. "Got more money than anything else. As long as nobody else has one like it, that's what they want." He turned toward the other object. "Suits me."

The second object was such a contrast that I had to adjust my thinking. More Asian in configuration than anything else, the curio was tall and slender where the table was sturdy. Graceful curves at corners added to the impression of elegance.

"What type of wood is this? It's different. So beautiful."

"Oh yes, it's different all right. That's black walnut. I had a hard time finding that one."

"Did the same people order this?" I asked.

"Nope. That one's for a lady in Atlanta. She's got a bunch of antique vases, and she wants to show them off in that curio."

Nick said, "You must be acquiring quite a reputation."

"Not really. I knew this lady from Asheville too."

"Your work is amazing," Nick admitted. "I wish we could see more of it."

"Any time. Any time you're up this way, come on in. I love showing my furniture, especially to folks who appreciate it."

I wondered how long that might be before we found our way there again, but I simply thanked this kind man for sharing his home and his work with two strangers. And as we rode toward Charity, I couldn't help wondering if all mountain people were like Paul. Whatever the answer to that question, we seemed to be batting above average so far, and we had yet to meet the residents of Charity.

We started up the mountain late in the morning. The road was rocky and narrow, but it would take us fairly close to the commune. I'd surrendered driving duties to Nick because I wanted the chance to look at the scenery. The hillside was thick with trees that, I was certain, provided a blaze of color in the fall. Beneath, ferns grew thick as the blackberry vines back home and provided havens for birds that flitted across the road before us as if totally unaware of our presence. Maybe they just didn't care if we shared their space.

Although we'd traveled only a few hundred yards, I felt removed from the rest of the world. The air was cooler, the sky bluer. We'd reached the halfway mark, and the road ended in a wide turnaround. Since we'd left the valley, we hadn't seen another vehicle or another human being, and as Nick turned the car around and parked, I'd never felt more at peace.

We'd brought along a makeshift backpack filled with bottles of water, snacks, and a digital camera. Those people on top of the mountain had figured out a way to provide the necessities, but we couldn't impose on their generosity. Whatever motivated them to seek such solace might also resent the intrusion of outsiders. All that the community below had told us about these people was positive, life-affirming. But still, they chose to live separate lives, and there had to be a reason.

Nick and I had both dressed in shorts for the climb, but the coolness was already significant, and I was glad to get moving. As we made our way up the steep path, the only sounds were the crunching of our feet as we struggled to maintain balance on the incline and, of course, the birds. I wondered if their twittering was some sort of alarm system. And I wondered if the people in Charity could interpret it.

We'd climbed for nearly an hour when we came to a small clearing. A fire ring in the center of it told us that we were getting close to the commune. I turned to look back down the mountain and at the town of Liberty below us. People in the town went on with their lives while life here on the hillside continued unabated since the primeval surge that had created these mountains.

After a brief break, we started up the trail again that soon disappeared into the forest. Air was distinctly cooler now, and I knew we had to be getting close. Then as sudden as rain on a summer day, we entered the commune known as Charity.

On the slope of the mountain, a landing had been carved out, and it supported a dozen or so small log cabins tucked beneath huge trees, and in the central clearing, a woman stoked the fire of a large brick kiln. Smoke billowed from the kiln, no doubt the smoke we'd seen from the town below.

We walked toward her, and when she sensed our presence, she turned around to face us.

I smiled and approached. "Hi. Hope we didn't startle you."

She relaxed and looked back at Nick, who'd remained at the edge of the clearing. "Not really," she said. Then she held out her hand to me. "Welcome to Charity."

"Thank you. I'm Lila Dawkins. I hope nobody minds if we visit for a while."

"Always glad to have visitors." She put another log into the fire, closed the door to the kiln, and turned back to me. "I'm Gerri Blackwell."

At first glance, I'd not realized how very pretty this woman was. Her skin, a flawless café au lait, bore no makeup, and her tightly curled black hair was cut close to her head, making the high cheekbones even more pronounced. She was taller than I was and more slender. She wore a man's white shirt over jeans but somehow made the outfit look glamorous.

"Glad to meet you, Gerri. I'm Lila Dawkins."

Nick joined us, and I introduced him. Then I asked, "So you're a potter?"

She glanced back at the kiln and shrugged lightly. "I try," she said smiling. "But sometimes the mud has a mind of its own."

We laughed with her, and then she asked, "So what brings you up here?"

Tempted to say something irrelevant like hiking, I dug out the truth. "We came looking for somebody that we believe may live in Charity."

"Oh?" Her black eyes turned to Nick. "Has this person done something wrong?"

"No, not at all," he answered. "On the contrary."

He drew a deep breath, but before he could finish, I said, "The truth is that she's done something quite wonderful. It was only after she'd left town that we discovered her work. And it's marvelous. So good in fact that an art professor has looked at it, and we all agree that it needs to be shown. But we can't do that until we get her permission."

The eyes appeared even more puzzled. "What makes you think she's here? Didn't she tell anyone where she was going?"

"We know now that her parents came here back in the sixties, and we thought she might have done the same."

"Who is this person?"

"Her name is Berniece Messer. Do you know her?"

Gerri shook her head. "No. I'm afraid we don't have anybody here by that name."

"Is it possible that she's using another name?" Nick asked.

"Sure, that's possible. Some people come here for the anonymity. But there are only two painters here right now, and one of them is a man."

"How old is the woman?" I asked.

"Hard to tell. Probably early thirties. How old is this person you're looking for?"

"Quite a bit older than that," I answered, my hopes sagging.

"Is it possible," Nick asked, "that she's working with some other media? I mean, she could have come up here to learn different techniques."

"Good idea, Nick. Maybe somebody else fits her description." I continued, "She's tall and dark-haired with pale blue eyes. I'd say Berniece is in her early sixties, but she's still extremely energetic like somebody who's worked on a farm."

Gerri listened as I spilled out the description, but the whole time, she was shaking her head. Finally, she said, "I'm sorry, but there's just nobody here like that."

"How long have you been here?" I asked.

"Nearly a year," she said rather sadly. "But come on, and I'll introduce you to the other artists anyway. They might know something that I don't."

Gerri took us past the kiln and the commons area, up a different path, to an opening in the trees where a thin middle-aged man worked at an easel he had set up in bright sunlight. He wore a white tee shirt dotted with the same colors of the canvass, but the thick spectacles perched on his nose coupled with the burr cut of his gray hair gave him more the appearance of a college professor than that of an artist.

Gerri stopped in the pathway, waited a moment, and then asked, "Tom, mind if I interrupt for a minute?"

He turned, apparently surprised that he had visitors to his hillside studio. "Sure, Gerri. What's up?"

She turned to where we waited on the path behind her and motioned us forward. "Tom, we have some visitors. This is Lila and Nick. They're looking for an artist who might have come up here recently. I told them I didn't know of anybody, but since you come up here off and on, I thought you might know this person."

He squinted into the sunlight, offering his hand first to me then Nick. "Tom Clewis," he said. "Glad to meet you."

"Same here, Tom," I said.

"Now who's this artist you're looking for?"

"Berniece Messer."

For a second, I could have sworn that he would answer in the affirmative. But then, slowly, he shook his head and said, "No, sorry. That name doesn't mean anything."

I wanted to ask more, but for Tom, the matter was closed, and he turned back to his canvass.

Gerri said, "I'm sorry. I guess he's wrapped up in his work right now. But I'm sure if he'd known anything, he would have told us."

I nodded. "Sure. I understand. We're just trying to touch all the bases."

"Well, let's go back to the commons, then," Gerri said quickly. "I think Laura's working there today."

I thanked her, and we turned to follow, but as we did, I glanced back at Tom who watched us as we made our way back down the path.

We found Laura in her cabin, which consisted of a single bed against the back wall and a large rough-hewn table in the center of the room, where she worked, her back to us as we entered. Around her lay several other tiles painted in stylized shapes from nature.

She stopped working and listened while we explained our purpose. But again, the artist seemed to know nothing of Berniece's whereabouts.

"Sorry," she said to me genuinely. "Is she a relative of yours?"

"No, she's not a relative."

Her expression softened. "A friend?"

"Yes, a friend."

"And I guess she's an artist."

"Yes, and a very good one." I looked across the beautiful tiles lying on the table. Any other time, I would have wanted to spend time with this talented artist, admire her work, and watch while she created. "And so are you," I concluded. "Thanks anyway. I'm sure we'll find her."

My disappointment was huge. Gerri escorted us back to her kiln and peeked inside at the fire. She chatted about her community, about how they financed the venture, and how they brought in supplies once a month. All these I had cared about only moments before. Now my only thought was that we were leaving without finding Berniece. Although I knew better, I realized I'd counted on it, and now that she wasn't there, I really didn't know which way to turn.

I tried to hide my disappointment from Nick during the trip down the mountain, but the knot in my throat grew with each step. Nick too must have been disappointed, but his motive was far different from my own. Why had I made the search for this woman so all-important? I finally asked, "Nick, will you keep on looking?"

"I honestly don't know. At this point, Ward will probably turn it over to the feds. They've got all the resources, which we don't. His grip on the steering wheel tightened. "I don't know if we'll ever find her, Lila. I'm sorry, but that's the way it looks. You wouldn't think that in this day and age, people could disappear, but they do. Sad to say, but it happens all the time."

"I know, I know. But aren't those usually people who get kidnapped or run away with somebody's husband? Why would anybody want to disappear like this?"

"Any number of reasons. Lila, you're right that most people never think about it. But occasionally it happens. Somebody can't cope any longer. And if you don't use cell phones or ATMs, you can do it. All you need is a little cash and the desire to disappear."

"But why?"

"If I could answer that one, I'd be the guru, wouldn't I? Who knows what makes people do what they do?"

I knew he was right. And I knew from the start that this might be a wild goose chase. But before we got to the bottom of the mountain, the tears slipped down my cheeks, and I wasn't sure if they were for me or for Berniece.

Home

The ride back to Knoxville was long and boring. Under normal circumstances, I would have enjoyed the hills and the bright sky of fluffy clouds that so mimicked Virgil's cotton fields. But on that particular day, I didn't care. All I wanted to do was go home to Antioch and figure out my next move if there was one.

Nick must have thought my moodiness unnerving too because he didn't flinch when I suggested we try to change our tickets to the flight leaving out of Knoxville that night rather than wait for morning. I couldn't blame him for wanting to get away from me. I didn't like me much either.

The plane touched down in Jackson about nine, and before long, we were headed back to Antioch. I was glad to be on the highway in the dark where I could hug my side of the car and stare out into the darkened but now familiar landscape.

Thankfully, Nick wasn't one of those men who try to talk about anything and everything to perk you up. And since he wasn't compelled to cheer me up, I gladly passed the miles in silence. I wanted to go home, slip into my cocoon where sleep would come and tomorrow everything would be all right again. Oh, I talked to him—passing comments, the kind of stuff you say to strangers. But my feelings were wrapped around themselves inside my cocoon, and I wasn't ready to share.

My house on top of the hill never looked better. A full moon behind the house outlined it like a tall sentinel against the night, and we drove around to the back porch, where I'd left the light burning. A tree frog screeched either welcome or warning as we got out of the car. Nick opened the trunk, but without giving him the chance to be a gentleman, I lifted my suitcase and headed for the steps. Then I turned back to where he stood by the trunk.

"Nick, thanks for letting me go along with you. I really appreciate it."

"Glad to do it. I'm sorry we didn't find her."

"That wasn't your fault. You did everything you could." I started to go in, but I felt he deserved more, some sort of explanation. "Nick, I swear I don't know why finding her is so important to me. And I apologize for being such a bore all the way home."

"You weren't a bore, Lila. You could never be a bore."

I managed a smile and turned once again, but this time, he reached for my arm and his fingers wrapped tightly around it. His voice sounded different when he said, "Lila, sometimes we can't explain why something's important to us. Like right now." And as he pulled me toward him, his lips touched mine first lightly, then more firm.

After the kiss, he released my arm, and I looked up at his face, illuminated by the porch light. I reached out to touch his cheek and moved closer. When he kissed me again, my heart pounded in my ears. His kiss tasted like sweet wine, and I wanted more.

My tiredness and disappointment gone, I returned his embrace. His body felt like I'd imagined it—firm and sensuous as he held me against him. His lips left mine for a moment, and he looked toward the house. "Think we could go inside?"

"Maybe we should," I said and picked up the suitcase.

The house was dark, but it felt like home. Our footsteps echoed on the wooden hallway as I led him into my bedroom, and when I turned around, his lips again met mine. This time we swayed together to a tune that only we heard.

"I've wanted to do this for days," he whispered into my ear.

"Me too."

"I'm glad," he said and then pulled me closer. His hands moved over my back in perfect rhythm to our song. Kiss by kiss, his lips moved down my neck and to my shoulders.

Once again, I took him by the hand, this time into the shower where our clothes fell into a heap on the floor. We stepped into the claw-foot tub and then pulled the shower curtain around us. Hot water ran over our bodies, and the aroma of soap filled my nostrils as we slid our hands over each other's bodies. We were in our own world, and it had never felt so right.

The Committee

I fell asleep in his arms, all concerns banished for the night, and when Sunday dawned, I was alone. I sat up and called to Nick but then saw the note he'd left on the pillow beside me.

You were sleeping, beauty, so I left before the neighbors got up. Call when you can. And, Lila, I'll go anywhere with you!

He was right, of course, to leave. As much as I didn't want to admit it, my little town would frown on seeing his car parked in my driveway in the morning. I also didn't want to admit that, at that particular moment, I didn't care. The attraction I'd felt for Nick since I first saw him behind the church must have been mutual all along. I was alive, and I was, after all, quite human.

Rare was the day when sunshine didn't fill my kitchen, but when I finally got up to make coffee, I discovered that this particular Sunday was one of them. A thick covering of pregnant clouds hovered low over the barn, and I knew we'd be in for it shortly.

I filled a mug with strong black coffee, but before I got settled in the rocker, the phone called me back to the moment, and I heard a familiar voice.

"Lila, did I wake you?"

"No, I was up. Clyde?"

"Yes. Sorry to bother you on a Sunday morning."

"Not at all. You could never be a bother."

"How kind, Lila. I tried to call you last night, but you must have been away."

Before I could ask what was on her mind, she plunged ahead. "I couldn't wait any longer to tell you. The Jackson Museum of Art is sending a committee out to Antioch. They want to see Berniece's work."

My grogginess disappeared in the instant. "A committee?"

"Yes. I know most of these people, and they're quite knowledgeable. I told them about Berniece's work, and they want to come and see it for themselves. Lila, these people have influence. And they have the connections to financially support a major show. Your Berniece could soon be a celebrity. Not to mention what her celebrity would do for Antioch."

I tried to soak it all in, but my mouth wasn't responding. I finally said, "This is wonderful, Clyde. How did you manage to contact them so quickly? And how many people are we talking about? When, when are they coming?"

"Which question would you like answered first, dear?" she asked with a laugh.

"Anything at all."

"Details are a bit sketchy thus far, but it appears you'll be getting a visit by the end of the week."

"Within the week? As in *this* week?"

"Yes, I believe so. Is that a problem?"

"No, no. I'll figure it out. But I've got to get the house ready. I mean, we can't let these people go in the house with boards over the door. And it needs cleaning. Nobody's lived there for a while. Then I've got to get her work from the church—"

Clyde interrupted, "Lila. Slow down. They'll understand if the house is not in perfect order. After all, wasn't that part of the charm of the discovery for you?"

"Yes, but they need to at least feel comfortable."

"Granted. Do what you can, but don't overdo. After all, they realize the circumstances."

"Okay, okay. But there are still the other matters."

"Yes, about those other matters. Did you say that she had some other works in a church?"

Yes, I said that. I hadn't done so on purpose, but she had caught the slip nonetheless. I drew a deep breath and plunged ahead. "Clyde, I'll explain when you get here, but for now, I've already said too much."

She was silent for a moment and then said simply, "Whatever you say, dear. I can certainly come to help if you'd like."

"If I'd like? You know the answer to that one. But I can really use you once they arrive—to pave the way with introductions and all. You speak their language, and I don't. I'll do the grunt work. But I might need help with arranging, so the sooner you can get here, the better off I'll be."

"Good. Then I'll ask for a couple of days when I get a firm date."

"Thanks. That would help."

"And, Lila, slow down. You have friends I'm sure. Ask them to help. All will be well, I assure you."

I thanked her again and finally put the phone down although my mind wanted to call everybody I knew and tell the news. We didn't find the artist, but the work would speak for itself. All I had to do was work the next five days at the pharmacy, clean and arrange the house, decide what to do about Berniece's work at the church, and prepare some type of reception for who knew how many guests. That's all.

I suddenly felt really rotten about my promise to Brother Sciple. And of course, that promise extended to Berniece. But hadn't I gone to all sorts of extremes to find her? At what point did her work fall into the realm of public domain? I didn't have answers for any of those questions at the moment, but I also didn't have time to waste. This visit could be the opportunity of a lifetime, and I wanted to make the best of it.

Clyde had promised to help, but my first priority was organization. That and to talk to Nick. As excited as I was about the committee, my thoughts kept returning to the night before. I'd been close to marriage and kids and the whole ball of wax. Now that I look back, too close, but at the time, having that door slammed in my face hurt like hell.

Costa entered my life right after graduation from college. A close friend threw me a get-together at her family's beach house in Destin, Florida, and he was there. Their families had shared beach space in Destin for years. I'd never met a Greek man before, and he knew all the moves and angles to charm me into believing that our marriage was meant to be. Before I knew it, I went home to meet his family in Tampa, followed by the presentation of a monstrous diamond ring in the company of the entire family.

I was flattered, and for a while, I was truly taken. He was good-looking all right. Thick black hair, rippling muscles, and all the right moves. He told me he loved me, and he said he wanted me to bear his children. I wasn't crazy about the plural sound of that word, but I accepted anyway. We planned a wedding on the beach, the site of our meeting, and I went home to Atlanta to tell my family and friends. My family's not one for merging well with other cultures, but neither are they bigots. Their reaction was less than jubilant although calmly accepting. I figured that with time, they'd come around, and I pictured our much-enlarged family gatherings that would now include baklava and lots of dancing.

A couple of weeks later, I arranged a surprise trip to Tampa where Costa worked. I'd already made wedding plans and wanted to share with him. But it turned out that he had the surprise for me. I thought I recognized my friend's car in the driveway, but I didn't really believe it until I let myself in and saw Costa's very naked body draped over another equally naked female one on the sofa.

Without a word, I backed out the door, got into my rental car, and aimed it toward Georgia. There was no way I was hanging around to wait for explanations or apologies. The enemy is what it is. I drove straight through to my apartment in Atlanta. The phone rang incessantly, that is, until I turned it off and lay across my own bed, staring at the ceiling, tortured by thoughts of what a fool I'd been.

When Monday came around, the tears had dried up, and I knew what I had to do: I insured the ring and mailed it by FedEx, cancelled any wedding plans, and went to work as if nothing had ever happened. When I walked into the store, Johnny was on the phone in the back, but his questioning eyes followed me.

I shook my head and whispered, "I'm not here."

Johnny said into the phone, "No, I haven't seen her, Costa. I'm sure she'll call you soon."

Then he put down the phone. "What in the hell happened, Lila?"

I answered simply, "The wedding's off." And I went to work. Until closing time, he never asked another question, but once he'd locked the doors, as if on cue, I headed straight for our little break room in the back and dropped into a chair at the table. The tears flowed again, and I couldn't stop until I had a big red nose and puffy eyes and looked about as lovely as any cabbage patch doll.

Johnny never said a word during my display. Instead, he sat down across from me at the table and waited. Male best friends listen, not sleep with your intended. When he felt it was safe, he said, "I'm sorry, Lila. But it's a good thing it happened now."

I knew that. Of course, I knew it was better to have happened then rather than when I had a house full of kids, a million-dollar mortgage, and maybe even the looks of some of his maternal relatives. I'd already sworn off baklava. I knew all that. In the final analysis, we both knew. But we also both knew that my feelings had been crushed and would take a while to mend.

Of course, what Johnny himself did to me a few years later made Costa's crimes pale in comparison. Somehow, I'd forgotten and forgiven, and now

I had to do it again with Johnny. Antioch was my chance to start over, and I wasn't about to screw it up.

So I called Nick. His easy voice held nothing of Costa's arrogance, and I told him about the committee. He sounded every bit as excited as I was and promised any help that he could offer.

"Don't say it if you don't mean it," I said. "I have the rest of the day off, and there won't be much time the rest of the week. Do you think you might take me over to the Sciples? There's something I have to talk to the reverend about."

He laughed. "As long as it doesn't look to him like work on the Sabbath."

We agreed to meet at the parsonage after I'd called the reverend, which I did and made a date to meet in the church that afternoon. I hadn't yet dealt with the possibility that the reverend wouldn't budge from his promise to Berniece. That would come after I'd had a chance to present the facts as they'd unfolded. Wherever Berniece had gone, she obviously didn't want us to find her. She had abandoned her work and her town. So did that give us the right to ownership?

That thought nagged at me as I drove to the church, but the moment I saw Nick waiting on the portico with the reverend, it slipped into my subconscious again. I met them on the portico, and we exchanged the pleasantries of friendship in a small town, including the familiar handshake, but when the reverend held open the door for me, I felt Nick's hand on my back, warm and familiar.

I told Reverend Sciple about our trip to Florida, and I told him about our trip to Tennessee. "We've done everything we can think of to find her," I concluded.

"And now you want to show her work," he surmised.

We were still standing in the vestibule, but then the reverend walked away from our little group. He walked to the front door, jangling the change in his pockets again as he gazed out the little window.

I said, "Brother Sciple, I know you promised Berniece, and I respect that. But look at her parents. They never showed up again. Chances are Berniece won't either, and all her beautiful work will go unknown. I think that would be a shame, don't you?"

His shoulders heaved with a sigh, and he turned around. "Who profits from showing her work?" he asked, his eyes drilling mine.

"The town. My thinking is that we could funnel any proceeds into a trust fund scholarship. Some local students may get a chance at college they wouldn't have otherwise."

His determination ebbing, he asked, "Nick, what do you think about all this?"

"What's the harm, Reverend? Nobody's trying to claim her work. I think we're making the most of the situation without hurting anybody."

I could have kissed him. The pastor nodded. "Let me think about it, Lila. I've sworn to keep her paintings a secret, and I can't take that promise lightly. But what you said also makes sense. I think maybe Berniece would like helping kids. For whatever reason, she never had the chance, and if it hadn't been for a generous church member where I grew up, I wouldn't have either. Just let me sleep on it."

Nick walked me to my car, and as he opened the door, he said, "Feel like a little outing?"

"Sure. I guess. What'd you have in mind?"

He said, "Follow me. It's not far."

Feeling like a schoolgirl again, I got into my car and trailed after him as the road wound back to Highway 49 and he turned back toward Antioch. We hadn't gone far though when he turned off the highway and onto a dirt road that meandered uphill into a hardwood forest, somewhat uncommon in the pine belt, and then leveled off. Sweet gums, oaks, maples, and dogwoods formed a near-perfect canopy over the gravel road, telling me that few people came that way. We went a few hundred feet, and he turned again, this time onto a much narrower road with barely room for a single car. Bright yellow wildflowers poked through tall weeds on either side, brushing my car as I crept past. Then he stopped and got out of his car.

Although the sun was still high in the sky, the forest cut most of the light before it made it to the ground. In spite of the day's warmth, I felt a chill in the air as I got out of the car and went to join him where he stood beside his car.

"I wanted you to see something," he said simply and started walking. "It's not far."

Again I followed, this time on foot as we left the gravel road and plunged into even thicker woods surrounded on all sides by kudzu that worked its way to the treetops. Eventually, it would win, but for now, the forest still breathed.

Nick led the way and held each branch until I could take it from him. We'd gone perhaps a hundred yards when he stopped again. "Here we are," he said.

I looked around. Sure, the woods were beautiful, but so they were nearly everywhere around there.

Then he parted the foliage in front of us until I could see through it. "Recognize anything?"

I gasped. There, another hundred yards or so down a gentle slope sat Berniece's house. But we were behind it. "How'd you know how to find this? I mean, I didn't know there was a road back here."

"Not many people do. Story goes, there used to be a house at the end of this road, but it burned a long time ago. I stumbled on the chimney one time when I was a kid. I'd forgotten about it until we started looking for Berniece, and I remembered and came back here to check."

"That means that if there's a way out behind the house, Berniece could have left this way and nobody would have ever seen her, doesn't it?"

"Sure. That could have happened. But why leave her car? It'd be a hell of a walk to anywhere from here."

"Have you checked the entire road? I mean, what if something happened to her way out here?"

"I checked as far as the road goes. Went all the way back to where I found that old chimney. Nothing but a family of raccoons."

"Could somebody else have driven up here the way we came in? If she'd walked back here, anybody could pick her up, and nobody would be the wiser."

"Sure. That could happen too. Are you thinking that maybe somebody met her here on purpose?"

"Isn't it possible she had a friend or relative that nobody knows anything about? Somebody who'd pick her up?"

"I suppose that could have happened."

"But why didn't she tell anybody she was leaving?"

"That *is* the question, isn't it?"

And I had no answer. "Nick?" I finally asked. "What if Berniece was simply taking a walk back here and somebody picked her up? Somebody who wasn't a friend."

"That's possible too," he said softly. "It's a strange world these days. Anything's possible."

That horrible thought sent an involuntary shiver through my body, and Nick put his arm around my shoulders. His presence was real and comforting, but something about this place wasn't. I continued, "Do you think it's possible that something unnatural happened in that house?"

"Unnatural? You mean supernatural?"

"I'm not sure what I mean, but when the rules as we know them don't apply, maybe others do."

"Lila, there's something else I need to show you first. Then you can decide for yourself."

I followed him out of the thicket, and we stood on a small rise that overlooked the house. He bent to pick up an object and held it up for me to see the spent firework in his hand. "Here's the lights around Berniece's house," he said and motioned to others lying about the ground. "Looks like they had a big old time up here."

"The Carruthers boy and his friends made all that up?"

Nick nodded. "Either that or somebody else was up here. Those boys looked too scared to me. I suspect what happened was that they came down Jordan Road all tanked up, and when they saw those fireworks, who knows what they thought they saw."

"That would explain a lot, wouldn't it?"

"Yep."

"Have you presented this idea to the boys?"

"No, I didn't remember about this place until this morning. I can't see it'd do any good to go to Mr. Carruthers with it." He smiled and added, "Besides, might do them a bit of good to keep wondering what they saw out here."

"I guess. But, Nick, I'm wondering about something myself."

He leaned to kiss me lightly on the lips. "And what might that be?"

"Do you think it's possible for people to wish themselves to another place?"

"You mean like I could wish myself to the World Series?"

"No, Nick. Be serious."

"I wasn't making fun, Lila."

"Okay. I know, but I'm trying to figure it out. Have you ever read anything about astral projection?"

"Some. I don't remember where, but I'm familiar with the concept."

"Me too. I even tried to use it once when I was going through a tedious dental process."

"Did it work?"

"Either that or the nitrous oxide," I laughed. "But, Nick, I can't help wondering if it's possible. When a person disappears like Berniece did, we're trained to think that she exists on another material level, only somewhere else either alive or dead. What if, just suppose, that's not always the case?"

"Do I think that people can disappear literally? Is that what you're asking?"

"There's nothing literal about my supposition. And as far as I can tell, there's nothing literal about her disappearance either." I drew away from him. "I'm thinking out loud, that's all."

I saw the hurt in his eyes, but I could do nothing about it at the time. We left the place and walked silently back to our cars, with the promise of getting together on Monday after work. We were new to each other, and I didn't know how to tell him the depth of my quandary. The basics of my faith said it was possible, but the world would say I was crazy. For the moment, I thought it best to keep to myself what I thought had really happened there.

A Cry in the Night

When we parted on the road behind Berniece's house, Nick asked me to call him later in the evening, but one thing led to another, and I went to bed without doing so. I'm not prone to pouting, and I was certainly interested in pursuing our relationship. Something though kept me from making the call, so when the phone rang around midnight, I thought it was Nick.

I'd gone to bed an hour earlier, but sleep still evaded me. I switched on the lamp beside my bed and looked at the identifying number. It wasn't Nick. It wasn't even local. Knowing that the call had come from somewhere in the Atlanta area, I swallowed the knot that had formed in my throat and answered, expecting to hear that somebody was in the hospital or worse.

The shaky voice said, "Lila? I've got to talk to you."

I eliminated any relatives' voices, and apprehension rapidly turned to anger. "Who is this?" I demanded.

"Lila, it's Shannon. I've got to talk to you."

"Shannon Crowe?" I asked incredulously. Johnny's wife was calling me?

"Yes. Something terrible has happened, and . . ." the sound of weeping filled the space between us.

"Shannon, what is it? I can't help you if you don't talk to me."

For several agonizing seconds, I held onto the phone and listened to her weep. I tried again, "Shannon, whatever it is, you've have to get control and tell me what's happened."

Finally, she responded in a weak voice. "Lila, Johnny's gone. And the police are looking for him."

"Gone? When?"

"He's been gone all day. They called me from the store when he didn't show up. We waited all day, and he never showed up. I even drove up to the cabin, but he's not there either. And, Lila, when I got home, there were police cars everywhere. They're looking for him too, Lila. The FBI's looking for my Johnny!"

Again, she succumbed to tears, and I held onto the phone as my brain spun with possibilities. If Johnny was on the run, that meant they were on to him. That also meant he could be coming after me.

"Shannon, I'm truly sorry about all this." Then I asked, "But how did you find my number?"

"I called your parents," she said sniffling.

"Oh. Does Johnny know where I live?"

"I don't know. Isn't it okay if we know where you live?"

I wrestled with what to say and finally answered, "Sure. It's okay. But I need to know if Johnny knows where I live."

"Why, Lila? We're your friends."

"Just answer me, will you, Shannon?"

The fear in her voice was palpable. She said, "Johnny knows where you live. He told me a few weeks ago that he'd found out you were living in Mississippi. We just thought you were tired of the city—that's what Johnny said. You left kind of suddenly, and Johnny, well, he had it all to himself. He's worked so hard."

"Okay, Shannon. I know." I had to know how much she knew, so I continued, "But why are the police and the FBI looking for Johnny?"

"I have no idea, Lila. Don't you think I'd tell you if I knew?"

"Yes, I suppose you would. I just thought they might have told you what's going on."

"All they tell me is that they need to talk to him about something at work. They won't even tell me if he's a suspect or a victim. And they're watching the house, Lila. They're parked outside my house watching everything I do. It's a nightmare, Lila."

"I understand. But whatever it is, I'm sure Johnny will show up, and everything will work out."

"God, I hope so."

"Trust me."

"I will, and will you call me if you hear from him? Please, Lila?"

I assured her that I would and added, "Try not to worry, Shannon. Johnny can take care of himself."

She tearfully agreed, and I pushed the little button that connected me to the rest of the world. The house was dark, and I couldn't remember if I'd locked the doors. Nobody in Antioch locked doors at night, a fact that had taken quite a bit of getting used to for me.

I got up and went first to the kitchen. The doorknob turned easily in my hand. I pushed that button and then took the key hanging over the door and locked the deadbolt. Nobody ever goes in or out the front door, but I checked it anyway and found it locked. Was I locking somebody in or out?

By that time, I was as awake as possible, so I went back to the kitchen, took the latest wine bottle from the refrigerator, and poured its remnants into a glass. Then I sat down at my table. I'd come to Antioch to find peace, and I had found it. Now my past threatened my peace and the way of life I'd struggled to create. I've never been one to mind being alone, but the moment called for a friend. Again, I reached for the phone.

A few minutes later, Annette's car crunched along the gravel drive. "Thanks for coming," I said as I opened the door. "Is Bart at home?"

"Yes, but he's sound asleep." Her hand reached out to wipe my cheek, and until that moment, I hadn't realized that I was crying. "Now tell me, Lila. What's happened?"

We moved automatically to the table. I poured her a glass of wine and sat down. "Do you remember my telling you about Johnny?"

"Of course. Your former partner. What about him?"

"What I was afraid of must have happened. The police and FBI are looking for him. But he's disappeared."

Her brow furrowed. "You mean he's missing? How did you find out?"

"His wife called me. Just a few minutes ago."

"Okay, Lila. Slow down. Talk to me. Why did his wife call you? How did she know where to reach you?"

I repeated what Shannon had told me and added some things about her in the process. "Shannon was my friend in college too, you know. I introduced the two of them. But Shannon always was a bit of a social climber, and it only got worse after we bought the store. I sort of understand why Johnny made the mistakes he did. He could never make enough money for Shannon."

"That's sad, but it doesn't excuse either one of them, especially Johnny."

"I'm not saying it does. I'm just telling you how it is."

"Well then, we may have a problem. I'd say one of two things has happened. Johnny's either gone underground or he's come looking for you."

I gazed back at her green eyes, now alight with excitement. So typical for her, she boiled it down to two possibilities. "I don't know what to think, Annette. He could have left the country for all we know."

"Yes, he could, but I doubt it. Think about it. If he found out that there was a warrant out for him, he probably already knew that they'd have the airports alerted, too. So that means he's probably still close by."

"I don't know, Annette. Cheating insurance companies is one thing, but murder's a whole different ball game. I can't imagine he'd risk his life to come after me."

Her eyes pierced into my own. "Lila, I'm not trying to scare you. But when a person's come to the end of his road, sometimes he loses touch with who he's always been. He does things that make no sense under normal circumstances. Fear may have warped him into believing that you're the cause of all his troubles."

I knew she was right, but I didn't want to accept it. After all, I'd already seen him pull a gun on me. "Okay," I said. "I understand what you're saying. But what can I do about it?"

"Tell Ward, for one thing. He can watch out for you. He's got Nick now too."

At the mention of Nick's name, my hand went to my face. I tried to cover by rubbing my eyes, but she knew me too well.

"Now that's a reaction if I ever saw one," she said flatly. She smiled and sat back. "What else are you keeping from me?"

"Nothing. Why?"

"Nice try, Lila. I didn't think you two gorgeous people could be around each other for very long without the sparks igniting."

I laughed out loud. "I knew you'd figure it out. But it didn't happen like you might think."

"Nothing happened in Tennessee? It was the perfect opportunity."

"I know. But he couldn't have been more of a gentleman. I even behaved myself."

She laughed and waited for me to finish. "It was late when we got back to Antioch, and he brought me home."

"I see." Again she waited.

"I'm still not sure where we stand with each other, Annette. All I can tell you is that I like being around him. He's different from anybody I've ever met."

"He's a good man, Lila. Nick's had his problems though. I'm sure he'll tell you about it in due time."

"I know about his bout with alcohol if that's what you mean."

"That's part of it. But I really don't want to talk about Nick. That should be between you two. Just be assured that he's a good man. You'll work out whatever problems together."

"I'm sure we will."

"Will you promise not to keep me in the dark this time?"

I promised but still wondered what she'd left out about Nick's past. Then we returned to the more pressing problem.

She said, "Tomorrow, you need to let Ward know what's happened. It's his job to keep the people of Antioch safe, and you're no exception."

"I will. I promise. But I'm okay now. Thanks so much for coming over. I can see now that I was panicking. Tomorrow's another day."

"That it is," she said and looked up at the clock. "Actually, it *is* tomorrow, and I probably need to get home."

She rose from the table and picked up her keys.

I stood up and hugged my friend. "Thanks for coming. You made me feel much better about all this. I'm not alone anymore."

"That's what it's all about." She turned to go and then stopped. "Come home with me, Lila. We've got all that space, and Bart won't even know you're there. He's got a meeting in the afternoon that could last all night. It'll be like a sleepover."

"As tempting as that sounds," I answered, "I'd better hang around here. I'm fine now. The goblins are all out from under the bed. Go home and get some sleep if you can."

She finally agreed, and I assured her that the doors would be locked and that I knew how to shoot. What I didn't tell her was that I'd never owned a gun and probably never would.

Somehow talking to Annette had indeed brought my fears into the open. Sleep eventually came, and although bleary-eyed, I went in to work at the usual time. But what I found when I got there took away all thoughts of sleep.

The Package

On my desk sat a letter-size box about two inches thick and wrapped in brown paper. The return indicated that it had come from Tallahassee, but I didn't recognize the address. Apparently, it had been delivered while I was in Tennessee. Nobody had said anything about a package arriving, and I wondered if Vivian had thought of something. Something that might help us find Berniece.

I unlocked the front door and returned to the back to open the package. Edwin entered through the rear door just as I slipped the paper off the box. We spoke, and he told me that he'd come in to check on some orders, but he managed to hover nearby long enough to see the lid come off the box.

On top was a letter in what I assumed to be Vivian's hand. It read,

Dear Lila,

I enjoyed so very much meeting you and Sheriff Johnston. After you left, I stayed with Pearl for another hour or so during which time she remembered something that I now deem worthy of your attention. I'm sure you could see that Pearl's attention wanders quite readily, so please excuse her for not remembering these papers while you were there.

The enclosed letters were apparently mailed to her years ago when Virgil was living in Tennessee. I had no idea that they existed, but Pearl told me exactly where to look to find them in her safe deposit box. She may forget what day it is, but she remembers with great acuity what matters most to her.

I was not aware until I read these papers of Virgil's inclination as a writer, and I certainly could never have envisioned him as the talent he most surely would have become had he not died so suddenly.

Yes, Pearl remembered that, too. Hopefully, you have by now found out about Virgil and Delores's stay at the commune.

I do also hope that these papers will shed some light on who these people were, and I fervently hope that you will find Berniece and in some way encourage her to share her work with the world.

Again, I am most happy to count you as a friend and wish you and Ward all the best in this pursuit.

Your friend,
Vivian Bastrop

I put the letter on my desk and lifted the stack of neatly typed papers from the box. They had turned yellow with the passage of decades, but the type was quite readable. The first page had a title: "Home to Antioch." Below began a story that drew me in like a moth to a flame. People had started coming into the store, and still I read.

The very first page enthralled me as Virgil Messer described the town I'd come to know as my own while his words took me down Main Street. It took me back to the first time I strolled down that little street, remembering Patti's café and its wonderful aromas, the old shops, where I gazed into the windows. I remembered my pulse slowing, and I remembered why I'd come to Antioch in the first place. Then Virgil led me through town, out a winding road, familiar now, and up the hill to my own little farmhouse. Then he continued the description all the way to Jordan Road.

"Lila?" Edwin's voice interrupted.

I tore my eyes away from the yellowed pages to where he stood at the counter. His smile was tinged with a question as he awaited my answer. "Hate to interrupt, but can you come help Mrs. Robbins?"

"Sure," I mumbled and then sadly looked back at the pages. "Be right there."

I tucked them back into the box they'd come in, slid the box into my desk, and went to the counter. Whoever said that life in a small town is slow hasn't worked in the only pharmacy within fifty miles. The manuscript had to wait. Each time I'd try to read a few more pages, somebody else would come in with a prescription, a question that needed answering or simply the craving for conversation. The result was that when I closed the door at six that evening, I had read no more than when I first came in, and I couldn't wait to get home and find out what else Virgil had to say about our town.

My cell phone rang as I opened the back door. "Feel like some company?" Nicky asked.

What could I say? "Sure. If it's you."

"I'm not interrupting anything?" he asked.

I set the box on my kitchen table and said into the phone, "No, of course not. But there's a condition."

"What's that?"

"We have some reading to do."

"What kind of reading?"

"I'll show you when you get here. But, Nicky, you won't believe this."

I poured myself a glass of wine and fixed him his standard sweet tea and then settled down in the living room with the manuscript. Ordinarily, I would have met him on the back porch, but the day was hot and sticky, and the lighting out there not so good. I sank into the sofa, and by the time he arrived, I was well into the second chapter.

He knocked and then called my name as he opened the back door.

"In here," I instructed, hardly looking up from the pages.

"What's all the intrigue?" he asked from the doorway.

I patted a place beside me on the sofa. "Come on. See for yourself."

He sat down beside me, and I offered him the first chapter. He started to ask something else and then stopped as he began to read. When he'd finished the first page, he turned to me. "Where'd this come from?"

"It was on my desk when I got into work this morning." I reached for the note. "Here, it's from Vivian Bastrop, the woman Ward and I talked to in Tallahassee."

He read the note, shaking his head as he did. "This is unreal. Who would have ever thought old Virgil was a writer?"

"And who would have thought a manuscript of his would surface after all this time?"

"I know," he said, turning his attention back to the pages. "Lila, I'm no expert on literature, but this sounds pretty darned good."

"Doesn't it though?" I picked up the remainder of the manuscript. "And there's more. I haven't had a chance to read much more than you have, but, Nicky, he's describing the Messer place."

"His old house on Jordan Road?" he asked and turned the next page.

I nodded. "See why I can't wait to read the rest? With what we know now about that house, I can't wait to see what he says about it."

He grinned his little "got me" grin and added, "I must admit I had something else on my mind other than reading a book tonight, but this is too good to resist."

"I'm glad you think so," I said. "It'll be more fun reading it together." I handed over the pages I'd finished, and when he caught up with where I'd left off, he moved closer to me, and we continued reading. The pages flew by as Virgil's story unfolded.

The main character, a man named Daniel, came to Antioch from somewhere up north, seeking asylum for as yet an unnamed offense. He had arrived in Antioch with little money but was soon taken in by a warm and generous couple Michael and Hannah who lived in a farmhouse on Jordan Road. The family gave him work on their large farm and even provided him with comfortable housing in their barn. He shared meals with the family at their kitchen table, and they spent twilight hours together rocking on the back porch.

The family had a single child, an eighteen-year-old daughter named Elizabeth, who was indeed the center of the parents' attention and the recipient of all their love. When Elizabeth first saw Daniel, it became apparent that she would fall for the stranger in their midst, but he kept a respectful distance, admiring her also but from afar.

Daniel had been with the family for nearly a year when everything suddenly changed. One day, while Elizabeth was in the garden gathering vegetables, a police car drove up the driveway and stopped at the back door. Billows of dust followed the tractor that Daniel drove, making rows in the farthest field. Michael, who'd gone in for lunch, came out of the house and went to meet the officer. They talked for a while, occasionally looking out toward the field where Daniel continued to work.

Elizabeth stopped picking beans and joined her father. She listened long enough to know that the policeman was looking for someone for the murder of a young woman. He said that the man had escaped and that he was believed to have taken refuge in their small town.

Elizabeth had heard enough. Without a word, she slipped away from the two men and went to her room upstairs where she gathered bits of clothing and a single heart-shaped necklace from her jewelry box. Then she left the house of her childhood and went to the barn where Daniel had returned on the tractor. He was getting off the tractor when he spied her.

Her father and the policeman were still talking in the driveway while Elizabeth and Daniel slipped out the rear of the barn and made their way into the woods bordering the rear of the property. Before long, they had crossed over the creek that separated their property from the neighbors' and headed east, toward Alabama.

We'd read nearly a hundred pages when I finally put the manuscript down. "What do you think it all means?" I asked.

"Does it have to mean something?"

"There must be some reason he set the story in his own house. Why didn't he just make up a setting?"

"I don't know a thing about writing a book, but if I were telling the story, I'd set it some place I was familiar with too. He already knew those details, so he didn't have to make up as much."

"You're right, Nick. Of course, that's what he did. I make too much of some things."

"I didn't mean that. All I said was why reinvent the wheel?"

Again I smiled at his simple, masculine explanation. "You're right, Nick. Sometimes I overlook the obvious."

"Look, I'm no literary scholar. You know more about this kind of thing than I do."

"I'm no scholar either. When we read more of the story, maybe we'll find out, but in the meantime, let's call it a night, shall we?"

"You're tired, aren't you?"

"I'm tired of *reading*, but not of being with you." I cupped my hand under his chin and turned his face toward me and kissed his lips. "Thanks for reading this with me," I said. "I can't help thinking that this story will tell us something about the family, about Berniece."

He returned my kiss and held me in his arms for a moment. "Glad to help if I can. I know this means a lot to you, so it's important to me too." He stood up from the sofa, stretching. "But sleep's important, too. And we both need some."

I walked him out onto the porch where we embraced again, more like two very good friends than two lovers who only a day before had made an indelible memory of passion. But friendship felt good too. And for that moment in time, it was more than enough. I told him good night, watched him drive away from my house, turned off the lights, and retreated into my bedroom. What had happened in the house on Jordan Road that caused three people to disappear? The more I found out about this man, the more questions I needed answered.

Choices

He held onto my hand as we ran through the forest. All around us was night, but a full moon illuminated the dense woods and cast a silver shadow across his face. He was handsome, exquisitely so. I had no fear as I held onto his hand, unaware of where we were going but following blindly, exhilarated by his mere presence. Although we ran at an alarming pace, my breath came in strong, even bursts, and I felt as if I could run forever.

We eventually came to a stream that made a sound not unlike the purring of a kitten as it coiled around my feet, cool and inviting. I wanted to give in to it, sink into the silver water. But wordlessly, my companion tugged again at my hand, urging me forward. We crossed the stream and climbed the bank on the opposite side. When I turned to look back, a huge black animal reared on its hind feet and opened its cavernous mouth, but no sound escaped, only hollow blackness. As I stared, the animal turned and slithered back into the darkness from which it had come.

Again, he tugged at my hand. I wanted to join him, to run forever through that silver forest. But for some reason, I stopped, dropped my hand from his, and turned away. Then as tears slid down my face, I turned back, and he was gone.

Very real tears filled my eyes as I lay staring up at the ceiling. The clock told me that the sun would shortly be up, and so I must be. But the troubling dream lingered all the while I made coffee and ate breakfast. I identified it as fantasy, but at the same time, I couldn't help thinking that it had some underlying meaning. I've never been one to try to attach deep meanings to dreams because I adhere to the theory that they are basically the neurons firing off at random. While they may produce some interesting, sometimes scary stories, they don't necessarily mean anything. However, by the time I got into the pharmacy, I'd convinced myself that I was avoiding something. The problem was that I didn't know what.

I had already dealt with several minor irritations, so I was glad when I spotted Ward's friendly face entering the store. Taking off his hat, he strode the aisle toward the back of the store where I worked at filling the latest batch of prescriptions.

He plunked the hat onto the counter with a smile. "Mornin', Lila."

"Good morning, Ward. I'm glad to see you."

"Oh? Anything wrong?"

"No, not really. Just one of those mornings when a friend's face is welcome."

"Yep. I know how that goes. But I came to tell you somethin' that just may make your day a little better."

"Oh yeah?"

His moustache twitched upward at the corners, and he said, "Thought you might want to know that a guy from the *Herald Reporter* is down in my office wantin' to talk to you. I told him he'd have to wait there till I had the chance to ask you whether or not you wanted to talk to him."

"You mean he works for the newspaper in Jackson?"

"Yep. Writes some column about the arts, he said. I figured it has something to do with your project with Berniece and all that."

"You're kidding!"

Ward shook his head and smiled broader. "Does that mean you want to talk to this fellow?"

I assured him that I did, but that I'd have to tend to some things first. Ward told me that he'd go back and tell the writer I'd meet him in about an hour, in time for lunch. Then I processed the remainder of the prescriptions, made sure my assistant could handle things while I was gone, and took off for the café. I wasn't familiar with the name Rich McMahon, but that wasn't surprising. I hardly ever looked at any local papers, depending instead on the Internet and nightly news from Hattiesburg. But if this man working for the largest newspaper in the state could give Berniece and her work publicity, then I'd certainly talk to him. What harm could come of that?

I spotted him in the café the second I went through the door. His was, of course, the only unfamiliar face in the room, but Patti made sure I knew by the nod of her head in his direction. He waited alone at a table, his black hair draped casually over his forehead. Two equally black eyes managed to appear bored although conversation in the room had reached piercing levels.

He stood up when I approached his table. "Rich McMahon," he said, offering his hand.

"Lila Dawkins," I said, returning the handshake.

"Good to meet you. And thanks for taking time to talk with me."

"Glad to do it," I said and pulled out the chair to sit down. "I understand you write a column for the *Herald Reporter*."

"That's correct. I write about what's going on in the arts and humanities community."

"I see. Sorry if I'm not familiar with your work, but we're not really close enough to Jackson to keep up with that sort of thing very well."

"Understandable," he said, ducking his head. "That's why I came up here to talk to you. One of my sources called and told me about some pretty important folks in the arts community who'll be making a visit to your little town, and I wanted to get the story first from your point of view."

"Did this source tell you what the visit is about?"

He draped his arm across the back of his chair. "My understanding is that you've uncovered a folk artist, a real eccentric with talent. It sounds like a good story, especially if we can let the people around the state see how she managed to do something good without any training. A human-interest sort of thing, you know. It could bring in a ton of money for the town. Folks love to buy souvenirs." His eyes scanned the café. "They gotta eat, too, you know."

My back stiffened against the chair. Before I could say something I might regret later, I decided to give him another shot. "Her work is quite remarkable, training or no."

"That's what I hear." He nodded. "Precisely my point. So I was thinking that if you'd show me around, you know, show me some of her work, then I could do a story on her."

"Mr. McMahon, I'm afraid you don't understand."

His brows raised. "Understand what?"

"That the artist isn't here. All we have is her work."

"Oh, I know that," he said nodding. "But it really doesn't matter, you know. My concentration will be on the town and the atmosphere that produced her personality. Her disappearance will just add to the story, you know. Makes people want to run up here and see if they can find her for themselves."

"Mr. McMahon, I thoroughly understand now what you're saying. I thought so from the beginning, but I let you finish all the same." I stood up from the table and glared at him. "However, if you want to do a story about some local yokel who up and disappears, I strongly suspect that you've come to the wrong place. You see, her work is seriously good, and it deserves a more dignified representation than images printed on tee shirts for tourists who came here to view both her and us as oddities and nothing more. Mr. McMahon, you've come to the wrong town, *you know*."

I turned away from the table and made my way through the café, blinding anger all but marring my vision. I could have sworn that the noise level dropped in the café, but I really didn't care. I stomped across the street and found Ward at his desk eating one of Dolly's giant po'boys. The hand holding the sandwich froze midway to his mouth.

"You through already?" he asked.

"I'm finished all right."

"What happened?"

I dropped into the wooden barrel-backed chair in front of his desk and tried to figure out exactly what had happened. Once I'd found the words, I said, "He wanted to make us look stupid. And he wanted to depict Berniece as some sort of freak."

Ward's eyes narrowed. "Lila, I'm sorry. I had no idea. If I'd known, I sure wouldn't a sent you to talk to this guy."

"I know that, Ward. It wasn't your fault. But you know how sometimes the press makes assumptions that aren't valid?"

He nodded. "Yep. I'm afraid it happens all the time."

"Not only did he severely underestimate Antioch, he never even tried to see Berniece's talent. All he saw was a chance to turn our town into some sort of a carnival. And I won't have that. Berniece deserves better, and so do we."

He nodded and chomped off a bit of lettuce hanging out the side of his sandwich and then stopped chewing. "Bet you haven't had any lunch, have you?"

"What?"

He picked up his half of the sandwich and slid the other on the paper toward me. "Here, have some lunch. It's fried catfish."

I protested mildly, "But you won't have enough."

"Are you kidding?" he said.

We both knew that half of anything Dolly made was adequate in the portion department and more than adequate in the taste department. So I acquiesced, thanked him, and started eating. Once my stomach had settled, I felt better about the whole irritating encounter, but something told me that we'd probably not heard the last of Mr. McMahon and the likes. Of course, there really were only two people in town who fully knew about her work, and I couldn't see the reverend talking to that jerk either.

I finished lunch with Ward and went back to the store, still seething below the surface. Whenever that happens, I have to be really careful not to take it out on somebody else, and you would know Ethel Downey had to test the waters. When I saw her coming, I wanted to duck out the back door, but I got a grip and stood my ground, with my smile plastered into place.

She began with the usual pleasantries, but of course, that was a cover for what she really wanted to know. She pretended to look for something on the aisle behind her and then stopped. "Oh, and Lila," she said, turning back to me, "what's this I hear about the paper in Jackson doing a piece on Antioch?"

"I'm not sure. What did you hear?"

"Well, I heard you met this reporter guy in the café, and that he wants to come to town and take pictures and write about Berniece."

"I'm sorry, Ethel." I said sweetly. "But that won't be happening."

"It won't? Why not? Did he decide we weren't interesting enough?"

"Oh no, nothing like that."

Her head tilted to one side, and she asked, "Well, if you don't mind my asking, what in the world stopped him?"

I could feel the darts of pressure building behind that tongue, so I tried to alleviate the situation while I still could. I didn't need to be the cause of Antioch's misfortune. I told her, "We didn't want the kind of publicity he was offering."

"I see," she muttered.

I didn't think she understood yet, so I added, "He wanted to make us look foolish, and that's not what we want. Is it?"

"No, indeed," she said, throwing her shoulders back. "Why would they want to do that?"

"That kind of stuff sells newspapers."

"Well, they'll just have to sell those papers somewhere else, won't they?"

I agreed although I knew we weren't talking about the same thing. I also knew that I could depend on Ethel to make the rest of the town aware that the deal with the paper in Jackson was off and that I was the reason. I only hoped that they wouldn't blame me for what they had perceived as the chance for Antioch to become more like their quaint counterparts with the mega stores and hot and cold running gawkers. All that goes in the name of progress isn't good.

I'd been reading Virgil's book whenever I got a break during the day, and I was more than halfway finished. Nick had asked to come by that night, and I looked forward to it—to talk about us or not to talk at all. I simply wanted to be near him.

He got there a half hour before dark, and I met him on the back porch even before he could get into the kitchen. His arms slid around me as naturally as breathing in and out, and I drank in the aroma and the feel of his body.

"Hey there," I said, turning my face up to his.

"Hey there, yourself." He kissed me on the lips then my neck. "I've been thinking about doing this all day."

"Oh? Is that all?"

"No, but it's a good start."

"I agree," I admitted. "A really, really good start."

The passion of our first night together had failed to wane in the intervening days, and we soon found ourselves lying across my bed, tired but completely at ease with each other, and I snuggled into the crook of his arm. Soft jazz played from the living room, and moonlight seeping into the bedroom window outlined his profile. I traced it lightly with my finger.

"I love your profile," I told him. "It's strong."

"Of course it is. I'm the big lawman."

We laughed and again fell silent, enjoying the feel of our bodies so close. I finally asked, "I guess you heard about my visitor today too."

"It's a small town, Lila."

"Which version did you hear?"

"Ward's version."

"Then that's probably the one closest to the truth."

"Probably."

I pushed down the anger that threatened to stir again and asked, "Did I do the right thing?"

He propped himself up on his elbow. "Of course you did. We didn't need that jerk's version of anything."

"Thanks for saying that."

"It's the truth, Lila."

"I'm not too sure. Maybe I jumped the gun. After all, I could use the publicity for Berniece's sake."

"Not that kind. Besides, I think there may be another way."

"Whadda you mean?"

He sat up and plumped the pillow behind his back, and I followed suit. When he was situated, he added, "I have a friend who works for the *Coastal Gazette* in Biloxi. Would you mind if I gave her a call?"

"No. Of course not. Do you think she could help?"

"Won't hurt to ask. She's done her share of coverage for the museums down on the Coast. She knows her way around that world."

"That would be great," I said, another thought occurring and asked tentatively, "Is she from Antioch?"

"No, she's a friend from a long time ago. We were two dropouts from med school. Cried in our beer together until she ran out of tears, and I ran out of beer."

I could see that the conversation was about to turn serious, so I added, "It's okay if you don't want to talk about it."

"Lila, it was a long time ago, and there wasn't much to it even then. Like I said, we were handy for each other."

"Why did she quit?"

He shook his head. "That was a puzzler. Sure, some old dudes on faculty gave her a harder time, being a woman and all, but she didn't let that stop her. And she's smart, damned smart. But she's something else—too kind maybe. Truth be known, I really think she wanted to help people, but she couldn't put up with the suffering that went with it."

"You mean she wasn't emotionally cut out for it?"

"Something like that. Anyway, I haven't talked to her in years."

"Nick," I said reaching for his hand. "I'm not prying. We both have a past. Nothing to do but let it remain in the past."

"Oh, I know. I just don't want you to think that's the reason I'm calling her."

I couldn't help smiling. "The thought never entered my mind, but thanks for saying so. Nick, there is one more question I need to ask you since we've opened the bag."

"I knew that was coming."

"Do you mind?"

"If I minded, I'd tell you. Besides, there's not a lot to tell."

When he'd adjusted the pillow at his back, he asked, "Have you met my father yet?"

"No. I've heard all about him, but I haven't met him."

"Well, when you do meet him, you'll understand better, but for now, let's just say he's a bit larger than life."

"Go on," I urged.

"He's from the generation that thought they could cure the world's ills, and they did so in some ways. When I was a kid, all the others respected me because I was Doc's kid. Even the grown-ups in town treated me differently because of that. So naturally, I wanted to grow up and be just like him. Who wouldn't want that kind of respect?"

"Naturally."

"So when it was time to choose a career, I didn't put a whole lot of thought into it. With Dad's pull and a lifetime of preparation, med school was practically a given. The problem came about halfway through when I realized I didn't want to be there." He stared across the room, his profile set in a strong line. "I didn't know what to do about it, so I hit the bottle. I'm not talking about having a few beers after hours. I'm talking about showing up drunk a couple of times. Could have been disaster. Lucky for me I didn't kill somebody."

"So what did you do about it?"

"First, I went home and tried to talk to Dad. But he acted as if he didn't even hear me. Told me to go back to school—that he'd make a few calls and do some repair work. I'd be back in the good graces in a flash."

"Did you tell him you had a problem with alcohol?"

Nick turned to smile at me. "Lila, you really haven't met my dad, have you? Doc Reynolds's son can't have a problem with alcohol. He doesn't, so I don't. That's what the problem always was—living for him instead of for myself. It just wouldn't work, so I walked out before I really hurt somebody."

"Has he forgiven you? Seen your reasoning?"

Nick looked down at his hands folded across his chest, his thumbs going round and round in little circles. "Not yet. Don't know if he ever will. I'm a failure, and that's not acceptable for a Reynolds."

"But, Nicky, why did you come back here to this town?"

"It's home," he said a bit surprised. "Where else do you go when you're trying to find yourself?"

"In that respect, I guess we're a lot alike, aren't we?"

"How's that?"

"We came here for the same reason. You just came *back*, I came here for the first time."

Virgil's Story

Nick left around eleven that night, and although I was tired, I wasn't particularly sleepy. Much against my better judgment, I picked up Virgil's manuscript and began to read. Although the opening had intrigued, I wasn't fully prepared for the impact the remainder of the story had on me. I felt as if I was peeking into a window in the house on Jordan Road, watching as a family, through no fault of their own, fell into horrible tragedy.

When Elizabeth followed Daniel into the woods, she did so with an innocence born of naivete, not spite, and for days, all went well. They had passed over into Alabama, and Daniel soon found work at a lumber mill. The company provided basic housing for the young couple, and Elizabeth set out to make their makeshift home comfortable. But one day, while Daniel was at work, she was cleaning and found among his belongings a picture. Wrinkled and faded, the picture still proved enough for Elizabeth to suspect its subject to be the murdered young woman in Daniel's past.

At that moment, she knew she'd made a mistake and planned to return to her parents in Antioch. And so it was that Michael could hardly believe his eyes when he looked across the field to see his daughter at the edge of the forest. Torn between the anguish he'd felt during the months of her absence and the love he'd given so freely over her lifetime, Michael rushed out to meet her. When he held his daughter in his arms once again though, his pride surfaced, and he demanded answers that poor Elizabeth couldn't provide. Tormented by conflict, Michael made a decision.

"Your mother is gravely ill," he told her. "Seeing you appear right now would be too great a shock. You must stay here until I think it's safe to see her."

And so it was that Elizabeth waited. To get out of the heat, she went into the barn, into the quarters where Daniel had spent nearly a year. Seeing the little cot where he had slept, she was overcome with regret once again. What if the picture was not what she assumed it to be? What had happened to Daniel after she left him? She lay down on the little cot, closed her eyes, and soon drifted off to sleep. And she still slept when the eastern diamondback rattlesnake sank its fangs into her body.

When Michael finally returned, she had managed to crawl as far as the door, but he found only a lifeless body. Michael's heart tore irreparably now. He could take no more. His gravely ill wife lay inside, and his dead daughter outside. He did the only thing he could think of and placed Elizabeth's body in the back of his truck, drove down the logging road behind his house, and buried her beneath a magnificent oak.

Hannah eventually regained her health, but Michael unfortunately did not. He never spoke a word to Hannah about the reappearance of their daughter. He thought it too cruel to tell his wife that Elizabeth had returned only to die moments later. And he never told another soul where his darling daughter's corpse remained. But he did leave a strange request with Hannah. Every spring, on the day of Elizabeth's birth, she should take a walk down the little road behind their house and stop beneath the largest oak. "Do that on every March 26," he said, "and one day you'll see her." And Michael died.

I put the pages down on the bed beside me and started to cry, at first a few tears then a river of them. I cried for every mistake I'd ever made and for every wrong done to me. I cried for every human who ever loved and lost. But most of all, I cried for whatever had happened to Virgil and Delores to make him write such a story.

When dawn finally slipped into my window, I was still awake and more exhausted than I can remember ever having been. I'd spent days crying for my grandmother's death when I was sixteen, and then I'd spent more days weeping for the silly romance gone sour. But for the first time in my life, I had suffered for another human being, one I'd never met and would never meet. How would I ever explain this to somebody else?

So I did the only thing I could do at the time and called Edwin, making some excuse about having spent the night ridding myself of a nasty bug and needed to come in later in the day. He was okay with that, especially since he didn't really have a choice about it all. Mine was the only game in town, but I'd certainly make it up to him later.

After that phone call, I slid back under the comforter on my bed and fell into a sleep the likes of which I've seldom known. When I did make it in to the store in early afternoon, I must have looked the part of the recently ill because Edwin let me fill the orders waiting for me and then ushered me out of the store to get some rest. I didn't argue.

I did indeed need more rest, but I needed to do something else first. Virgil's story had hit home with a vengeance. I called Nick and asked him to come over as soon as he finished his shift.

"Anything wrong?" he asked.

"No," I lied. "You just need to see something."

By the time he arrived at the back door, he'd worked up a goodly share of curiosity, so I didn't have much trouble convincing him to read the remainder of Virgil's book. Because I wanted him to get to the burial scene first, I filled him in on the intervening action and then flipped the pages open to the scene.

He read in silence, his head getting lower and lower over the pages. When he finished, he frowned and looked at me, shaking his head. "What do you make of this, Lila?"

"Probably the same thing you make of it. Somebody's buried out there on the logging road."

He lowered his eyes back to the words on the page. "That's the conclusion I'm drawing, but who could it be? I mean, why would Virgil write a story about some daughter being buried out there? As far as we know, his only daughter is still alive."

"I know, Nick. But I do think that Virgil had to be sending some sort of message. He sent the manuscript to Pearl thinking that she would maybe get it published, at least get somebody else to read the story and find out about the grave behind his house. I think it was Virgil's way of exculpating himself for some crime."

Nick's face looked as blank as my mind felt. We were stunned with a revelation that seemed so right for us to know, but we didn't know what to do with it. He said, "Maybe it's just a story."

"You don't believe that any more than I do."

"You're right." He studied the pages for a moment and then asked, "Do you think we should go out there and poke around?"

"You mean look for a grave?"

He nodded.

"Would we be able to find anything after all these years?"

"If there's a body buried out there, bones could be unearthed. But how do we go about convincing Ward that after all these years, we read a book, and we think Virgil killed somebody and buried her out there?"

I had to admit it sounded implausible. I said, "Let's go back to the part where he buried her. See if he gives us any specific clues. When I read it, I wasn't paying that much attention to the details, but you know that place better than I do, and maybe you'll notice something I didn't catch."

He agreed that sounded reasonable, and together, we reread the section. About halfway through, he stopped me, pointing out a detail I had indeed missed. We were both fairly sure of the magnificent oak he mentioned. It was the one where Nick had stopped his car on the day he showed me the view to the Messer's house. But this time, he caught another detail, a slight one, but one that would make all the difference. It was afternoon when Michael buried his daughter, and it was late March. He talked about the sun's position in his face as he dug the grave, and he mentioned sitting against the tree and staring into the grave before he placed his daughter in the ground. That meant that he had to be facing west, where the sun would be at that time of the year, and he had to have left enough room between the grave and the tree for him to sit.

It wasn't much, but it was something. The time of year had changed, but we could calculate its position a month earlier. We wouldn't have to search the entire area beneath the tree, only a sector of it. And both of us felt strongly that once we went out there again, Virgil would surely have left some sort of message. He would never have left his precious daughter for eternity in that place without also placing the tiniest marker. That's what he was talking about in his instructions to Hannah. She would have recognized his message. And now that we'd read his book, maybe we could too.

A Parable

As much as Nicky and I wanted to go right that moment and search beneath the old oak, it wasn't possible, and we realized that it might not be for a while. Other things had to take priority: somebody had to prepare food for the visiting committee, the house needed a good cleaning and some repairs to make it safe for visitors, and I still needed to secure the reverend's permission to show Berniece's other paintings.

One of those needs was met unexpectedly. I'd been in the store for only an hour or so when Brother Sciple came through the door. When he headed straight back to my counter, I knew that he'd made a decision, just not what it was.

"Reverend Sciple," I greeted with a smile. "Nice to see you."

"Nice to see you too, Lila," he said and then glanced around the store. We seemed to have it to ourselves for the moment, and he asked, "Do you have a minute?"

"Of course," I assured. "Would you like to come around here and sit down? It's a little more private."

"Sure. That'd be nice."

When we were seated at the break table and I'd supplied him with the inevitable cup of coffee, he began, "Lila, I've thought long and hard about Berniece's pictures. You surely know that this hasn't been an easy decision. I take promises seriously."

"As do I," I agreed. "We all should."

"Indeed," he said, nodding. "That's why I'm sure you'll understand."

"Understand what?" I asked, my hopes flagging.

"Why it took me so long to decide to let you show her paintings."

My sigh could have been heard at the front of the store. What I said was, "I'm glad, Reverend. I wasn't sure."

His smile told me that the scare may have been intentional, but he continued, "As I said, I thought a long time about it, but then I remembered the parable from Matthew about the servants who were given talents."

"Wasn't that about how they used them?"

"It was. Two of the men doubled their master's talents while the third one was insulted by being given the smallest amount, so he buried them instead of using them and making them grow. When accounting time came, he had nothing to return except what he was given."

"I think I understand what you're saying."

"I'm sure you do," he said. "Berniece may not have been able to share her work with others, but there's no doubt she was given a talent, quite a good one. For me to refuse to let her work be shown may just be the equivalent of burying it. And that would be an injustice not only to Berniece but also to the maker who gave her the talent in the first place."

I was nearly speechless. In my world of work, I'd seldom had much contact with people who gave so much thought to anything apart from money to be made on a venture and how succeeding at it would increase his reputation. I thanked the reverend and made plans to retrieve the paintings that very afternoon. I knew Nicky would help me with them, and I planned to take them back to my house until the day of the showing. The house on Jordan Road had sat empty for a long time, and I couldn't risk their being harmed by some animal, a leaky roof, or just the heat. And the heat in Antioch by that time could blister paint as easily as it burned my fingers on the steering wheel in the middle of the day. I didn't know how sturdy these people coming from Jackson might be regarding the heat, so I couldn't risk their having a meltdown.

I wasn't sure what I would do about all that, but I did know where to start. When I drove up to Annette's house, she was outside watering the abundant flowers around her patio. Lush zinnias and geraniums competed with marigolds and something purple and lacy bordered all around by a row of impatiens thick with pink and white blooms. Among her many other talents, Annette could put a toothpick in the ground and not only have it grow but also soon produce gorgeous flowers followed shortly by a world-class crop of toothpicks. She flashed me a grin and went to the faucet to turn off the water.

"Hey!" she said. "I wondered when you'd get by here."

"Am I that transparent?"

"Whatever do you mean?" she asked in her best Southern Belle imitation.

"Woman, you know me too well."

"Don't worry about it. I knew you'd need help, and that's what friends are for. Mind if we go inside?"

The patio felt good to me at the moment, but her face was red, and I suspected she'd been outside all day. So we sat down at her kitchen table, and I poured out my need to her. "Annette, you know you said that if there was anything you could do to help with the visiting committee, and since you know all the good cooks in town, could you get some of them to help out? I thought about having them eat at the café, but they don't really have a place for everybody to sit down and talk. All we need is one meal and a few snack things. It doesn't have to be anything fancy, just good."

Annette's expression never changed. "I would have been disappointed if you hadn't asked," she said simply. Then she got up from the table and reached to a bowl that she keeps on top of the refrigerator. She brought back a lined tablet, shuffled through a few pages, and said, "I made a few notes about what you'll need."

And that was that. As usual, she'd anticipated my moves. She had the dinner all lined up at her house. And it seemed that the entire community had already followed suit in offering their specialties. The menu included a salad made with Mr. Ellsworth's pampered tomatoes and cucumbers, followed by Bart's famous braised short ribs, Mimi Jenkins's scalloped potatoes, Annette's own yeast rolls, and a variety of fruits to top off Laura Halston's cheesecake.

"Think that'll be enough?" Annette asked sincerely.

"To quote a famous redhead, we're not takin' em up to raise."

"Good, then," she continued. "And here's the list of goodies we'll have ready when they get here," she said, shoving the tablet over to me.

At that point, I didn't even have to look at it to know that it would be a veritable feast in itself. One thing people in our town are good at is food. And this was a chance for them to show off. It was also the first time I felt like a permanent member of the community. They had already done all this planning for Berniece's benefit for sure, but I like to think they'd done if for me as well.

"I'll have the dining room set up for lunch. Don't worry about a thing except showing off Berniece' work. It's all under control." I must have looked surprised because she added, "But if that's not okay, we'll do something else."

"Oh no. That's fine. That's wonderful. I just can't believe you're doing all this. And how about the others? Did they volunteer?"

Annette gave me that told-you-so smile and answered, "Of course. They wanted to help."

I made the drive out to Poorhouse Creek where Brother Sciple met me and helped me carry the paintings out to my car. I was thankful for all the paper wrapped around them because we had to stack them in the trunk and in the backseat, sixteen of them in all. As I drove back to my house, I couldn't help wondering how many hours Berniece had worked on them to depict her little town. And I couldn't help wondering what she would think of this show with her as the featured artist.

When I rounded the drive to the back of the house, Nick's car was already there, and he got out as soon as I stopped.

"Hey. Thought you could use some help."

"Thanks. We need to get these inside."

He helped me carry the paintings into the house, propping them against walls. I had no intention of attempting to hang them all since I knew their stay would only be temporary, but we needed to take off the papers covering them so the visitors could see them. One by one, we removed their coverings and folded the paper neatly to be reused and put them away in the kitchen closet.

When we returned to the living room, I was struck anew by their vitality. "Nick, look at this."

He followed my path around the room, gazing at the paintings that he was seeing for the first time. "Lila, I thought you might be exaggerating, but this is something."

"Aren't they beautiful?"

"It's more than that." He stopped in front of the one depicting my farmhouse. "There's something uncanny about these pictures." He looked at me as if he needed help finding the right words. "You can almost *feel* these paintings."

"They are alive, aren't they?"

He turned back to the painting. "That's a good way to put it."

We marveled a bit more about her work and, then returned to the kitchen where we sat down at the table. "Okay," he began, "so what's the plan?"

"What plan?"

"Don't look at me all innocence. Whoever's buried under that oak tree has to be driving you as crazy as it has me." He shook his head. "You can't help it."

Laughing, I agreed and then added, "But there are eight important people coming here in less than three days, and I'm responsible for everything that they see and do here. I can't let it get to me right now."

"I know," he said and came around the table to stand behind me and put his arms around my shoulders. He kissed the back of my neck and said, "I have to razz you a little. Besides, maybe we got all worked up about nothing. Maybe old Virgil is laughing in his grave at us because he made up a mighty good story."

I looked up into his face. "Do you believe that?"

"Not for a second. Do you?"

"No."

"Good. Then it's settled."

"What's settled?"

"We still have an hour of daylight left."

It took a second for his words to register. "Nick, we don't even know what to look for."

"That's true. But remember Virgil's story said that if Hannah walked by that tree often enough, sooner or later she'd see their daughter. I don't see any harm in going out there. See if we can figure out what he's talking about."

"Nick. I've got so much to do."

"Okay, let's sort it out. Is the food taken care of?"

"Yeah. Annette's got that under control."

"What about the house?"

"You and I are going out there tomorrow night—with your friend Andy, remember?"

"I remember. And so does Andy. What else?"

"Well, I suppose those are the major things."

"Don't you want to go, then? It may be the last chance we have for several more days."

I stood up from the table and reached to kiss him. "I've created a monster," I mumbled and started toward the door.

"I believe the correct term would be a *ghoul*."

The drive to the logging road takes about twenty minutes, and by the time we got there, very little sunlight remained, but it was enough to easily find the oak in Virgil's book. It stands alone on a little rise at the rear of the property, larger and fuller than any of the others. I thought back to the day Nick had led me out there, and I remembered thinking then what a great place that tree would make for having a picnic or hanging a swing. What I didn't think about that day was what might be buried beneath it.

We parked the car on the side of the road in some tall grass mixed with yellow and lavender wildflowers. Long shadows crossed the logging road in irregular patterns, giving it the appearance of huge pieces of a jigsaw puzzle. We walked toward the tree, and tall seeded Bahia grass brushed against my legs. It tickled and made me think of insects instead of grass. I struggled with the concept that anything unusual, least of all a possible murder, could have happened in such an innocuous spot.

This tree had caught my attention the first time because it was a water oak. I'm told that they usually grow near the Coast, but occasionally, they grow up this far north, especially if they have a good water source. And this one would have stood out, even among others like it because of its size. It was massive, with branches that dipped near the ground in places and a canopy thick enough to hide most anything. Surrounding trees were red oaks, maples, sweet gums, and a few dogwoods, now green only, having spent their blooms weeks before. But this oak stood its ground on a rise that overlooked Berniece's property. She must have admired it for most of her life, and I was willing to bet that she'd played there as a child.

I began to feel slightly foolish, but we were there, and I did want to find out if Virgil's story had any basis in reality. All that made it tough for me to concentrate on anything other than the spectacular sunset winding down at the end of the road.

Nick went ahead of me, pacing off steps from the trunk of the tree to where he imagined that a grave might have ended. I leaned up against the tree where a thin column of large black ants crawled down the trunk. The column seemed to continue behind my back, so I moved away and looked behind me. The line, broken for a moment by my presence, quickly reformed, and the ants resumed their path down the trunk and outward onto a large root that ran above the ground for seven or eight feet and then intersected with another one. I stood back a bit, surveying the roots. About eight feet from the trunk, the roots formed a nearly perfect cross.

"Nicky, look at this."

He walked over to where I stood looking down at the cross. "Do you see anything unusual?" At first, he stood over the single root coming from the tree. "No, come back here where I am."

He moved, and I watched his eyes trace the same route my own had done a moment before. "A cross," he finally said. "The roots make a perfect cross."

We looked at each other in the dim light that remained, and I asked, "Do you think it has anything to do with Virgil's story?"

"I have no idea," he admitted. "It could be a clue. But where do you look? I don't think it could be in the center of the cross because if the roots were that way when Virgil buried her out here all those years ago, there's no way he could have dug below them."

"What about the apex of the cross?"

He shrugged. "Could be, I suppose."

From somewhere in my memory, something connected, and I shivered as we stood there in the heat of a Mississippi twilight. "Nicky," I asked. "When Jesus ascended, what direction did he go?"

His brow furrowed, and he asked, "What makes you ask that?"

"I just had an idea. Jesus ascended straight up the cross. I remember that from somewhere. That's where she's buried," I said, pointing toward the top of the cross.

He put his arm around my waist and drew me to him. We stood there huddling beneath the massive oak for long seconds. The sun was completely gone now, and darkness was claiming its own. He finally said, "I think you're right. That's the way Virgil would have done it."

"When do you think we'll get back? When can we start looking?"

"That I can't answer yet. I'll have to talk to Ward and convince him we're not crazy. Then if he agrees to look, we'll have to get a team together. I don't know, but I'm guessing we may have to bring in the state police. Who knows what else."

I looked up at him, his face dark except for the moonlight that filtered through the old oak. "Nick, thanks for doing this. You don't have to, you know."

"Oh yes, I do," he said and kissed my forehead. "Somebody's buried out here, and that person deserves to be known."

Surprises

Nick and I returned to my house and made a couple of salads for dinner and then sat down to talk. Berniece's pictures were still propped up against the walls of my house, which I began to see wasn't my best idea. The visitors would be on a fairly tight schedule, and a trip by my house was another stop. I asked Nick what he thought about their location, and his reply confirmed my own belief.

"They should be viewed in context with her other work."

I agreed, and he helped me wrap them up again. He and Andy would pick them up on the way to Berniece's. Piece by piece, our plan fell into place. We knew how tiring the next night would be, so we said good night, and I was walking him to the door when my cell phone rang. I looked down at the number and recognized a prefix from the Coast.

"That's my cue," he said. "Have fun."

Julie sounded friendly and professional, and she sounded young.

"You're driving up from Biloxi on Friday morning?" I asked after we'd chatted for a few minutes.

"Yes, but that shouldn't be a problem. It's less than two hundred miles, and I'll allow plenty of time to get there."

Conscience tugged at me, and before I could stop it, my mouth was at it again. "Julie, there aren't any motels close by, so if you'd like, you're welcome to stay here with me."

A brief silence, and she asked, "Would you mind?"

I wasn't too sure of that myself, but my answer was in the affirmative. "Besides," I added, "you won't miss anything this way."

She agreed, and I turned off my cell, wondering exactly what I'd done. Nick's former girl friend was coming to stay in my house. Unable to process that information at the time, I simply started getting ready for bed. "This should be interesting," I said to the reflection in the mirror. "Nick will get a kick out of this."

But when I told him about the arrangements the next day, I saw little humor in his eyes when I dropped by the office to tell him about it.

"But you said it didn't matter anymore."

"Lila, it doesn't. But put yourself in my place."

"Nick, I can't do that right now. I'm up to my eyeballs in details, and this is one less I'll have to worry about now. Julie will be in town and won't have to worry about missing a thing. She doesn't know about us, and I can't see any reason to tell her otherwise. If that's okay with you."

"I'm not worried, Lila. But you have to admit the arrangement's a bit awkward."

"Granted," I said and let the matter drop for the moment.

We had bigger fish to fry, not the least of which was the cleaning of the Messer house scheduled for later in the day. I'd begun to feel really bad about depending so much on Nick. He was already doing double duty between his garage and the part time work as deputy, but he swore he didn't mind. On top of that, he'd rounded up the help of an old high school friend, Andy Travers, who worked in Hattiesburg at a bank but who also kept up his parents' old place in town. We figured that the three of us could handle the job. Then it hit me.

No one had lived in the house for a long time, and no one had paid a power bill in an equally long time. That was enough of a problem with our cleaning to take place at night, but an even bigger problem would be the smothering heat. How could I expect these people to concentrate on artwork when they were melting?

As usual, more heads together came up with a solution. Andy would bring his generator capable of handling a small air conditioner and all the lighting we would need. That meant that I now only had to find some five-gallon containers, fill them with gasoline, transport them to the house, and find a soul willing to refill the generator at strategic points in time. Things only got better.

As I suspected, Nick volunteered for the job of monitoring the generator, and he also volunteered to find enough extension cords to connect the generator to the air conditioner and lights placed strategically around the house. While I considered the prospect of getting Mississippi Power to reconnect the house, I was wasting time, so I decided that the present plan would have to do.

Edwin had agreed that until the doings at the Messer house were finished, I really didn't need to be in the store all the time. If some emergency came up, he'd call me. Otherwise, I could concentrate on matters that needed my attention.

The list of visitors finally arrived by fax, and a real lump formed in my throat as I read it. True to expectations, five of the visitors were bound to the artists' community: the curator of the museum in Jackson; her assistant, a young man named Dennis; my friend Clyde Kennedy; and two other art instructors, one who taught on the Coast and one from Jackson. The surprise came with the remaining three. It seems that the governor of the Magnolia State is a huge supporter of the arts, and as such, she was coming herself along with her husband and his close friend who, among other talents, had racked up a Pulitzer Prize for Literature.

I nearly dropped to the floor. I wanted coverage for Berniece, and I was surely going to get it. The governor's limousine would arrive in Antioch at ten on Friday morning, where they would meet up with the rest of our guests and the hostess, me. Because our governor also happened to be the first woman in the state's history to hold that office, and because she also happened to be African American, she created news from the time the first ballot was cast. And I knew this would be no exception. We could expect an influx of reporters and cameras the likes of which had never been seen in Antioch. Wherever Kathryn Burroughs went, the press followed. Only two days before, I'd been concerned about having a single reporter on the scene. Now I couldn't wait till Julie found out what a windfall scoop she'd walked into.

I called Edwin, told him that if he could handle it, I needed to be out of the store until Saturday. "I'll gladly handle Saturday alone," I told him. "This has gotten larger than I expected."

"Oh?"

I wanted to blab it all right then and there, but I needed the time. Although I knew it would be perfect, Annette still wanted me to come by her house to make sure all was to my liking. And I wasn't at all sure what surprises we might find at Berniece's.

"Yeah, you know how things look easier on paper."

"Sure. Glad to do my part."

As for Edwin and the town, they would find out in due time. If they knew ahead of time about the governor, they may have tried to plan something else, and I was sure the governor would be on a tight schedule. I didn't like hiding things from the people of Antioch, but they would surely find out in time to sneak a peek at the famous lady and her staff before they left. And after all, maybe they wouldn't be angry with me when they saw Antioch on the evening news.

I was the first one to arrive at Berniece's. Ward had gone out that morning to unlock and to make sure no unwanted guests waited for me in the house, but he'd adjusted the schedule for Nick, and somebody had to stay on call. Although I would only be there a short time before Nick and Andy showed up, I still felt shaky when I turned down the lane that leads to the house.

Berniece had neighbors on either side, but each was a good mile or more away, so it's a lonely place any way you look at it. To chase the ghosts away, I went through the farmhouse room by room, pulling up shades and windows. What was left of the screens over the windows would surely let in insects, but at that moment, I preferred them to the idea of staying alone in that house.

I was about to turn my attention to the kitchen when I heard Andy's truck in the front yard, and I went to the front door to meet him. Andy is a pleasant guy but good-looking in a different way from Nick, his fairness quite a contrast to Nick's dark hair and complexion, and his short stature in juxtaposition with Nick's height. But they'd been friends for practically a lifetime, and I soon found out why. I'd never really been around the two of them together, but I could see the two little boys in grade school, snickering over their latest joke or plotting their next move.

And all that energy they stirred up soon came in handy. The generator Andy had loaned looked heavier than the truck they'd arrived in, and getting it in place on the back porch took some real effort. Once it was in place, Andy fed it some fuel and started it up. The quiet was gone, and the drone equivalent to a jet engine took its place. I could see that any talking would have to take place in the house behind closed doors.

Andy assured me that he would put the air conditioner with its gentle humming in the living room where guests would remain the longest. Anyone wandering near the generator on the back porch wouldn't stay for long.

Then we started on the myriad of cobwebs draped from light fixtures, in corners, and even over the furniture. I'd remembered to take along a vacuum cleaner, which, although it added to the noise, surely made the task easier. Next we tackled the accumulation of dust on every surface in the house. Every surface of furniture was covered with a thick layer of it. By the time we finished with that chore, the house began to smell and look almost habitable.

A final task was the rugs. The house had wooden floors throughout, not the fancy kind people use today but old rough, wide-planked floors. And throughout the house, somebody, supposedly Delores, had scattered rugs in the hallways, beside beds, and a larger one in the living room in front of the fireplace. And all of them looked as if they contained the dust of decades.

We took them outside to beat away months, even years, of accumulated dirt. The night was dark since the moon had waned to a fraction of its former self and no lights from town had ever made it out that far. Nick produced a broom from the hall closet, and as we beat dust from the rugs, an orchestra of frogs and cicadas kept time. One by one, satisfied that we'd done the best we could do with the rugs, we took them back into the house. The last one went in the back bedroom.

I was taking it back into the room, and Andy was busy cleaning the mantel over the fireplace where the angel beckoned. When he picked up the old clock on the mantel, something fell onto the floor.

"What's that?" I asked.

He stooped to pick it up and then examined it. "Looks like a necklace," he said, holding out his hand to me.

In his palm lay a small heart-shaped necklace. The chain was simple gold, and the heart made of the same. No jewels or gemstones adorned the necklace, but I knew in the instant what it meant.

"Nick!" I called. "Come back here, will you?"

"Does this necklace mean something to you?" Andy asked.

"I think it does," I said as Nick entered the room. "Look at this," I said holding it out to him.

"Where'd you find it?"

Andy said, "I picked up the clock on the mantel, and it fell out on the floor." He picked up the clock again and turned its bottom up. "There's a little compartment under here," he added, moving the closure back and forth. "Maybe somebody had it hidden. People used to do that a lot."

Nick nodded and then asked, "Anything else in there?"

He poked a finger inside the compartment, shaking his head. "Nope. That's it. Guess whoever put it there forgot about it."

"Could be," I said. "But I think it may have just been put there to hide it forever."

Nick looked at me, understanding in an instant what I meant. "You don't think this belonged to Berniece or her mother?"

"Well, of course it could have. But, Nick, why would either one of them hide a necklace in there? Why not wear it?"

"I can't answer that. But it does add another piece of the puzzle, doesn't it?"

Andy looked mystified, and Nick explained, "We found a story that Virgil wrote. It was about some young woman who got killed on this property, and she wore a necklace like this one."

"So you think it's the same necklace?" he asked jokingly.

"It's not quite that simple, but yes. It might be."

Andy watched his longtime friend and then asked more seriously, "So who was this young woman who got killed?"

"That we don't know yet," I answered. "But," I added, looking from Andy to Nick, "you two have been here a long time. Has anybody ever disappeared from Antioch? I mean anybody other than Berniece and her parents?"

"Not in my lifetime," Andy answered and then stopped. "Wait a minute. I remember hearing something about . . . some story or other about a woman who disappeared. Nick, you know what I'm talking about?"

Nick shook his head, but as he did, his expression changed, and it was clear that he had indeed remembered something. "We were kids, weren't we?"

"Yep. I remember my folks talking about it, but you know how it is when you're little, and grown-ups talk about stuff, then shut up when you go into the room."

"Would Ward know?" I asked.

"If anybody does," Nick said.

"Then I'll ask him," I said. "Let me take the necklace to him and see if he knows anything about it. Or about a girl that went missing."

We all agreed that Ward was our best source, so I put the necklace away in my jeans pocket while we finished up our cleaning. We turned off the generator for the night, locked up the house with the new lock that Ward had provided and started back into town.

"Want to come by the house?" I asked Nick as I got into my car.

"When is your guest arriving?"

I looked at the clock on the dash and said, "In about an hour."

He grinned and leaned over to kiss me and then added, "If it's all the same to you, I think I'll wait for another time."

"Chicken," I said and kissed him again.

"Better part of valor." He glanced back at Andy waiting in the truck and then bent down to whisper, "Lila, we gotta get back to that logging road. I wasn't so sure before, but evidence is piling up. Somebody's buried under that tree, and I think Virgil knew who it was."

"Do you really think Virgil was a murderer?"

"I don't know what I think, but something happened out here. Ward will be really interested, and we need to bring him up to date."

"I agree, Nick. But we can't right now."

"I know. I know. But as soon as all this stuff with the governor and all is over, we've got to talk to him. Find out what he knows and take it from there."

I agreed, but as I gazed back at the old house sitting forlorn in the dark, I still couldn't bring myself to think of Virgil as a murderer. There had to be another answer.

I drove back into town and straight to my little farmhouse. I'd left enough lights on for it to resemble a lighthouse perched as it is on the hill, and for that, I was thankful. I was expecting a visitor that I'd never met, and she would be there any minute. The last thing I needed was to be scared of the dark.

The Big Day

I wasn't prepared for Julie. While I'd known all along that Nick's ex-girlfriend would no doubt be attractive, nothing could have prepared me for Julie. By the time she arrived at my back door, it was after ten o'clock, a fact that seemed to escape her attention. She bounced into my kitchen, grinning like a kid at recess, taking it all in with obvious approval. Her light brown hair swished about her shoulders, and she turned a pair of deep brown glittery eyes to me.

"I love your house. It's sooooo authentic."

"Thanks. It really was a farmhouse, you know."

"And you're so sweet to let me stay with you," she added, tracing a hand over the kitchen table. "Oh, I love antiques."

"I like them too," I said, hoping to get a grip on the conversation. "Especially Americana."

"Absolutely." Then she stopped in front of Berniece's picture, studying it. "Did you paint this?"

"Actually, that was done by Berniece, the woman whose work you're going to see tomorrow."

A frown crossed her face, and she whirled back to face the picture. "But I thought you said you haven't been here long."

"I haven't. The picture was in the closet when I bought the house."

"But isn't that you in the picture?"

"It looks like me, but we all think it's a coincidence. I never knew Berniece, and anyway she did that long before I moved to town."

"Wow!" she said, facing me and rubbing her arms. "That gives me goose bumps."

"Wait till you see her other work."

"Is it all this good?"

"Better. I think you'll love it. But for now, let's get you settled. Can I help you bring your things in from the car?"

She assured me that she had it under control and returned in a couple of minutes with a small bag and some hanging clothes. I led her into the guest room upstairs, made sure that she had all that she needed, and I turned to go back downstairs when she asked, "Lila, are you a close friend of Nick's?"

"We're friends," I said.

"I was so surprised when he called me. You know, we haven't talked since he left school." A cloud passed over her face, and she added, "Oh, he didn't flunk out or anything like that."

"I'm sure he didn't," I assured.

"Well, anyway, maybe I can say hello to him while I'm here."

"I'm sure you'll have the chance. He's helping with the activities tomorrow."

"What does he do here? He didn't tell me much when he called."

"Nick has a garage here, and he's deputy sheriff."

"Nicky's a sheriff?"

I nodded, biting my tongue. "I'm sure you'll have the chance to talk to him tomorrow. He can tell you all about it then."

"That's great. It'll be so good to see Nicky."

"I'm sure."

We agreed that the time had come to get some sleep for the busy day to follow, and I returned downstairs to my own bedroom and picked up the phone and then decided that it could wait until tomorrow. Nick would see for himself soon enough, and I really didn't know what to think of my houseguest except that she was about as likeable as I'd expected her not to be. Good. I never wanted to think that Nick had fallen for some bitchy type, but the aggressive woman he'd verbally painted hardly fit the one sleeping upstairs in my guestroom. At best, events of the next day should be interesting.

To say that I hardly slept would be an understatement. I was up before dawn, made a pot of coffee, and sat down at the kitchen table to call Annette. Bart, a notorious early riser, answered.

"Not nervous are you?" he joked.

"No more so than Annette probably is. Speaking of which, is she up yet?"

"You know she is. Hang on."

Hardly a second had elapsed when she answered, "Ready to party?"

"I'm not too sure about the partying. But I'm ready to get this show on the road and over with. How about you?"

"As long as our girl Kathryn likes country food, we're good."

"Annette, I have no earthly idea what she likes. I've never fed the governor and a Pulitzer Prize winner before, but I assume they eat just like the rest of us. Besides, everything you do is wonderful."

She sighed. "It's probably just another rubber chicken lunch for them. They won't even notice what they're eating."

"They'll notice. It's nowhere close to rubber chicken."

She chuckled and added, "Let's hope not."

"Annette, how can I ever thank you for doing all this?"

"We'll think of something. Not to worry. But I gotta know—how's the reporter who's staying with you?"

"Interesting," I said simply.

"Interesting? How so?'

"I like her. But I'll tell you all about it later. Is there anything I can do, anything you need?"

"Thanks, but no. It's all under control."

That, too, is Annette. Bart had declared that he would remain home to help too, and all I had to do was show up with our famous guests, who I knew would be entranced by her personality, not to mention the town's best food. Now I could concentrate on simply meeting the VIPs and showing off Berniece's artwork. Nothing to it.

When we got into town, it swarmed with SUVs bearing call letters from stations across the state, and Patti's café had a line outside for the first time in my memory. We went straight to Ward's office where we met him headed out the door.

I made introductions to which Ward said, "Glad to meet you, Ms. Donovan." Then with a nod in my direction, he added, "Make yourselves at home, Lila. I'd like to sit and talk, but things are kinda busy today."

"We understand," I told him. "The governor's car should be here any minute, so we'll just hang around here if you don't mind."

He shook his head. "Help yourselves. I'll be around if you need me." He'd no sooner left than Nick's outline crossed the window, and the door opened again.

Julie's face lit up with sheer delight as she jumped up to greet him. He pecked her cheek lightly and then glanced over her shoulder to look at me. "How've you been, Julie?" he asked.

"Great, Nicky! And look at you! You look wonderful. Antioch must be good for you."

"It's home," he said. "Thanks for coming."

"Thanks for asking me. I had no idea how big this thing was going to be. I thought I was coming up here to cover some art teachers, and now it's turned into a list of important people in the state. Nick, this could be a big break for me, you know."

"It's a big break for Berniece and her work too. Let's hope everybody likes what they see here today."

Julie said, "Lila's told me all about her. My cameraman should be here any minute, and then we can start making pictures. You know, Lila's promised me the only interview with the governor. Can you believe that?"

"That's Lila," he said, winking at me. "She'll do anything for a friend."

At that moment, the noise level on the street rose to a new pitch, and Nick went to the window. "I think our guests are arriving."

I swallowed the knot in my throat. "Let's go, Julie. They're here."

Three cars lined up in front of the Sheriff's Office, but attention immediately focused on the one in the middle, a long black Mercedes. Security appeared from everywhere—uniformed officers and several men wearing perhaps the only suits in Antioch on that day. When the signal had been given, a driver got out of the Mercedes and opened the back door. Cameras rolled on the streets of Antioch as a pair of attractive long legs swung out of the Mercedes, and the governor of the state of Mississippi exited, smiling and waving to her constituents.

Kathryn Burroughs was even more impressive in person that she had been in the many film clips and news photos I'd seen. For the months of her campaign, it seemed that the national news sources couldn't get enough of this attractive woman in her forties. Even international news had picked up on the possibility of an African American woman running for the highest office in a state once shamed by its bigotry, and when she was actually elected by a wide margin, the nation gasped in surprise. Still, hardly a day went by that her image didn't grace some day's press.

Then she spotted me standing there in front of Ward's office, Julie at my side, and walked straight toward us. She held out a slender hand, and in the distinctive pace of the region, said, "You must be our hostess."

"Yes, Governor Burroughs. I'm Lila Dawkins. Thank you so much for coming."

"I wouldn't miss it."

"Still, it's very kind of you. And, Governor, I'd like for you to meet Julie Donovan from the *Coastal Gazette*. She writes a column for the arts in Biloxi. Julie agreed to cover this event even before we knew you were coming, so I hope you don't mind if she goes along with us."

"Not at all," she said and offered her hand to Julie. "Happy to meet you, Julie."

"This is an honor, Mrs. Burroughs. Quite an honor."

"Julie, if there's any honor here, it's mine in being part of the discovery of a new talent. You see, I'm not really a politician—just a would-be artist in disguise."

"Oh, do you paint too?"

The governor leaned closer to Julie and whispered, "Only in secret. Please, let's don't mention that to anyone, shall we? I'd die of embarrassment if anybody should ask to see my work."

Julie's grin widened. "It'll be our secret, then," she said. "But I'll bet you're good."

The governor laughed. "Only my intentions, Julie. But it doesn't stop me from trying."

"I know what you mean. After I went to the George Ohr Museum, I took a course in pottery because I just knew I could do that. But," she said with a slump of her shoulders, "it was hard, you know?"

"Yes, I do know," Kathryn said. "I guess that's what separates the real artists among us, isn't it?"

Julie agreed, and the matter settled for the moment, Governor Burroughs asked, "Well, then, Lila, shall we go? I'm anxious to see this artist's work."

My pulse quickened as we got into the Mercedes and pulled away from the curb. I instructed the driver, a young man named Terrence, and we were on our way to the house that had started it all. Clyde had agreed to escort the group from Jackson, and they would meet us at the house at precisely ten thirty.

The trip to Berniece's could have been awkward had the governor not been as able a conversationalist as she was a politician. Before we knew it, we had discussed the latest exhibit at the Walter Anderson Museum in Ocean Springs, the finishing of the Ohr Museum after Katrina's destruction, and the state's acquisition of some renowned paintings for display in the state capitol. I found it no small wonder that she'd captured the hearts of Mississippi.

Clyde's silver Toyota waited in front of the house, along with another long red sedan bearing plates from the capital city. Our entourage of three cars was followed by the parade of press that had tailed us out of Antioch and down the gravel lane, throwing up clouds of dust across the countryside. Although we'd hired local teenagers to mow it, the front lawn showed neglect, and blackberry vines mixed with elderberry and honeysuckle crept through the wooden fences that had once surrounded Virgil's cotton fields.

As people hurried out of vehicles, aiming cameras toward our car, the governor got out and began making introductions. I recognized her dignified yet somewhat older husband, Maurice Burroughs, when he got out of the car in front of us. Maurice kept to the background during his wife's tenure in the state capitol, but he was never far behind. He'd made a small fortune creating computer parts in our state, back when they weren't all that common, so everyone assumed that he could well afford to support a political campaign. It hadn't been necessary. Even before she announced her candidacy, supporters lined up from the Mississippi Delta to the Coast.

With him was an equally familiar face around the state and, for that matter, the nation. What Faulkner had done for literature, Charles Allenby perpetuated. I have to admit that few works have ever stirred me like *High Ground*, so I found it hard to believe that the round little man who approached our group was the literary giant, but the face said I was right. In demand because of his irreverent sense of humor, he knew all the right people and spoke their language.

Clyde brought her group over to our car, and introductions began anew. She had brought with her Dr. Jenny Whitcomb, a vibrant redhead, and Dr. Tim Holliday, older but with an equally red beard, both art professors at the nearby University of Southern Mississippi. She then introduced Dr. Suzanne Lu, curator of the Mississippi Museum of Art, and her young assistant, Dennis Graham, currently on loan from the Metropolitan Museum in New York. Then Kathryn introduced her husband and Charles Allenby whose fame far exceeded his stature, but not his personality.

"Charmed," he said as he kissed my hand during the introductions.

I felt that if anybody there had been charmed, it would have been me when I read his work, but I figured he'd heard that a million times, so I let the matter drop. After all, we were there to look at another form of art, and I knew he wouldn't mind.

The group followed me onto the porch. I held open the door and stood aside as they entered Berniece's living room. Without exception, every head turned upward in much the same way I'd first seen Oscar's that day when Ward and I went to Berniece's house. Quiet except for the "Ah's" and an "Oh, my" or two, the only sound was the humming of the little air conditioner in the window. I hadn't known exactly what to expect, but the effect was hard to disguise. They were overwhelmed, as I had been, and as I knew, admirers would be for generations. Berniece was a true artist, a fact that could no longer be denied.

The group stayed in the living room for quite a while as they examined the content and the technique of Berniece's work. As I might have expected, these artists saw things I either failed to notice or didn't know to look for, and when they'd seen enough, I led them toward the rear of the house and into the room where the angel beckoned.

I moved aside to let them enter. Again, their response was unanimous. Each in turn reached out to touch Berniece's hand. "I expected to feel a pulse," Suzanne murmured. "I've never seen anything quite like it."

Others agreed, but Charles perhaps summed it best. "I think something rather miraculous happened here," he surmised, looking to the others. "This woman's spirit is in this room."

"That it is," Kathryn agreed.

One by one, the little group left Berniece's bedroom and gathered again on the front lawn. Some had been strangers when the day began, but now they were a community with a common spirit, joined by what they had witnessed in an old farmhouse.

I found Nick in the backyard propped up in a folding chair, reading, and he looked up from the book when I came out the back door. He must have seen my enthusiasm because he began to smile even before I said a word. "How'd it go?"

I threw my hands into the air and said, "Spectacular!"

"They loved it?"

"That they did. I knew they would."

"So what happens now?" he asked.

"I'm not sure, but I know they'll pass the word. Berniece is on her way!"

I had to leave Nicky out there in the yard because I had a luncheon to attend, but I kissed his forehead and said, "Leave the generator and come on to Annette's. I don't want you to miss this."

He said, "I can't barge into the luncheon. Annette's counting on so many, no more."

"I know, I know. I don't want you to miss anything. It's all too wonderful."

"From the looks of that crowd out there, I'll see plenty on the news tonight."

"I know, Nicky, but as hard as you've worked, you should be part of it."

He took me into his arms and stroked my back. "You win," he said. "I'll be the guy in the kitchen, washing dishes."

True to his word, he did show up at Annette's house where with the press parked all over the road and the caravan of official vehicles in the driveway, her usually peaceful home looked like a movie set. Annette, as I knew she would, charmed everybody there while the food did its part to convince our guests of the good life in Antioch. Nick, I knew, would be waiting for me when they left. For the moment, the important thing was that Berniece's work would eventually get the recognition it deserved, and I would have lots of help in that endeavor.

Afterglow

By two in the afternoon, our guests had exited Antioch, leaving behind that day after Christmas feeling. And the debris in their wake did somewhat resemble the clutter after all the presents have been opened and the new worn off. Julie was the last to leave, having thanked me for the thousandth time, and I assured her that I would surely read her story online when it appeared in the Sunday issue. Her interview with Kathryn Burroughs had been more spontaneous than we'd imagined, but they definitely took a liking to each other, and I knew the result would be good.

I tried to help Annette and her crew in the kitchen, but they had a system in place. Eventually, all the leftover food was distributed, her best silver and china washed and put away in her grandmother's glass cabinet, and the linens started in the wash. Claiming that I would simply be in the way, they shooed me out where I joined Nick on the patio talking to Bart.

"They won't let me help," I said, taking a seat beside Nick.

Bart laughed. "Be thankful."

"But they did all that work, and all I did was show up."

"That's the way that bunch is," he assured me. "You don't want to get into the club, believe me. I insisted one year at a benefit, and they nearly worked my tail off."

I decided to let the matter rest and leaned back in the chaise. A huge oak kept the patio relatively cool in the afternoons, and the strain of the day gradually eased. We talked about the day's success, and we talked about how impressive our governor was. Then the conversation took a different turn.

Nick asked, "Bart, you've been around here a little longer than I have, so let me ask you a question."

"That's a sneaky way of saying I'm old."

"Not what I meant, and you know it. We just need somebody who's lived here a long time to help us out with something."

"Truth hurts. So what's the question?"

"Did you ever hear any rumors about there being a grave out on that old logging road behind the Messer place? This would have been about twenty-five, maybe thirty years ago."

At first, he shook his head, but he stopped and said, "You know, maybe I do remember something, but I didn't give it any credence at the time."

"Can you recall any of the particulars?"

"No. I dunno. I'll ask Annette. She's better at remembering stuff like that than I am. Why do you ask?"

I answered, "We think somebody may be buried out on that logging road behind the Messer place."

"There's never been a cemetery out there that I know of."

"That's not what I meant. Remember that manuscript of Virgil's that I told you about?"

"Yeah, but what's his manuscript got to do with a grave?"

Nick explained, "In his story, the main character buries a girl, and the way he describes the place, it sounds just like that big water oak out on the logging road."

"Well, I'll be," Bart said simply.

I added, "It may be a stretch, but there are clues in the story too."

"How did the girl in the story die?"

"She ran off with a worker who was staying on the farm, and when she came back, her father made her wait in the barn while he prepared her sick mother for the shock. But while the father was gone, a snake bit his daughter, and she died before he could get back out there. He never told her mother that she'd come back. The character in the story died with the secret."

"Damn, that sounds like a cheerful story."

"Yeah," I admitted. "It wasn't too cheerful, but it was good, Bart. I'm telling you, the man could write."

"Damn," he said again. "'Scuse me, Lila, but I just remembered something. When you said that about writing, I remember a little problem my girls got into one time about a story they wrote. Beth was in the third or fourth grade, so that would have been about the time Nick's talking about. Anyhow, Bethie wrote a story that got her into all kinds of trouble."

"Why? What for?"

"Gosh, I'll have to ask Annette, but the best I remember, she made out that Virgil Messer killed this young woman and buried her out behind their property. I have no idea where she got the idea, but I do remember punishing her for writing the story. And the whole time, she kept crying and saying she was telling the truth, which I ignored because she was supposed to be making up a story. We couldn't have our daughter spreading tales about innocent neighbors. Just because the Messers stayed to themselves didn't give little girls the right to make up stuff about them."

I asked, "Do you think Beth would remember why she wrote the story?"

"She's more likely to remember the details. She stayed mad at me for the longest after that."

I looked at Nick, and I could tell that he was thinking ahead of me. While it is true that children like to make up stories about somebody different in the community, perhaps they also have an ear to the ground that adults don't. Whatever Beth knew about the story, I wanted to know too.

Annette eventually came out onto the patio and sat with us for a few minutes, but we could see that she'd had enough excitement for one day and needed some down time. We excused ourselves and headed back to my place where the subject came up once again.

I asked, "Nick, do you think I should contact Beth?"

"You probably want to think about that one. If we go asking her, however innocently, she might tell somebody else, then the thing gets blown out of proportion. On the other hand, if we go out there just the two of us and do some more looking around, who knows? Maybe we'll find something, maybe not. But I think that at this point, it's better to keep the lid on it, don't you?"

I had to agree. What purpose would be served if we besmirched Virgil's name for nothing? Too, it could backfire and hurt Berniece. After all, I was proceeding on the supposition that she wasn't coming back. What if she was living somewhere nearby and found out that her father was being called a murderer?

I finally agreed. "You're right. But we need something to go on. We could dig under that tree till the cows come home and not find anything, that is assuming that there's anything to find in the first place."

"Lila, I've got an idea that may help us out on that problem. Remember what Virgil said in the book about walking by there every day, especially on her birthday?"

"How could I forget?"

"Exactly. He wanted to make an impression on somebody. I've thought about this a lot in the past few days, and what if Virgil wanted people to walk by the same place many times for a particular reason?"

"I assumed that he thought that if she wanted to see their daughter badly enough, the power of suggestion would kick in and she'd either imagine that she saw her or, at least, feel closer to her there."

Nick nodded again. "But what if he had another reason? What if the walking by there might eventually expose something?"

"To quote Julie," I said, rubbing my arms, "that gives me goose bumps."

He grinned. "That's Julie."

"Seriously, you may have a point. It's been a long time, but nobody much goes out there anymore, do they?"

"No, and that's *my* point. Delores wouldn't have had much chance to go walking back there because apparently right after whatever happened, they left town and went to the commune. Then the house burned out at the end of the road, and people quit going by there completely. Isn't it possible that he buried a clue just beneath the surface under that tree?"

"At this point, I'd believe most anything. It's worth a try, don't you think?"

He shrugged. "Most we could lose is time."

"Then let's go," I said, the tiredness of the day suddenly evaporating. "Let's go look around under that tree some more."

We still had at least an hour of sunlight left when we got there. Nick's idea made sense to me, but still it was a long shot. Virgil Messer didn't fit what I knew about murderers, and it had been a long, long time. But then, Nick was right. If we found something, we could answer a lot of questions about the disappearance of the family; if we didn't, we'd keep it to ourselves and count the afternoon as one spent rather pleasantly under the old oak.

Again, Nick paced off steps from the tree to a point where he imagined a grave might have been dug. I followed him, scanning the earth beneath my feet for anything that appeared out of the ordinary. While I was scanning the earth beneath the tree, Nick searched through the underbrush nearby and came up with a long straight stick. Then he retraced his steps of the last time we were there, poking the stick into the ground every few inches. Nothing appeared out of the ordinary.

And once again, the curious crossing of the roots caught my attention. "Nick, try the stick out there," I said.

"Where?"

"Follow the apex of the cross straight out. Start at the end of the root and go straight out."

He drew a line in the soil that began where the root stopped and went out for about three more feet. Then he went back to the beginning of his line and gently prodded the stick into the dirt. He'd made several prods into the earth when the stick met with resistance. "Something's under here," he said and knelt beside the pointed end of his stick.

I knelt beside him. "How deep is it?"

He gently prodded the stick once more, but the tip would only go into the earth for a half-inch or so. "It's not deep, but there's definitely something here." He looked around. "We need something to scrape the dirt off in layers."

I looked back toward the road. "How about a flat rock?"

"Yeah, that'll do."

I returned with a flat rock no more than six inches long, and he began to gently wipe away the top layer of dirt. Within moments, we could see what lay beneath, a small box made of some dull metal. He continued scraping until he'd removed the dirt entirely from the top of the box. Then with the pointed end of the stick, he carefully created enough space around the box to lift it from the dirt and place it on the ground between us.

"My god, Nick, this is unreal."

"It is, isn't it?"

"Do you think Virgil buried it here?"

"Only one way to find out," he said and picked up the box. He tried to lift the lid, but decades of lying beneath the moist earth had sealed it. He took out his pocketknife and traced the edges, prying until it finally released, and the lid lifted to reveal a sheet of thick folded paper, molded and heavy with the moisture of many years beneath the earth. He lifted it from the box and laid it on the ground. "I'm afraid if I try to unfold it, it'll disintegrate."

"Yeah, it looks pretty fragile," I agreed. "Maybe if we took it home and dried it out?"

"I don't know. That might make it worse, and then we couldn't read what's on it."

Again I agreed. "But we've gotta try. Nicky as crazy this sounds, I think Virgil was sending a message. Maybe he didn't intend it for Delores. After all, they left town apparently right after the rumor, so she would hardly have had time to find it. I think he was sending a message to whoever read his book. But he had no way of knowing that Pearl would keep it secret all those years. He wanted somebody to find out about this girl, whoever she was. He wanted somebody to find her."

Nick carefully picked up the folded paper and handed it to me. "You may be right, Lila. But whatever it is, we can't figure it out here. Let's go back to your place and see what we've got. Maybe then we'll know if we need to get Ward out here to start digging."

Hidden Words

I poured us both a glass of sweet tea, and we sat down at the kitchen table. The fragile paper remained folded where I'd laid it there between us on the table when we came in, its words taunting but indecipherable. On the way into town, we'd discussed how to proceed and had come to the agreement that we needed to find somebody expert in the field of preserving old documents. Before we did something that could keep us from ever reading the words, we'd take whatever precaution the experts advised. I suspected that Clyde could advise us, but after her grueling day, I wouldn't call her until the morning. In the meanwhile, Virgil's note would stay in my house.

Each of us pretended not to notice, but the whole time we sat there, we could scarcely keep our eyes off the paper. We finished our tea, and when Nick got up to leave, I followed him to the door. He kissed me and said, "Don't let that note drive you crazy."

"Thank you so much for reminding me. I'd almost forgotten." I laughed and closed the door, safe in my farmhouse. Whatever message Virgil had sent from the grave would have to wait for the morrow. I needed sleep in the worst kind of way, and the note would be perfectly safe there on my kitchen table. Nobody ever broke into houses in Antioch, and should they do so, the last thing they'd be looking for was a piece of moldy paper.

Secure in that knowledge, I went to bed. I had no dreams of messages from the dead, only fond remembrances of the day's events. As I drifted off, I realized that I'd made friends with the most powerful woman in the state. I'd made contacts with the very people who could make Berniece known. Nothing could have gone better, so why then did I wake up with a start at exactly 3:03 a.m.?

The noise, or supposed noise, came from the living room. I reached for the flashlight that I keep on the table beside me, but I waited before turning it on and reached instead into the drawer for the .38 that Nick had insisted I keep. If whoever I thought was in the living room saw my light, he would then know that I was awake. But if I continued to lie there, he might take that as a sign that I would be a willing victim.

Wanting neither to be a victim nor to become a murderer, I waited there in the dark to be sure after all that I'd heard something. When I'd almost convinced myself that a fragment of a dream had awakened me, I heard something else, something far more distinct. The back door opened and clicked shut again, an unmistakable sound in my house.

Flashlight in one hand and pistol in the other, I felt my way down the hallway and into the living room. As I expected, it was empty. The floodlight on the barn cast shadows over the room and it lit up the solitary figure that ran across my yard and into the trees that separate my property from the neighbor's.

I went to the door, tried to turn the knob, but found resistance. What kind of burglar locks the door when he leaves? And better yet, what in the world did I have that somebody was willing to break in to get?

Then another thought occurred, and I raced to the kitchen. But the simple folded paper lay where I had placed it hours before. After checking again to make sure the doors were locked, I returned to my kitchen and sat down again at the table. "So much for sleep," I said aloud. I thought about calling Nick, but then what could he do? One of us needed to get some sleep, and I knew my night was over. So I did what I'd wanted to do ever since we unearthed the little box.

The stove's lowest temperature registers at 150, and that's where I set it. Figuring that paper might absorb moisture better than metal, I placed the note between two paper plates, and I put them all into the oven and closed the door. "This better work, Lila," I said and sat down again at the table where I could monitor my project. After checking for the umpteenth time, I decided that the oven had done all it could, and I removed the paper plates with their folded message. The mold had not disappeared, but now it wasn't so prominent. When I tentatively picked up the corners and pulled them away from each other, the note began to unfold.

Words spread across the page in the kind of script that nineteenth century textbooks used as examples of how we all should write. At first, I wasn't sure it was handwriting at all because of its perfection. But I hardly thought that a computer could have produced those letters buried long enough to produce the mold. But the words had come from a pen, and the signature at the bottom of the page said that Virgil Messer wrote them.

Some words were too obliterated by time and the elements for me to read, but the gist of it was clear, and I mentally filled in the pieces as I read.

March 26, 1968

> *Having just performed the saddest duty that has ever befallen my lot, I write this in the hope that once I am sufficiently away from my dear town of Antioch, someone will find this letter and will do what I should have done but could not do.*
>
> *In the ground below this letter lie the remains of a young woman named Elizabeth Samuels, who came to our farm on this day in search of a mother she had never known. It was by the merest coincidence that she found me alone at the farm because had Berniece or Delores been here, either one would surely have recognized her as belonging to our family and would have taken her into our home. However, they were not, and what happened as a result is unalterable. Through my own carelessness and the idiocy of accident, not through any harbored violence or resentment, they will never have the opportunity, and Berniece's child is gone forever.*
>
> *Elizabeth came here looking for the mother who, in her sixteenth year, had been forced to give up her baby girl. In all innocence, this beautiful young woman appeared at the doorway of my barn, and I knew in the instant who she had to be.*
>
> *I welcomed Elizabeth, and we sat down on a woodpile beside the barn. Then she told me how she came to find out about her adoption, and she expressed no resentment toward her mother. As we talked, the air around us stilled as if in anticipation of the horror to occur. I didn't see it happen, but when she screamed, I knew, and I could not stop the poison already coursing through her body. I killed the creature cursed by God, but it was too late, and my granddaughter died in my arms.*
>
> *To share this knowledge with my wife and daughter would only bring more sorrow. Thus, I did the only thing I could think to do and placed her body in her car and brought her here to her final resting place. Then I drove the car to the end of the road and set fire to the house that once stood there. Nature took care of the rest.*
>
> *One day perhaps my words will bring her discovery and the recognition of the child Berniece could never know. May God forgive me.*

Virgil's unmistakable signature crossed the bottom of the page.

A chill entered my kitchen in spite of the sun that had lifted above the horizon and filtered in through the windows. The fact that I'd been right brought no satisfaction. The simple woman nicknamed Devil Lady had indeed lived a tortured life, much more so than I could have imagined. I realized that at that moment, Berniece could be somewhere out there lacking the knowledge that her child had come looking for her without resentment and without malice, only to meet a horrible, untimely death. And what torture Virgil must have endured for the remainder of his life.

The mysterious intruder in my house suddenly seemed faraway and unimportant. I was glad now that I didn't call Nick because I had bigger news to share. There was someone buried beneath the oak, and I knew who it was.

He answered on the first ring and swore that I didn't awaken him, but I knew better. Just being kind, he was in for another shock. "Nick, I need to see you. When are you going in to the office?"

"I'm due there in an hour." His voice lost the grogginess, and he asked, "Has something happened?"

"Yes, a couple of things. But I need to see you in person. And then we need to talk to Ward."

"Meet you at the office then?"

I agreed to meet him and hung up. I got a folder out of the desk in the living room and went back to the kitchen. I gingerly placed the letter between the covers of the folder and then made myself a pot of coffee. Only then did I realize what a chance I'd been taking by heating the letter. Nick and I had discussed the what-ifs, and we'd both agreed that the best thing to do would be to let an expert advise us. Then I remembered why I'd gotten up in the middle of the night in the first place. I had more than one thing to share with them when I got to the office.

Nick was waiting for me when I got there. He was supposed to work the early shift because Ward had done double duty of late, but I had a feeling that I'd see him before long, too.

He was on the phone when I came in, so I sat down on the other side of his desk, gripping the folder. He hung up the phone, and I said, "Thanks for seeing me, Nick."

"Lila, you know I'm always glad to see you, but I am surprised. I figured you'd be out for the count after yesterday."

"I probably would have been, but something woke me up, and then," I placed the folder on his desk. "Well, look for yourself."

He opened the folder and realized what I'd done to the folded paper. "How'd you do this?"

"I dried it out in the oven at the lowest temperature. But read it, Nick. You'll see why I couldn't sleep."

He turned his attention to the letter, shaking his head as he read. "Son of a gun! Somebody really did die out there, just like we suspected."

"Yeah, but that letter contains a double whammy."

"No kidding. I've never heard anything about Berniece having a daughter. Not a single rumor."

"I know. But somehow, Bart's daughter picked up on enough to write a story about it. My guess is that some kids must have seen Virgil doing something weird, and they added their own details to make the story interesting. That's how Beth got into trouble. Who knows. Maybe she was there, and her way of dealing with the reality was to make up a story about it."

Nick stared at the letter again. "Old Virgil had to deal with some grim stuff, didn't he?"

"And that's the saddest part to me. He probably spared Berniece and Delores a bunch of grief, but I hate to think about that poor man dealing with it all by himself."

"I can't imagine," he said and then looked up. "By the way, not that I mind, but I thought we were going to let the experts advise us before we did anything about opening the letter."

"I was going to, but I was up anyway, and just on the spur of the moment, I figured it wouldn't hurt to put it in the oven to dry. I used the lowest temperature and really kept watch. And it worked pretty well, didn't it?"

"Yeah, it did. Good job. When did you have this brainstorm?"

I shifted in the chair and finally said, "It was a little after three this morning. Something woke me, and I couldn't go back to sleep, so I tried it. I'm just glad it worked."

"What woke you?"

"I heard a noise in the living room and got up to investigate."

"Did you take the pistol with you?"

"Yes. But he'd gone by the time I got there."

"How did you know that?"

"Because I heard the door close."

"A burglar took the time to close the door?"

"Nick, I'm telling you what happened. When I got to the living room, he'd already gone. I went to the window and saw somebody running across the yard. He disappeared into the woods over by the Pattersons."

Nick leaned forward, pressing toward me. "You had somebody in your house, and you didn't call me?"

"I told you, Nick. He was gone. He even locked the door on the way out."

"What? You didn't have the door locked in the first place?"

"I live in Antioch, Nick. Nobody locks their doors. You told me so yourself."

He gave me that sideways grin of disbelief that I'd come to recognize. "But I do hope you consider that most of those people live with somebody else who has a gun and knows how to use it."

I started to argue that he'd given me lessons on the use of the .38, but thankfully, Ward opened the door, and the conversation started all over again. This time, however, it began with my intruder in the middle of the night. His sentiments ran about the same as Nick's but with them added, "I'll drive by there myself tonight. In the meantime, lock the doors, Lila. Times aren't what they used to be."

Then Nick showed him the letter. "Well, I'll be damned," he muttered as he read. "I sure never knew anything about all this."

Nick added, "They kept it a secret from the whole town. I guess the only other person who knew would have to be the father. Any ideas on that one?"

"Absolutely none. Berniece went to high school right here with everybody else, and you know how that goes."

"I remember, but usually word got out around school if somebody was in trouble."

I asked, "What if he wasn't from Antioch?"

"That's a possibility, but no way to find out now, is there?" Then Ward added, "Tell me again how you figured where to find this letter."

I explained it once more, and he asked, "Have you told anybody else about this letter?"

"Not about the letter. We found it after we left Annette's yesterday, but Bart already knew some of it. We asked him if he'd ever heard any rumors about Virgil."

"And what'd he say?"

"He told us that Bethie got into trouble when she was in grade school for writing a story about Virgil burying somebody out on the road. But they figured she was making up stuff on the family like kids in town used to do, so they punished her. Apparently that was the end of it."

Ward said, "Okay. Maybe it was. But at any rate, let's keep a lid on this for now. I'm gonna have to get a crew of state police out here and probably a state medical examiner, not to mention the local coroner." He held up the letter. "This here is just the beginning. Lord knows what else we'll find when we go digging out there."

The shock of his meaning coursed through me. "Ward, you don't think he killed her on purpose and covered it up with the letter?"

Ward didn't comment but laid the letter back on the desk. "I don't know what to think right now. But I'll tell you this: stranger things have happened. We'll know more once we go dig up whatever's lying under that tree. Until then, let's just keep it between us. You two understand?"

Oh, we understood all right. But neither one of us had thought through the ramifications Ward was talking about. I guess that's the difference for somebody who's spent his life in law enforcement even in a small town like Antioch and the rest of us who haven't. I'd heard all the ugly stories of serial killers, but to me, they were still just that—stories. They couldn't happen for real, especially in my town.

"How long do you think all this will take?" I asked.

"Don't have any idea. I'll make some calls today. We'll know more then." His brown eyes bored into mine. "And in the meantime, both of you stay away from the Messer place. And stay away from that logging road. I don't want some fancy lawyer coming back later and suggesting that you planted evidence."

"But her paintings are still out there in the house along with some other things that need to be returned."

He scratched his head and finally said, "Then take Nick with you. You'll need a witness." He reached for the door to his office and then turned around. "Oh, Lila. Did your intruder take anything that you know of?"

"No," I shrugged. "Nothing seems disturbed at all."

"Hmm. A burglar doesn't take anything after he's taken the risk of going in while you're home? And the son-of-a-gun locks the door on the way out. Sounds to me like somebody you know. You wouldn't have any ideas on who that might be, now would you?"

For the second time in a few hours, I shivered involuntarily. Annette was the only person in town who knew about Johnny. I'd thought about telling Nick, and Ward too for that matter, but the time hadn't been right yet.

"I guess I need to tell you something," I finally said. And as the two of them listened to my story, their expressions changed to anger. "It could be Johnny," I concluded.

Ward said, "Sure sounds like it. When was it his wife called you?"

"A few nights ago. I didn't think too much about it because Johnny had gotten selfish like that. He would have run away to save himself and left Shannon to deal with it on her own."

"Nice guy," Ward said.

Nick added, "Who else would have broken into your house, Lila? Ward's right about it being somebody you know, especially if you have an idea what he might be looking for."

"That's just it. I don't know what he could be looking for. Why would he break into my house and just leave? If Johnny came looking for me, wouldn't he try to shut me up, not steal something from me?"

"I can't answer that one yet," Ward said. "But in the meantime, we're gonna keep a real close eye on your place, and if you think of anything he might be looking for, give me a call, okay?"

I promised that I would, and when Ward retreated into his office, we saw him talking on the phone. No doubt he'd have a busy day. Nick said softly, "Lila, you could have told me about Johnny."

"I know, Nick. But it wasn't a matter of trust. You should know that. I do trust you, of all people. Johnny's just part of my past that I thought didn't need attention any longer. I would have eventually told you, but it wasn't important to me at the time."

I could see he was hurt, but there was no use trying to salve feelings. Other things demanded our attention at the moment. Nick and Ward would have a full day explaining the evidence to authorities and deciding who should be called out to Antioch. And I had spent too much time away from the job that brought me to Antioch in the first place. I went back to the store and dug into the pile of prescriptions awaiting me. By lunchtime, I was fairly well caught up, but the lack of sleep caught up as fast, and I left the store in midafternoon and went home to rest. But rest would be the last thing I got that afternoon.

Forgiveness

I pulled down the shades in my bedroom and turned on the ceiling fan. Removing the comforter seemed too much trouble, so I kicked off my shoes and lay down on top of it fully clothed. Strange as it may seem now, by that time, the intruder in the middle of the night seemed far away and impersonal, and I drifted off to sleep almost immediately. For perhaps a half hour, I basked in that dreamless state of complete relaxation.

Then the gears in my brain ground into action, and I could do little to stop the process. One line of thinking led to a second then a third. I tried my old trick of playing a song tape in my head. Usually that works because when I'm forced to remember words, the brain can't think of anything else and eventually gets tired enough to let go. But that afternoon, every time I came to a phrase I couldn't quite remember, the brain filled in the void with another concern. Finally, I gave up. Some things still had to be done before I could let go.

I remembered Ward's admonition about going out to Berniece's alone, but some things still needed to be done, and Nick had his hands full. I also thought about asking Annette, but she too was still recuperating from all the activities and trying to catch up on her own affairs that she'd let go in order to do the luncheon for me. The paintings were my concern. I was afraid that exposure to the heat in the house might damage them, and now that the story of Berniece's work had been broadcast around the state, I couldn't be sure that some nut might not destroy them for kicks. I needed to wrap them up again and take them back to the safe at the church. Time for showing them would come soon enough. And Bart's air conditioner needed to go back into his workshop, where he spent a lot of time. To Ward, these matters may have seemed small, but they were important to me, and I needed to get them done before the state police arrived and wouldn't let me near the house.

I put on a pair of old shorts with a tee shirt and headed out to Berniece's place. All those cars from the day before had trampled down what grass remained, making the place look even more forlorn than usual. I parked there beneath the group of trees and made my way to the porch. When I unlocked the front door, I knew I'd done the right thing. Heat inside the house was nearly suffocating. We'd thought about leaving the air conditioner on, but that would have required keeping the generator running, and that couldn't happen. Andy had to be back in Hattiesburg, and besides, it would have been silly to run the thing without anybody present.

I started in the living room and took the paintings one by one to the family's dining table where I had some space. I was going to the hall closet to get out the brown paper I'd left folded there when I heard a noise outside the window. Suspecting that my imagination still played tricks on me from the previous night, I shrugged it off as an animal moving about in the yard. The area around the house was still covered with winter's accumulation of leaves, particularly those large magnolia leaves, and they magnified every sound.

I went back to the dining room and wrapped the pictures one at a time with the brown paper and then stacked them by the front door that I'd left open, with only the screen door to keep out the insects. Then I picked up three of the paintings and headed for the car, the screen door banging against the house as I left. Using my key fob, I opened the trunk and put the first load of pictures down. I realized then that I needed to put Bart's air conditioner in first because it would fit into that little space nearest the backseat. I reached down to pick up the first load when a hand cupped around my mouth, and a voice said, "Don't scream, Lila."

I knew that voice, but the reality of what was happening couldn't sink in, and I struggled to free myself from the arm that wrapped around my shoulders. Again he said, "Don't scream, Lila. I'm not here to hurt you."

I finally stopped struggling. The hand slowly dropped from my mouth, and the arm released its grip. The person I turned to face was much thinner than the one I'd known for much of my life. His eyes looked anxious and tired, and his face hadn't been shaved for days.

"I knew it was you, Johnny," I said, turning to face him.

"You knew I'd come, didn't you?"

I nodded. "And that was you last night, wasn't it?"

"In your house?" He turned his eyes away from me. "Yes, I was there. But it's not what you think."

"Johnny, I don't know what to think. What were you looking for? I don't have anything of yours."

He turned back to me and said softly, "Lila, I didn't come to take anything from you. I've done enough of that already."

"Well, why did you break into my house? Tell me, Johnny! Why did you follow me here and ruin the peace I've created for myself in this little town?"

He started to say something, but our attention turned to the road where a car approached the lane.

Johnny grabbed my arms and leaned closer, saying, "Lila, I had to talk to you before they took me into custody and it was too late. It was important enough for me to take all kinds of chances. I wasn't in your house last night to steal something from you. I went there to leave you a message, but then you heard me, and I didn't have the nerve to stay. I wanted to see you in person, and that's not exactly the way to do it, now is it? I came out here to talk to you face-to-face, not like some coward sneaking in to leave a message in the middle of the night."

I pulled away from him and tried to run toward the car that barreled down the lane. He drew me toward him, shaking me until I looked back into those eyes. "I saw the news, Lila. I knew you'd be back, so I waited."

Nick's SUV stopped at the edge of the trees, but Johnny maintained his grip on my arms, his voice desperate. "Lila, I came here to apologize. I've screwed up everything I ever wanted, including our friendship." He shook me as the last words fell out in a torrent. "I just wanted you to forgive me."

As his words hung in the air, another voice demanded, "Back off, or I'll shoot."

Johnny shook me again, and Nick repeated, "Let her go, or I'll shoot."

When Johnny didn't move, a louder sound pierced the quietness of the countryside, and Johnny slumped to the ground. His shoulder was covered in blood, and he lay motionless save for the eyes that followed Nick as he moved toward us.

Nick asked, "Are you all right, Lila?"

"I'm okay, Nick. I'm fine." Then I knelt beside my onetime friend and said to him, "Hold on, Johnny. We'll get you some help."

"This is Johnny?"

"This is my friend. And we need to get him to a hospital."

"Lila, this man came here to kill you. I know he's hurt, but let's not forget why he's here."

"He didn't come here to hurt me, Nick. I thought so too, but he came here to ask my forgiveness."

"Well, he's got a strange way of doing it," Nick said.

"Think about it, Nick. If he'd wanted to kill me, he had every chance."

Johnny held onto the shoulder wound, grimacing in pain. "She's right," he said. That's why I came here."

The arm holding the pistol dropped to his side. "If what you say is true, then I guess we'd better get him some medical attention."

We helped Johnny to his feet and walked him to the white SUV and then got him inside. "Where are you taking him?"

Nick started up the car. "My dad's office," he said. "He's the closest help."

"I can't leave the paintings here. I'll put them in the car and meet you there."

Nick nodded, and the car headed back up the lane and then turned onto the road in the direction of town. I returned to the house where I picked up the pictures and loaded them into my trunk. The air conditioner could wait. The pictures were safe for the moment, but a friend needed me.

I'd seen Doc Reynolds's house. Everybody pointed it out to me when I first moved to Antioch as if it were a local shrine. One of the few who actually lived within the town limits, Doc had maintained the house with the same kindness he'd apparently given to generations of patients. Too bad he couldn't do the same for his only son, I thought as I pulled into his driveway.

Nick's car was already there with the passenger door still open. I shut it as I passed by and then stepped onto the porch. I thought about knocking but instead tried the door and found it open as I knew it would be. I stepped inside where it was cool and dimly lit. Formal furniture told me that this room didn't see a lot of use, and the only sound I heard was the ticking of the grandfather clock in the hallway. I called out, "Nick! Doc Reynolds!"

A cat peered at me around the corner and then disappeared beneath the sofa. Again I called their names, again with no response. I followed the hallway until it ended with a doorway and then stepped out onto a small patio. The drive led around to the back where decades of patients had parked and gone into the smaller building in the rear.

When I opened the door, Johnny lay on an examination table with Doc Reynolds bent over him, intent on the job at hand. Nick stood by, holding a mask up to his face as his father worked to retrieve the bullet that his son had put into the man's shoulder. Nick's eyes followed me, but neither of us spoke.

"That's pretty ugly," Doc said and held something covered in blood up to the light. "But I think you'll survive, son."

Johnny tried to smile, but it turned into more of a grimace.

"You take it easy. I'm gonna get you bandaged up, and after you sleep it off, you can tell me all about it." His eyes met Nick's. "This should be a good story."

When he finished, Doc Reynolds looked at me for the first time.

Nick put down the mask and told him, "Dad, this is Lila Dawkins."

I held out my hand but realized he still wore gloves. I said, "Glad to finally meet you, Doctor Reynolds."

"You're the new pharmacist, huh?"

It wasn't a question, but a statement, and I began to understand Nick's dilemma. Doc Reynolds was in person even larger than his reputation. Taller still than Nick, he was an imposing figure, septuagenarian or not. White hair had replaced the earlier duplicate of Nick's dark brown, but the face gave him away. The piercing blue eyes were the same as was the strong profile. Sure the chin wasn't as firm, but Doc Reynolds could never deny his son. I wanted to tell Nick that if he wanted to see himself in forty years, he needed to look no further, but I didn't know how much either one of them wanted to hear that at that moment.

Doc asked his patient if he was comfortable, and Johnny managed a nod and then closed his eyes.

"He'll be fine for now," Doc said and motioned toward the door. "Let's go into my office."

Again, this was no question, more of a command. Nick motioned me ahead of him as we moved into the adjoining room, and Doc closed the door that separated us from the patient. "Have a seat," he ordered again, and the three of us sat down around the doctor's desk.

Glaring at Nick, he said, "Before the police get here, suppose you tell me why you shot that fella in there."

I could see Nick's temper rising, and I interrupted, "Why don't I tell you about it."

Doc raised his brows, but I continued, "Nick thought Johnny was going to kill me. He was holding my arms and shaking me, and Nick thought he was trying to hurt me. He ordered him to let me go, but he didn't. Nick did what he had to do, as simple as that."

Nick added, "There's more to the story, Dad."

"I'm sure there is." His eyes remained on me.

"Doc, sooner or later, you'll hear the whole thing," I began. "For now, suffice it to say that Johnny was hiding from the law. Nick knew that. And Nick had good reason, as I did at the time, to believe that Johnny had come to kill me to keep me from testifying against him."

"I see," Doc said. "Did that man kill somebody? Did he hurt a child?"

"No, nothing like that. His crime was the oldest one in the book, greed."

Doc nodded. "Son, you did the right thing then."

"I know, Dad. But thanks."

A siren sounded not too far from the office, and Doc got up from his place behind the desk. "Guess I better go meet them," he said and left the room.

Nick asked, "Are you ready for this?"

"To talk to the police?"

"Yep. They're gonna ask you the same questions a hundred different ways, but don't let them shake you. Tell the truth, and everything will be fine."

"I know. We have nothing to hide."

"Thanks, Lila."

"I'm the one who should be thanking you. For all either of us knew at the time, Johnny wanted me dead. You only did what you thought was right. Truth is, you could have killed him, Nick."

"I appreciate the vote of confidence, but you never know how these things might go. I'm a rookie and, on top of that, no training. It could turn ugly."

"Something tells me that your dad won't let that happen."

"He's a pretty influential man in these parts, but I'm not sure even he can smooth this one over."

What Nick said worried me more than a little, but I wasn't about to let him know. He'd acted on my behalf, and I'd do anything I could to defend him. Of course, there was no telling what Johnny might say. Although he had come to Antioch to apologize to me, I couldn't be sure that he wouldn't press charges or, at the least, file some insane lawsuit. After all, he had no weapon when Nick fired on him. My guess was that if anybody could make a difference in Johnny's thinking, it would have to be me.

Nick was right about the questioning. The police separated us as I expected, and I repeated the story from every angle time and time again. But I couldn't change my story because it was the truth. I knew that Nick was going through the same thing, only worse, so I maintained the degree of patience needed to get through it without losing my temper. When they finally released me, I didn't even try to talk to Nick. I figured that might look bad for him, and there was somebody else I needed to see anyway.

They had taken Johnny to the hospital in Hattiesburg, and I wanted to visit him to talk some more, but I knew somebody else who was waiting to hear about Johnny. I called Shannon to let her know where Johnny was and told her that although he was in some deep legal trouble, he was physically okay. And I told her that Johnny had come to apologize to me.

"For what, Lila?" she wanted to know.

"You'll find out soon enough, but I wanted to call and let you know he's okay."

"I'll come right down there. I want to see him."

"I'm not too sure they'll let you do that," I advised.

"Why not? I don't understand."

"Shannon, it's better if Johnny tells you himself. For now, just wait. He'll contact you as soon as he can."

Then I drove to Hattiesburg. The guard at Johnny's door told me that I could have a few minutes with the prisoner, but that he would also have to be present. That was okay by me. The more witnesses, the better.

Johnny was awake when I entered the room, but he still looked a lot worse for the wear. "Hey." I went to stand by his bed. "How are you feeling?"

"Like I've been shot," he said with a faint grin. "Thanks for coming."

"Yeah, well, I'm sorry all this has happened."

"Me, too, Lila. I got greedy."

"It happens."

"Mostly I'm sorry I dumped on the best friend I ever had."

"Thanks, Johnny. It took some guts to come here to tell me that."

He gave me a weak smile and added, "Lila, your friend did what I would have done. I shoulda been shot a long time ago. Maybe then I wouldn't have hurt so many people."

"Do you mean that?" I asked.

"As far as I'm concerned, it's over. I'm already facing years in prison, and I don't want to spend them with any more on my conscience than I already have."

I reached for his hand and told him, "I'll be there, Johnny. I'll do what I can."

Truth from Fiction

I didn't leave Hattiesburg until nearly midnight. Bone tired, I was still anxious about how the questioning had gone for Nick, so I called him on the return trip. He sounded tired, perhaps more so than I'd ever heard him.

"How'd it go?" I asked.

"Good, I think."

"No charges filed?"

"None so far. I guess that depends now on Johnny."

"In that case, you can relax." And I told him about my conversation with Johnny.

He thanked me and then added, "The day hasn't been all bad. Dad called me tonight. Asked me to come have dinner with him."

"That's wonderful news. I'm happy for both of you, Nick."

"Yeah, I'm happy too. It must be true that good can come from a bad situation. Oh, and that reminds me. What do you have planned for tomorrow morning?"

"I haven't thought that far ahead. Why?"

"Ward has a crew going out to the Messer place first thing in the morning."

"My god, that's fast. How'd he pull that off?"

"He's been on the phone all day. I guess he called in a few favors."

"Must have. So they're going to try to find the grave tomorrow?"

"Yep. Ward convinced them that somebody's buried out there, so they're bringing in a whole team." He chuckled and added, "I think he mentioned the words *serial killer*. That got their attention."

"You're kidding?"

"I don't know whether he did or not, but Ward does have some old pretty powerful contacts. You'd be surprised."

"I bet."

"So would you like to be there?"

"Of course, you know I do. But will they let me near the place?"

"I'm not sure. I'll call you in the morning and let you know what I find out."

"Nick?"

"Yeah?"

"How tired are you?"

"Still running on adrenaline," he said. "Would you like some company?"

"Only yours."

He was waiting for me when I turned into the drive. We talked for a few minutes, but for the most part, enough had been said. I poured myself a glass of wine, and he lay down across my bed while I got ready to turn in. When I came back from the bathroom, he was snoring softly, and I turned out the light. Nick was already gone when I finally woke up to a stream of sunlight around the shades.

I went in to the store late, but Edwin assured me that was understandable under the circumstances. I started work on my backlog again. This time it was Ward's call that brought things to a halt. He said, "I hate to interrupt, but I thought you might want to be part of the activities today."

I thanked him for calling me and tried to look pitiful as I looked at the young assistant, who had no doubt begun to think of me as temporary help rather than the other way around. "I'll be back as soon as I can," I assured her and hurried out the door.

Berniece's front yard was filled with cars again. This time, police cars had taken the place of news reporters and cameras, but the effect was the same. Something important was about to take place, and thanks to Ward, I would be a part of it.

The crew's leader for the day appeared to be Dr. Mark Everson, the state medical examiner from Jackson. He was a rather short man with a boyish face whose speech told me he'd not spent much time out of the state. But behind the thick glasses was a seriousness that demanded respect. Our county coroner, David Houston, stood beside him, nodding in accordance with each point that Everson made. David, an older soft-spoken man I knew on a speaking basis, looked uneasy in the suit donned for the occasion. Although I'd always gotten the impression that he was competent enough to fulfill the requirements of his job, it was easy to see that he felt overshadowed by the man from Jackson and would no doubt accede to Everson's demands and priorities.

Detective Pritchard followed with his expectations. Red-haired and freckled, he too looked younger than his words would indicate, but the eyes said he'd seen too much already. Somebody had been killed and buried out there. He intended to find out whose remains lay beneath the tree and, most importantly, find the person responsible.

The little group had met for convenience's sake on the front lawn, but it soon would adjourn to the logging road behind the house. Since the only way to get to that road required going back to the highway and then turning onto smaller and narrower roads, Ward thought it best to lead the way along the circuitous route.

Ward's car led the way followed by Dave's with Everson as a passenger. Pritchard insisted on driving alone followed by two police vehicles. Finally, Nick and I brought up the rear. Once we arrived at the spot, Ward got out and motioned the group toward the oak. As the group convened beneath the tree, Ward commented quietly, "Haven't seen this many cars in a line since Old Man Martin's funeral."

"Yeah," Nick added, "Around here, funerals do that."

"Huh! Hadn't thought of it that way, but you're right. This is a funeral. Only thing is we don't know yet whose it is."

Ward turned when a pickup truck pulled up behind us and then announced, "All right gentlemen. Let's get on with it. Nick, why don't you show us where to start digging?"

Once more, Nick traced out the roots that formed a cross, explaining that this formation had caused us to look in that particular spot. He then pointed to the small hole where we'd uncovered the box. "The letter says that the body is buried under the box. So it should be right here."

Detective Pritchard motioned to a couple of uniformed officers who went to the pickup truck and brought back shovels. With repeated warnings from the medical examiner to move cautiously, I was surprised to see that within thirty minutes, they had a sizeable hole dug beneath the oak. I moved closer to the would-be grave with that same mixture of emotions we always feel when we're about to witness something terrible. Although we're repulsed and filled with dread at the same time, we can't turn away. I'd talked to myself all the way out there about the possibilities that we might unearth, and I thought I was ready. But nothing could have prepared me for standing beside what should be a grave and seeing firsthand what lay beneath the earth.

One of the men stopped. He tentatively poked the shovel into the earth once more and then announced, "Got something!" Pritchard squatted down beside the unearthed grave. From my place behind him, I could see what appeared to be part of a skull.

"Easy now," the detective repeated and then instructed, "get the other tools we brought. We have to get these bones out of here in as near a whole as possible. Everybody understand?"

I was about to discover that the digging was the easy part. Now came the sifting away of dirt and the gentle moving of anything that lay on top of or beside the skeleton. Bit by bit, dirt fell away from the bones, and a form began to take shape. But hours would pass before the skeleton was completely unearthed, and nobody knew at that point or would say how many days might pass before we found out who lay beneath the oak.

Nick put his arm around my shoulders and whispered, "Do you want to stay here for this?"

"I've seen enough for now."

Nick walked me to the car and told me that he'd stay in case Ward needed him. For once in my life, I was glad to be away from the action. From that point on, I would be happy to hear about the evidence, not to see it. I didn't need to be part of the agonizing process of lifting a woman's bones from the ground and testing every available particle through modern science. The experts could do that. The hard part for me would be the wait. I'd heard stories about the underfunded staff of our state and the months of wait required for any positive identification. So I went back to the store, my touch of reality in an otherwise unreal day, and went to work. There I might help the living.

As I expected, the curious filed through the store all afternoon. Everybody had heard about the goings-on out behind the Messer place and that I had been present when they dug up a woman. And everybody had a theory about who it was and how she got there. For the moment, I didn't want to hear any of them. The poor woman buried out there on the logging road deserved better. And so did Virgil. He was no murderer, and I wanted desperately to prove that.

The day cried out for my favorite drink, and I stopped by the little grocery store out close to my house in hopes that they'd have some limes. I'm still not sure what set off the thought process, but when I entered the store, something clicked, something that I should have recognized long before. Maybe it was the fact that this little store reminded me of the one where Nick and I had stopped in Tennessee, but whatever it was, the idea became crystal clear right there in the middle of the store.

I paid for my limes and got back into the car before I called Nick. "Are you still out at the oak?" I asked.

"We're finishing up right now. What's going on?"

"Nick, I remembered something, something important. Can you come by here before you go home?"

He promised that he would, and I returned to my house. While I waited, I turned on the computer and went to Amazon.com. I typed in Books by Author followed by the name. And there it was. I didn't know yet what it meant. I couldn't wait to share the discovery with Nick, and I didn't have to wait long.

When he knocked at the back door, I called for him to come on into the living room where I still had the information on the screen. "Look at this, Nick."

He stood behind me and leaned over me to look at the screen. He shook his head and asked, "What am I looking at?"

"Does this name mean anything to you?" I asked, moving the cursor beneath the name on the screen.

"Tom Clewis? That is familiar, but I can't place it. Do I know—wait a minute. Wasn't he the man up at Charity that was asked about Berniece?"

"Exactly." Then I told him about how I'd stopped by the store when something clicked. "Nick, this Tom person either knew Virgil or he knows Berniece. I'd bet on it."

"He did change his attitude pretty fast, didn't he?"

"Yeah. When I mentioned Berniece, he shut down."

"At the time, I just thought he was the eccentric artist type, but now that you mention it, he did change. I wonder why."

"I don't know, but let's see what this book he wrote is about."

We searched the site and soon found a synopsis for a novel called simply *Choices*. Nick pulled up a chair and sat down beside me. I began to scroll down as we read, the implications becoming clearer with each word.

"Nick," I said, "This is Virgil's story."

"It does seem that way. Click on the author, see if it tells us anything about him."

I did, and the usual blurb accompanied nothing really personal except for one rather important fact. Tom Clewis was a professor of American literature at a large Southern university.

"God, Nick. No wonder he blanched when we mentioned Berniece. He had to put two and two together with the last name. All these years, he's gotten by with publishing Virgil's story. Then he heard that Virgil not only has a daughter, but that she also might come to live in Charity. Who knows, maybe he even thought we'd found out about him and gone up there to look for him."

"That creep. Wonder how long he's been going up to Charity whenever he feels like it and steals another idea from somebody else."

"I doubt too many people would share ideas with him. But when Virgil died, I guess he thought he'd be safe forever. He didn't know Virgil mailed that manuscript before he died."

Nick agreed that I was probably right and then he asked, "Has he written anything else?"

We returned to the main page and scanned for other works by that author. Only two other things showed up though, both nonfiction and scholarly in nature. "Kinda makes you wonder if his research is genuine too, doesn't it?"

"That it does. And, Lila, it makes me wonder about something else too. If that book's been fairly successful, he's made some real money off it. Who do you think deserves that money?"

"Virgil's family of course." My words were hardly out of my mouth when I realized why Nick had asked. "Of course!" I pulled his face toward me and kissed him. "You brilliant man, you. I suspect that our friend Tom Clewis just may want to make a generous contribution to the showing of Berniece's work."

Nick grinned. "That's a distinct possibility."

"And," I said, clicking the screen back to the biography page. "I do believe that with a little more research, we can find this large university. After all, the man hails from Tennessee. He can't be that hard to locate. And with just a little prodding, Dr. Clewis and the school's wealthy alumni could provide a lot of publicity for Berniece."

"That's true," Nick agreed. Then his face changed from a grin to something more akin to shock.

"What?" I demanded.

"What if plagiarism is not all he's guilty of doing?"

"I don't get it, Nick. What're you talking about?"

He sighed and said, "Lila, what if he does know where Berniece is?"

His intent finally sank in. "Murder? Why didn't I think of that angle before? Of course, if Berniece showed up and threatened his little tea party, he could have done anything."

"He could have, but from plagiarism to murder is a long stretch. Let's don't get carried away at this point. After all, nobody else up there had seen her either, so that doesn't necessarily make him guilty of doing away with her."

"True. Okay, let's focus on what we do know."

Nick said, "Would you like to bet he's already turned tail and gone back to his university?"

"I don't bet on sure things," I said and began typing in the address bar. "The University of Tennessee would be a good place to start."

After wading through the introductory phases of the Web site, I came up with the university's instructors listed by academic colleges. First, I tried the College of Education and found nothing. Then I went to the College of Arts and Sciences. Bingo. Dr. Thomas Clewis, professor of American literature and associate director of independent studies. "I bet he does independent studies," I said.

"How do you want to approach him?" Nick asked.

"I'm not sure. Let's think about it. We want to make sure we have our ducks in a row, so the first thing I need to do is get a copy of his book and read it."

"Good idea. We don't need to make accusations that aren't true."

"There's always the possibility that he used Virgil's basic idea and wrote his own story from it. Even though that's still plagiarism in my book, it would be harder to prove. And murder's even harder than that. But if he's done something to Berniece, rest assured that I will keep poking around until I can prove it."

"I'm sure you will, Lila. Feel like a ride into Hattiesburg tomorrow after work?" he asked. "I've been wanting to see the new Barnes and Noble there."

Green Lights

The whole world believes now that modern science can do anything, so it was with that expectation that I waited on news from the exhumation of our mystery lady. The examiner's first conclusions coincided with what we had expected—that the bones belonged to a woman somewhere between the ages of eighteen and the early twenties. But we've become accustomed to clever characters working round the clock to put together the most random of clues, and they seemed to work with amazing speed. I knew that in reality, the process grinds out much more slowly, but it didn't stop me from hoping. Any day, I expected news from Jackson that would confirm what Virgil had told us in his manuscript. And quite naturally, when you're expecting something to happen, time slows to a crawl.

Nick and I talked about it on our ride into Hattiesburg. I asked the same rhetorical questions all over again, and the conversation took its usual turn. Berniece's daughter and Johnny's most recent circumstances seemed to be at the center of all our conversations of late. Federal and state charges against Johnny were imposed, but after spending a minimum amount of time in jail, he'd posted bail and awaited trial. Shannon had come to his aid, but unless she miraculously grew up in the interim, I doubted how much help she might be. When the money ran out, I suspected so would Shannon.

I would no doubt be called to testify, a fact that I wasn't looking forward to but would do nonetheless even if I were not required to do so. I wanted to do what I could to help Johnny. A call from his lawyer told me that my testimony could go a long way in convincing a jury of his remorse and the almost nonexistent probability that he would be a repeat offender. All that was somewhere in the offing though, and again, there was little to do but wait.

That and find out whatever we could about Tom Clewis. We had called ahead to the store, and Clewis's book waited for us at the information desk. Rather than opening it instantly though, I wandered off in another direction.

"What're you looking for?" Nick asked.

"Forensic science. They should have something here."

He went to the desk and typed the word into the computer. After several sources came up, we located one on the shelf and sat down to read. As I said, everybody's seen enough television and movies to know that you have to have some basis of comparison when using DNA for identification, but I wanted to know more than that. What kind of objects might be used for comparison? How long could DNA remain intact in human bones buried beneath the soil? Could it identify both male and female parents?

I thumbed briefly through the thick forensics book, filled with complicated drawings and processes. "This may be more information than I wanted. And I sure don't want to pay for this."

"I'll make a deal with you," Nick said. "Give me that book and tell me what you want to know. While I'm finding the answers, you can start on Clewis's novel and see if the story's the same. You're more familiar with it than I am."

"You've got a deal."

We swapped books, and while I read the increasingly familiar story, Nick took notes on forensics. Probably thirty minutes had passed when he said, "I think I'm done here. Have you reached a verdict yet?"

"No doubt about it. Clewis used Virgil's story almost exactly. He set it in Tennessee, and the name of the town is different, which explains why nobody in Antioch picked up on it. But the really funny part is that Virgil's a better writer."

"Somehow that doesn't surprise me."

"Yeah, when Virgil describes Antioch, I can see the places, hear the people. I don't think Clewis has ever even been there. And it shows."

"I have to admit I was hoping it wouldn't be quite so obvious," Nick said. "But I guess if you're gonna steal somebody's work, you go all the way. He thought Virgil and Delores were dead, so nobody would ever be the wiser."

"And that makes me sad to think that Virgil wrote the story so somebody would find out what happened to Elizabeth. And look what happened instead. That's the part that really makes me mad."

"I know," he said, looking down at his note. "But let me run this by you before we leave. I think I found out what you wanted to know, but let's be sure."

"Okay."

"There are several processes used, but for samples that lack nucleated cellular material, such as hair, bones, and teeth, they use a process called Mitochondrial DNA Analysis. With samples that are very old and have been exposed to the elements like a buried body, this is really the only reliable method."

"Okay. So far so good. What about the comparison to a male relative?"

"From what I can tell, the father's sperm contributes only nuclear DNA, so this test works only with the maternal relative, which in our case is good. Other methods are used in paternity cases and rape cases primarily. If we have a sample of Berniece's DNA, they should be able to tell us if it matches the bones."

"In other words, we'll know if the body could be Berniece's daughter?"

"Exactly. But don't get your hopes up too soon, Lila. This thing may take a year or more. With funding problems and a huge backlog, I suspect they'll be concentrating on more current problems."

"I know," I assured him. "In the meantime, I need to talk to Ward again. See if he's made any progress on finding out who adopted Berniece's daughter."

"He's doing what he can, but with the adoption records sealed, I don't know how much he'll be able to find out."

"I realize that, but what if it wasn't a formal adoption?"

"That makes it even harder," Nick said. "If it was just an agreement between the parties, there'd be no records. The only thing we'd have to go on then would be word of mouth."

"True, but, Nick, somebody should have come forward when she went missing. Surely, there's a missing persons report that matches up with the time she arrived in Antioch."

"There probably is, but searching for it takes time. And it was more than twenty years ago, long enough for changes to take place. People die or move away. Just give Ward some time."

I vowed that I would, but one thought nagged at me all the way back to Antioch. Time seemed to be the key to everything in this case. And it occurred to me that although we couldn't locate Berniece, her father still had relatives in Florida who needed to be brought up-to-date on their family's happenings, and before Nick and I approached Tom Clewis with our allegations, I needed to inform those relatives. They needed to know that his words had catapulted the entire town into the midst of an investigation. And they needed to know that the very same man whom state police might accuse of murder was also the victim of plagiarism and that had he not died, his work could very well have won the acclaim attributed to Tom Clewis.

Keeping in mind that the simplest approach is often the best approach, later that night I called Vivian Bastrop. I called her once before to let her know that the manuscript had arrived and to thank her for sending it, but I had not called since, and that conversation was way overdue.

Vivian answered with the same placid tone that she'd used before. We chatted for a minute, and then I got down to my purpose.

"Vivian, this novel is very well done. I'm no expert on literature, but I've done enough reading to recognize talent. Did you read the manuscript?"

"I must say I did not. Not because I didn't want to, but sometimes I don't handle things like that very well," she admitted. "If it's family, I get all melancholy, so I sent it on to you."

"And I'm so glad you did. But Vivian, this manuscript has opened all kinds of cans of worms."

"Oh? How so?"

Then I told her. I told her how we recognized the place where Michael buried his daughter, and I told her how we found Virgil's letter there and how we now waited for DNA tests to confirm our theory on identification of the exhumed body.

"I can't believe it. Berniece had a daughter! We had no idea."

"There's more, Vivian."

"Good grief! Next you'll tell me that my family spawned a serial killer, and he's on the way to Alligator Point."

"No, actually this is the milder part. Okay, you know about Virgil's manuscript, but what you don't know yet is that it's been published as a novel."

"Published? When?"

"It came out about ten years ago, and it was quite successful. But, Vivian, here's the thing. Somebody stole your cousin's story and published under his own name."

With that revelation, she asked me a hundred other questions, all of which I too would have asked under the circumstances. When I asked her whether she wanted me to proceed with the investigation into Clewis's plagiarism, she said she wanted a few days to think that one through. She'd contact me when she'd made a decision. On the matter of Virgil's granddaughter's identification, she wanted to know the minute I did.

We agreed that for two people who hadn't even known each other a few months ago, we now had quite a strong connection.

"Must be the town," I said. "It makes us all kin sooner or later."

For the remainder of the week, I did my best to go on with life as usual. Friday came, still without any word from the lab, and I still waited for Vivian to tell me what she wanted to do about Clewis. Something else though had gained my attention for the evening, and although I did look forward to it, I was also a little nervous.

Doc and his son had made those first steps toward repairing their relationship, and he'd decided that it was time to invite me for dinner. "Is this like taking your girl friend home to meet the parents?" I'd asked Annette when I stopped by on my way home from work.

"Lila, that's exactly what it is," she said. "The difference is that neither one of you is in high school anymore."

I pumped her for information. "You've known the man forever. I met him one time for a few minutes. What's he really like?"

"What you see is what you get, Lila. He's as good a man as ever lived, but there's no middle ground for him."

"What do you mean by that?"

"Well," she stopped for a second and then asked, "have you ever met Nick's sister, Lynn?"

"No. Nick talks about her some, but she lives in Arizona doesn't she?"

"Yes, she does. But do you know why?"

"No idea. I assumed she married somebody from Arizona or she got a job out there."

"That would be a logical conclusion," Annette said. "But when it comes to Doc and his daughter, logic doesn't enter the picture. That girl is exactly like her dad—either-or, all or none, black or white. Doc wanted her to be a cheerleader, so she played on the soccer team, would've gone out for football if the school had let her. When she was a little girl, the family went on vacation to Arizona, and she loved it. Came back telling everybody that she would move to Arizona any day. We all thought it was cute, but sure enough, when she graduated from high school, she got a scholarship to Arizona State, and she hasn't turned back since. She runs one of those guest ranches down south of Tucson now."

"That explains the picture of her in the Western outfit. I asked Nick about it, but he just smiled and told me she lived in Arizona."

"He would. They were real close as kids. And she was also close with her mother. Truth be told, I always wondered how she and Doc got together in the first place."

"Whadda you mean?"

"She was headstrong, and so was Lynn. Louise had a degree from some Ivy League school in archaeology, of all things. I remember when she went with a group to Peru. Thought Doc would split a gut."

"So what happened? Did she give it up?"

"Sort of. She tamed it down, but she'd go every now and then to some site around the South."

"I can see where Lynn got it, then."

"Yeah, and she got by with more because she was a girl, Daddy's sweetheart. Nicky wanted to please his dad, but she was too much like her mother and didn't care whether he agreed with her choices or not."

"I guess that's why Nick's had a few problems along the way."

She reached over the kitchen table and squeezed my hand. "Don't let any of this scare you, Lila. Doc will love you. After all, you're a bit of a rebel like his daughter."

I thought about that on the way home. No wonder Nick had some trouble figuring it all out. His sister had rebelled against everything her father tried to make of her, so naturally, Nick, being the older child and the son, felt an even greater responsibility to follow in his father's footsteps. I told Nick that I'd feel more comfortable if we went together, so he was to pick me up at seven. It was early summer, and darkness didn't come until some time after eight. The day had been cloudless, and I could see the nighttime being the same.

Nick and I were on the way to his father's house when my cell rang. I didn't recognize the number beyond the fact that the prefix was from the area around Jackson. A dignified voice, albeit friendly said, "Lila, this is Kathryn Burroughs."

"Why, Governor Burroughs," I said for Nick to hear. "How nice of you to call."

"My pleasure, Lila. But please, that title makes me feel old."

"I don't want to do that."

"Good, then Kathryn it is. And I called you with a bit of good news."

"I'm always in the mood for that."

"Aren't we all? I've been in touch with the group that came to see Ms. Messer's work, primarily Suzanne Lu, and they've worked out plans for an exhibit to feature Mississippi women artists. It's not scheduled until next spring, but Suzanne would love to have Berniece's work in that show."

Although I was nearly speechless, I found words to thank her and then asked if I could be of assistance. "I'm glad you asked," she said. "The exhibit will need some biographical information about the artist, the type that would make an interesting brochure to hand out to patrons. I recommended you to write it up. Did I speak out of turn?"

"No, not at all. I'd love to do that."

We concluded our conversation, and I filled Nick in. "It's happening," I said and told him about the exhibit.

"Congratulations, Lila. You've worked hard for this."

"No, Berniece deserves it. That makes finding out about her daughter even more important now. Think what that will add to her story."

"It won't be dull, that's for sure."

Dinner at the Doc's house was fun, a term I'd not expected to use in reference to the good doctor. While he certainly didn't fawn over me, he also didn't treat me as an outsider, the situation I feared most. He had planned dinner by the pool, which I loved. Conversation outdoors is always easier, and the night turned out to be one of those that you think about the following winter. The moon was full, and as it rose over the house, it had a whiteness reminiscent of Virgil's cotton fields. The back of Doc's house looks out over an open field covered at that time of year with someone's crop of corn, already grown to chest level. I wanted to take my shoes off and go tromping through the stalks, maybe get lost in the moonlight. But I'd save that for another time.

Doc and I got along famously. Our common backgrounds in medicine probably gave me a leg up, and we chatted away on a variety of related subjects. Several times, I caught Nick watching the two of us engaged in conversation, and I caught the encouraging smile. I liked Doc, and he liked me. But more importantly, I could see firsthand the admiration that Nick and his father had for each other, despite the gap that a temporary setback had created.

When it came time for the pouring of the wine, Doc stopped by his son's chair, the bottle held in abeyance. Nick said simply, "No thanks, Dad."

And instead of making an issue of it, Doc set the bottle down and resumed conversation. I wanted to kiss the man at that point. It could have been awkward, but it wasn't. More than that though, I wanted to kiss Nick. We hadn't seen much of each other the past few days, and I looked forward to being alone with him in my house.

When we got ready to go, I thanked Doc again for inviting me as well as for his hospitality and turned to leave. "Lila?" Doc called out.

I turned around. "Yes?"

"Take good care of my son. He's pretty special."

Nick looked first at me then his dad. And he smiled at us both. "Thanks, Dad. Call you tomorrow." And we went home to what was fast becoming *our* house.

For the second time in a night, a call changed everything. I suspected that Nick was as interested in lovemaking as I was, and the moment we got inside the door, he proved me right. Our hands were all over each other, and he pulled me close and pressed his lips against mine. "God, you were beautiful tonight," he whispered into my ear. "I've never seen you look so good."

I reached up and took his ear lobe into my mouth, pressed my teeth lightly on it, and then held it between my lips. "You look pretty wonderful yourself," I said and moved closer to him. "Shall we move this party to the bedroom?"

But before he could respond, a cell phone interrupted with that irritating little tune. This time it was Nick's. "I thought I turned the damn thing off," he said, reaching for it and looking at the number. "Better take this one."

And he listened intently, his face unreadable. He concluded with, "Thanks, Ward. This will be good news for Lila."

I could hardly wait for him to push the button. He said, "That was Ward."

"And?"

"And they've got the reports back."

"Did he know what they say?"

"No, only that we should get them first thing in the morning."

"They're going to make us wait all night?" I asked incredulously.

"Apparently so. They didn't want to send it over fax, so they're sending it by delivery service in the morning."

"I can't believe this. We wait all this time, and now we have to wait until tomorrow. Nick, this is agonizing."

"Maybe I can help entertain you while you wait."

He had a point. One touch from him, and I knew he was right. The morning was only a few hours away, and we certainly knew how to fill them.

DNA

DNA doesn't lie. And because of that, Nick and I were at Ward's office when he opened the door the next morning, all three of us eager to learn the results of the testing. While we waited, we told him about the governor's call from the night before.

"Can't say as I've ever gotten a call direct from the governor. I reckon that makes you an important person around here."

"What that makes me is happy," I answered. "Just to think that Berniece's work will be on display with all the other women artists in the state. I only wish she could be there to see it herself."

"Something tells me she wouldn't enjoy that part of it too much," Ward said. "But then I have to admit I didn't know too much about the lady. And I'm sorry for that."

"It's not all your fault," Nick added. "Sure, she was tough to read, but she could have reached out a little too. That's what's going to make Lila's job hard."

Ward's brows raised. "What job is that?"

"They asked me to write up a biography of her to use in a brochure."

"No kidding?"

Nick grinned. "That was the other reason Kathryn Burroughs called last night."

"Now that's one brochure I'll read," Ward said and then added, "Guess our town might become famous for something good after all."

His simple comment served to remind us why we were there, and our mood turned more somber. I asked, "How much longer do you think it'll be?"

"Best I can tell you is they said the paperwork should be here by eight," and when we all glanced up at the clock behind his desk that registered eleven minutes after the hour, he added, "Guess they're gonna be a little late."

And the waiting turned to agony as the clock moved forward to nine o'clock then nine thirty. Knowing that I was expected and needed in the store, I couldn't stand it any longer. "I'm wasting time just sitting here. I'm going on to the store. Call me the minute it arrives, will you?"

Ward agreed, and Nick excused himself to make an appearance at his garage. Although he'd hired two capable people to run the station, he too felt the sting of missing out on what was his primary concern. The days had been extraordinary in so many ways, but the absence of routine took a toll. We needed some normalcy.

When Ward hadn't called me by eleven, I began to panic. I picked up the phone to call him, but he beat me to the punch.

"It's here," he said simply.

"Be right over."

I stopped Ethel in the middle of a sentence. "I'm sorry, Ethel, but I've got to run to the sheriff's office for a minute. Let Sherri take your information, and I'll fill this the minute I get back."

I left before even Ethel could think of a reply, and Nick met me in front of the office. We didn't sit down or wait for preludes, and neither did Ward. He handed the papers to me while Nick read over my shoulder.

As usual, there was some medical gobbledygook, which we scanned rather quickly. Then it got down to business. The body exhumed on the logging road belonged to a young woman between the ages of eighteen and twenty-four. Death had occurred at best estimate twenty to twenty-five years before. Cause of death could not be determined with certainty as there were no marks to the skull or to the bones. However, trace amounts of hemotoxic snake venom remained in the bones, sufficient to suggest snakebite as the cause of death.

Another paragraph of medical jargon ensued, and then I finally saw what we were looking for. Tests conclude that DNA taken from the hair sample provided by the Sumatanga County Sheriff's Office matches that taken from the exhumed skeleton with a probability high enough to ensure that these two persons are related maternally.

"Yes!" I screamed, and the reaction around the room was unanimous. We had a nearly positive identification of the person lying in the grave on Virgil's property, but more importantly, now we knew that Virgil Messer could not be a murderer.

I picked up the phone and found Vivian's number. I knew she'd want to know the news. On the other hand, I needed to know how to proceed with Clewis's book. When she answered, I went straight to the purpose of the call and told her that not only was Virgil no murderer, but that she also had a great niece that she'd never known anything about. "We're in the process now of trying to track down who her adoptive mother was. I'll let you know when we find anything."

"I appreciate that, Lila. I can't tell you how much I appreciate all you're doing for a family you didn't even know."

"No more than you've done for a lot of children."

"Thank you. Then I can understand your motives."

"Which brings me to the second reason I called."

"Yes, I know. Please, Lila, go ahead and talk to this Dr. Clewis if you still want to pursue the matter. I've thought long and hard about what he did, and it's not right."

"No, that kind of theft is despicable even though Virgil will never know himself."

"I'm not too sure about that," she said. "Sometimes I get the feeling he's directing the show here."

I laughed, but I also felt something deeper. She had a point. Why now after all these years? And better yet, why me?

I went back to the store with a new determination to finish what I'd started. The last piece of the puzzle lived in Tennessee, flourishing and probably unaware that his life was about to take a dramatic turn for the worse. I wanted to shout from the tallest mountain what Tom Clewis had done. Virgil deserved it, and I needed it. What I decided to do, however, took a milder approach, although as it turned out, a much more profitable one.

During the week, I continued my research on the computer with the goal of returning to Tennessee. Nick would again go with me, but this time, we wouldn't be looking for Berniece. I waited until the university's offices should all be closed and made the call. I didn't expect him to answer; in fact, had he done so, I would have made up an excuse and hung up. I wanted to leave Dr. Tom Clewis a message that would give him plenty to think about without scaring him into hiding.

After I'd identified myself, I said for the machine, "Dr. Clewis, the town of Antioch, Mississippi, where I live, will soon celebrate its one hundredth birthday, and because the town in your novel *Choices* reminds us so much of our little town, we'd like you to be our guest speaker. I'll be in Knoxville next week and was hoping that you'd find room in your schedule to talk with me. Don't worry about returning the call. I'll get back in touch with you soon. I look forward to meeting you, Dr. Clewis."

I put down the phone. Tom Clewis had a surprise waiting for him when he went in to work. Make that three surprises. Nick and I would be there too.

We took the evening flight from Jackson to Knoxville and checked into a motel near the university. I'd checked his schedule online and knew that he taught a class at ten in the morning, which probably meant he'd check into his office before that. Time enough to drop a bomb and let him have to teach a class. The man deserved some torture, and I was ready to administer it.

The office opened at eight, but we wanted to give Clewis time to hear our message and stew a bit. We figured he'd recognize us from our visit to Charity, and since we didn't want to spook him, we waited across the hallway, trying to blend in with the assortment of students that waited for a nearby classroom to be opened. When time was right, we'd pay Clewis a visit.

A few minutes after nine, Clewis stepped off the elevator and started toward the opposite end of the hallway where a suite of offices looked out over a courtyard. Clewis must have done all right by himself. We watched him enter the common area of the suite and then go into his office.

Seconds elapsed, and the longer we waited, the antsier I got. I finally asked, "Think he's listened to the message?"

"I'm sure. Are you ready?"

"I've been ready," I said but the uneasiness in my stomach denied that. "Let's go meet our author."

The common area was a pleasant sunny room painted in the palest blue. I told a pretty receptionist, probably a student herself, that we would like to see Dr. Clewis and, rather than wait for the inevitable question, said, "We don't have an appointment, but it's quite urgent that we see him."

She studied us for a second and then lifted the phone. "Just let me tell him you're here," she said. "Who may I say is calling?"

She repeated our names to him and waited and then looked up at me. "May I ask the nature of your business?"

"Sure. I left him a message last night, but we got to town sooner than we'd expected. I was hoping he might have a minute this morning."

She repeated what I'd told her into the phone, waited again, and then said, "Doctor Clewis wants to know if you can come back this afternoon. He's really busy and has a class in a few minutes. But he can see you at one o'clock."

"Sure. We can do that," I said.

"Good. Now what was that name again?"

When we'd made the appointment, we left as far as the hallway where we waited for what we knew would happen. Within a minute, the door to his office opened, and Tom Clewis rushed by the pretty receptionist and nearly ran into us as we waited in the now-empty hallway.

His face registered surprise but also something else closely akin to panic. Without speaking, he brushed past Nick then me, and I called out to his back, "Dr. Clewis!"

He stopped and looked back. "Do I know you?"

"We met at Charity," I said.

He gave us a fake smile and said, "Oh, I see."

"Yes, I think you do see," I told him. "That's why you're running from us."

He shook his head as if confused. "I do remember meeting you, but why are you here?"

"We're here to talk to you about your book, Dr. Clewis."

"Ah, then, you probably need to talk with my publisher's representative. He handles all my appearances."

"It's not an appearance that we came to talk about," Nick added. "We came to talk about a man named Virgil Messer and a manuscript that you stole from him."

Clewis drew back. "I have no idea what you're talking about, and if you'll excuse me, I have a class to teach."

"Didn't you forget your notes?" I asked, looking at his empty hands. "Or were you just in a hurry to get away from us?"

"Look, Ms., uh, what did you say your name is?"

"My name is not important right now. But the fact that we can prove your book was written by somebody else is. Now would you like to discuss this out here in the hall, or would you like to go back to your office?"

He looked quickly down the hallway toward the elevator, and I think for a second, he considered running. But the reality of his situation sank in. He nodded and then said, "My office. But I don't have long."

The receptionist looked up inquisitively as the three of us went past her desk and into his office. Still not looking at either of us, he sat down behind a cluttered desk while Nick and I took the chairs no doubt usually filled by supplicant students.

I started the conversation again. "Dr. Clewis, very recently, a manuscript written by Virgil Messer came into my hands through a distant relative of his. I read it and found it to be quite good. Then by accident, I remembered your face and your reaction when we asked you about his daughter, Berniece Messer."

"So?" he asked, hands upturned.

"So from there, it didn't take Sherlock Holmes to Google your name and find out that you'd written a book. You know, the Internet is a wonderful thing. You can even get summaries of novels online."

His shoulders sank, and his eyes closed. When he looked back at me, the face had lost some of the arrogance. He asked, "What do you want from me? If it's money, I don't have much."

"No, Mr. Clewis," I said. "We don't want money. That would be blackmail."

"What then? Why did you come here?"

"First, we wanted you to acknowledge what you've done. You took advantage of a man dying with cancer. You stole his work and put your name on it. For at least ten years, you've enjoyed the money and the fame gained from somebody else's work."

Clewis looked up at the ceiling then back at me. "All right. I borrowed the idea for my story. Is that what you wanted to hear?"

"No, you didn't borrow it. You stole it. There's a difference."

"Let's not quibble over connotations, Ms. Dawkins."

Nick said, "There's more than a connotation involved here, Clewis."

I added, "I read your work, and I read his. And I know that you stole his story. Sure you placed it in Tennessee, but it's Virgil's story, and you need to make compensation."

"I thought you said you didn't want money."

"Oh I don't. But his daughter needs it."

"Did you find her?"

"No, we didn't find her. We probably never will."

"What then? I really don't understand where all this nonsense is heading."

I began to explain. "Berniece's work is excellent, and I now have the opinions of several experts to back me up on that. What I want from you is your influence around the university to help show her work. Under the circumstances, Mr. Clewis, I think that's asking very little of a man who made himself part of a commune with the expressed intent of giving back to the community. Or did that point evade you?"

He looked from me to Nick, unable to answer. I continued, "I see no reason why we should both have to go through a lengthy court battle where, in the end, nobody wins and nobody loses. I think our request is quite reasonable."

Nick added, "This way, your reputation remains intact, improved even. You raise money to show some extraordinary artwork, and the community thinks you're a saint. In my book, that's a win-win situation."

Clewis stared back at us and then lowered his head. "Okay, you win. I'll do what you're asking. I'll do what I can." Then his eyes drilled into mine as he asked, "Was my work better than Virgil's?"

"No, Dr. Clewis, it wasn't. But then I'm no literary critic like you are. What do I know?"

Eagle Valley

When we left his office, I was as exhausted as I can ever remember being. Nick and I both felt that we'd have Clewis's cooperation, but I'd still keep close tabs on him. We had the proof, and he knew it. But his reputation could do a lot to bring in the money we'd need to make Berniece's work known, and I felt confident that once that happened, buyers would appear. That money could, in turn, be used to train lots of talented youngsters who hadn't the funds to go it alone.

We found a quiet restaurant with a view of the Tennessee River and sat down to a leisurely lunch. For the first time in weeks, we had some time on our hands, and although I enjoyed the feeling, I also couldn't quite shake the notion that as long as we were that close, there was something else I wanted to do.

Nick was driving back to the hotel when I asked, "Do you really want to spend all afternoon in a hotel room?"

He turned slowly toward me. "Why do I get the feeling that I'm in trouble?" he asked.

"Aw, Nick. You know me too well."

"Where is it you want to go, Lila?"

I told him, and he asked with a sigh, "Are you sure you want to do that?"

I assured him that I did, and he pulled the car off the road and into a parking lot. "Then I guess we'd better turn around. Lila, I don't mind going up there, but why? What's there for us now?"

"I've been thinking about what Paul Cranley said about the place where Virgil and Delores are buried. And I'd really like to see it. If for no other reason than to give me some closure. I guess I sort of need to see something real, something that tells us Virgil was a real person, and all the work we've done isn't wasted on a figment of my imagination."

"I can understand that," he said nodding, "but I'm not sure seeing a couple of graves will make you feel any better. It might even make it harder to accept how he was cheated, knowing that he was a real person."

"I've thought about it, Nick. I've never been one to make regular visits to gravesides, but this time I just might need to go there."

"Well, your instinct's been on target so far, so why stop listening to it now?"

I thanked him for understanding, especially when I wasn't too sure I understood myself, and we passed the rest of the drive with more pleasant topics. We made it to the crossroads where we'd stopped once before, and again I went into the little store to ask directions.

The woman behind the counter was the same one who'd given us directions to Charity, and she seemed to recognize me, at least in the way that you know you've seen somebody before, but you're not sure where. We exchanged pleasantries, and I asked, "This may seem a little odd, but I understand there's a little cemetery somewhere around here next to a church."

"Unhun," she muttered.

I realized that probably all cemeteries around there were connected to a church, and I started again. "This one is in a valley. There are mountains all around it. Does that sound familiar?"

Her face brightened. "You must be talkin' about Eagle Valley. Prettiest little church you ever did see, and the cemetery's right next to it. They have a big festival up there every fall when the apples come in."

I thanked her and got directions, this time making sure that they didn't include climbing a mountain on a dirt trail. She was right about the distance, ten miles exactly, and she was right about the valley and the little church posed in the middle of it more like a post card than the real thing.

The small white frame church with clear glass windows occupied an idyllic spot beside a meandering stream surrounded by lush grass and clusters of apple trees with tiny green fruit. We parked next to a small park of sorts, complete with wooden picnic tables, a pair of swing sets obviously made by local craftsmen, and a brick barbecue pit that looked well used. The cemetery occupied the opposite side of the church, but the way it had been cared for made it appear more like a park itself.

Each gravesite had been maintained with loving care. There were no plastic flowers or sentimental displays. Perfectly trimmed grass covered all but the most recently dug grave, which would no doubt soon have its own rich covering. I'd always wondered why we feel compelled to build fences around cemeteries, and apparently people in Eagle Valley felt the same way because this little plot of ground looked as normal as the stream that passed by it. There was no need for fencing in or fencing out.

We had no idea whether there would be markers for Virgil and his wife, but we started looking closest to the church and moved outward. Walking down the rows, I got a sense of the people who had called this place home. Family names repeated with regularity—mothers, daughters, fathers, and sons, grouped together for eternity.

We'd made what we thought a complete sweep of the grounds, but we hadn't seen anything resembling the name Messer. We were standing at the edge of the cemetery, where forest threw all into shadows, and I said, "Maybe we missed it."

I was about to suggest that we make another round when Nick stopped me. "Wait, Lila. Somebody's in the church."

I looked back at the little church, and through the clear windows, I saw a tall figure moving about inside it.

"Let's go talk to him," Nick said. "If he's been around here for a while, he can probably tell us where to look."

I agreed that was a good idea, and we carefully retraced our steps and then stepped up onto the porch of the church. Nick opened the door, and the man who'd been moving about the church looked up in surprise. His white hair said that he must be older than I'd assumed. Dressed in a dark blue suit, starched white shirt, and bold red tie, I assumed he was the pastor of the church.

"Sorry," Nick said. "Didn't mean to startle you."

"You didn't," the man said. "I didn't realize anybody was around. Is there something I can do for you?"

"We're looking for somebody," Nick said and then smiled. "Actually, we're looking for a grave."

It was the stranger's turn to smile. "Then you may have come to the right place," he said and gazed out to the cemetery.

Nick chuckled. "Let me start that again. We're looking for a particular grave, but we didn't see it. Are you the minister here?"

He glanced down at his suit. "No. But I can see why you'd think so. I'm the local mortician. I was in here checking on a few things." He held his hand out to Nick. "Grant Waldrop," he said.

"Nick Reynolds," he said, taking the outstretched hand. "And this is Lila Dawkins. We came here from Antioch, Mississippi, hoping to find a particular gravesite. We'd like to pay our respects."

"That's kind of you."

I added, "It's kind of important to know for sure that they're buried here. Do you know everybody?"

"Not too many folks live here that don't eventually pass through my place too. Who are these folks?"

"Virgil and Delores Messer. They lived up at Charity."

His eyes clouded over, and I thought the man might fall. Nick reached out and took him by the shoulders to sit him down on a nearby pew. "Goodness," Grant finally said. "I don't know what happened there. I must be getting old or something."

Nick and I looked at each other, waiting for him to continue. He took out a white handkerchief and mopped his brow. When some color had returned to his face, I asked, "Are you all right now?"

He gave me a bright smile and assured, "Oh, I'm fine. That gave me a little start when you asked about Virgil and Delores."

"Why is that, Mr. Waldrop?" I asked.

"In all these years, you're the first people who ever asked about those two. And I can tell you why you didn't find any headstones or markers. They didn't want any. Said it didn't matter who they used to be, only what they would become."

"So they *are* buried out there?" Nick asked.

The man nodded. "They are. And so's their daughter."

He could have punched me in the stomach and had less impact. For a moment, I couldn't breathe. Nick repeated the phrase. "Their daughter? Berniece is buried here?"

Again, he nodded. "There were three of 'em. Virgil and Delores died a long time ago, but I remember because the circumstances were kinda strange, and I was fairly new in the business. But the daughter died just a while back. She came to me about six weeks ago and introduced herself. Said she'd come home to be with her parents, and then she paid me for my services. 'Ahead of time,' she said. I buried her out there beside her parents, but there wasn't anybody else—just me and the crew." He mopped his brow again and then added, "But I had to ask the preacher to say a few words. Hope she didn't mind. Apparently, the woman didn't know a soul in town."

I sat down beside the older man and tried to reason out what I'd heard. "Mr. Waldrop, how did Berniece die? Was she sick?"

"All I can tell you is that I got a call one day from a lady that rented her a house. She told me that Berniece had passed away, and she left a note tellin' me to come and get her. Said I'd know what to do."

I was stunned. All the time that we thought Berniece had run away, I never considered that she might really be dead. Nick reached for my hand, and I whispered to him, "Nicky, we were so close. We almost found her."

"I know. But she didn't want us to. Did she?"

"I guess not," I said as tears fell down my face. "She had so much to share with the world, but she didn't know how. And the world was too busy to ask."

Grant Waldrop looked away, out over the cemetery, giving us the moment to ourselves. I cried again for someone I never knew but someone I felt closer to at that moment than perhaps anyone else in my life.

Grant excused himself but not before he pointed out their graves to us. Nick and I left the little church and returned to the cemetery where I knelt beside the newest grave. Long shadows covered the plot, and I shivered in the coolness, but I also felt an uncommon peace descend on us as we sat there beside Berniece's unmarked grave. I had finally found her. Berniece would live on.